Father's Wings

sequel to

Father's Choice

Book Two in the Father Series

by
Rhonda Hanson

$$\textit{Father's Wings}$$

sequel to
$$\textit{Father's Choice}$$

Book Two in the Father Series

by
Rhonda Hanson

ISBN 979-8-218-33103-0

Dedication

This book is dedicated to my mother, who loved my first book, Father's Choice, and who made me realize that I wasn't through telling this story.

It is dedicated to my father, who made me laugh, who took me fishing, and who worked hard all his life, at whatever his hand could find to do. He was a simple man, in bib overalls, with a penchant for snuff and parched peanuts.

It is dedicated to all my siblings, particularly to the memory of six of us ten, who have gone on to join our parents.

All of these are in Heaven now, and can see Father's Wings for themselves.

Rhonda Hanson

*"...and in the shadow of Your wings I will take refuge
until destruction passes by."*

Ps. 57:1

The story continues...

Darcy Decker smiled in amusement, as her soon-to-be sister-in-law fumbled frantically with her veil.

"Hailey, don't, you're going to rip it!" Darcy reached up and gently unlocked her desperate grip.

"It looks stupid!" Hailey moaned.

"It sure does." Hailey's best friend and matron of honor strolled over, and inspected her with disapproval.

"Meredith, do something!"

Meredith Etheridge continued her skeptical analysis. "Well, for one thing, you've got it all pulled around, like a tobacco-spitting outfielder. Here."

She unpinned the veil's cap and set it back to a more attractive advantage.

"That's it," Darcy breathed softly.

Meredith cocked her head to one side. "Are you sure this is the one we picked out?"

Hailey's eyes widened in horror, and Meredith giggled softly. "It's a joke, Sissy. Relax, you're a knock-out."

"Are you sure?"

"You're beautiful," Darcy agreed wholeheartedly.

"So am I." Meredith looked down and patted her pregnant stomach in peaceful satisfaction. She and her husband, Joel, had been floating around in some sort of ethereal fog, ever since she discovered she was going to have his baby. They were both sure Father had told them to expect a son, which so widened Joel's constant grin, that it threatened to decapitate him.

"Merry, I know you said the nausea has been a lot better, but I still really appreciate your standing in for me," Hailey said.

"Are you kidding?" She gave the bride a playful grin. "Joel's so excited about this kid, he wanted me to wear a dress with a see-through tummy. I thought about it, too, if I could have talked Mrs. Powell into making it. But when I saw all those straight pins and scissors sticking out of her, I wouldn't let her anywhere near my midsection."

Hailey laughed at her friend's blissful state and turned to look up at Darcy. "How do you feel, honey?"

"Me?" She lifted her brows in surprise. "Fine, I guess. I think the important thing is how *you* feel."

"Well, I mean... " Hailey hesitated. "It hasn't been that long since you broke up with your boyfriend, and I was just hoping a wedding wouldn't trigger any painful memories."

Darcy smiled and gave her shoulder an affectionate squeeze. "No, it's not like that. I mean, there were some pleasant moments but, now that it's over, I can see that Bruce and I weren't meant to be together. I really wasn't in love with him."

"And who can blame you?" Meredith flopped down on the sofa next to Hailey, and threw one leg inelegantly over the armrest. "He was a geek. Besides, I never knew anybody named Bruce, who wasn't."

Hailey gave her a sideways look of mild reproach. "That's sort of a broad commentary, isn't it?"

"I didn't say *all* Bruces are geeks. I just said I personally never knew any, who weren't. While we're talking," she added, closely inspecting her cuticles, "what kind of name is Bruce Spillers, anyway? You can't tell where the first name ends and the last name begins. Say it!"

Hailey tried it. "I never noticed that before!"

Meredith shrugged. "You should never end a first name with the same sound that the last name starts with. They get all meshed together. It's bad enough to be a geek, without your name sounding dumb. And then there are *some* of us, who come into life with a fairly decent last name like Clark, then not only fall in love with a another name that just doesn't work, but *marry* it! We get exactly what we deserve.

"Mere-*dith Eth*-eridge. '*Thay*' that. '*Thee*' what I mean?"

Darcy chuckled appreciatively. One of the things she loved most about Meredith was the random nature of her irrepressible opinions.

Meredith was a well-known, chart-topping, Christian musician and songwriter, who loved God, or "Father", as she called Him, with all her heart. Still, no one ever knew what she might blurt out, at any given moment. Her husband Joel, who was also her manager, always kept one hand over his heart when she was in concert, and it wasn't because he was patriotic.

She glanced down at her watch. "Well, in this case, I'm afraid Meredith's right. There did seem to be a subtle 'geekness' about Bruce."

Meredith flashed Hailey a smug look. She ignored it and noticed, instead, the wrinkle of confusion on Darcy's forehead.

"What is it?"

"My watch says the same thing it said when you were getting dressed." She shook it and held it up to her ear. "It's dead!"

"I shouldn't have asked Mom to go check on the cake!" The flustered bride began to wring her hands. "Only, she kept calling out the time every two minutes, and she was making me nervous!"

Meredith got up and cracked open the door. She didn't see anyone out in the hall, so she crossed over to the men's suite and rapped loudly.

"Yeah!" someone yelled abruptly.

"What time is it?"

The door flew open, and a tall, handsome man with astonishing, blue eyes and a mane of premature, gray hair caught her up into his arms.

"Time to kiss your husband." He locked her more securely in place, and charged her pulse rate.

She pushed herself back so that she could look up at him. "Besides that, I mean."

"Heartless female." Joel smiled down at Meredith's beautiful face. He lifted the weight of her long, dark hair in one hand, and studied the coronet of tiny flowers that crowned her. "This is nice. Like our wedding day."

Meredith caught his face in loving hands.

"What... *time*... is... it?"

He glanced at his watch. "Uh oh! Five 'til."

She stared at him. "*Two*? Five 'til *two*?"

"Afraid so."

"Why didn't somebody come for us? Isn't there supposed to be a wedding lady, or something?"

Joel grinned down at her annoyed, little scowl. "I don't know, but we'd better scoot, in any event."

"You guys are supposed to go first," she instructed, checking his wrist for herself. "Make 'em hurry, honey!"

"I will, calm down." Joel lifted her chin and dropped a soft kiss on her mouth. "Don't be upsetting my boy," he added, caressing their baby tenderly.

Meredith gave him a swat and shooed him back into the room. "Hurry, Joel!" She turned and darted back across the hall.

"It's almost two," she announced breathlessly. "Up, up!"

Hailey leaped up in alarm. "Are you sure?"

"Hailey, why do you always ask me if I'm sure, whenever I tell you something? Stand right there." She surveyed her carefully. "What do you say, Darce?"

"I say she's gorgeous."

"I concur." Meredith opened the door again and peered out. "Good, they're going down the hall. Ready, baby?" She turned and looked at her friend.

Hailey nodded nervously. "Where's the bouquet?"

Darcy scooped it out of its box and placed it in her shaking hands. "Here you go. You're all set."

The bride hesitated. "Well... I mean, couldn't we have prayer or something, first?"

Meredith cocked one eyebrow. "We're late! You wanna pray *now*, Sissy?"

Hailey smiled feebly, and she sighed and shrugged.

"Fine. But let's hurry."

"You do it," she suggested.

Meredith rolled her eyes. "This is like asking the blessing. No one ever wants to do *that*, either. Okay..." She held out her hands to the others. "Just like the Waltons."

Darcy smothered a giggle as Meredith began.

"Father, would You please go down the aisle with Sissy, here? And, while You're at it, would You go ahead and help her light the candles, and cut the cake, and throw the bouquet, and pose for pictures, and... wait a minute... "

She broke off and opened one eye. "Do we need help at the punch table?"

Hailey bowed her head even lower and tried not to laugh.

"Just kidding, Father. You're good at what You do, so please do it for Hailey. You know... that 'Father' thing.

Thanks, love You!" She gave their hands a little squeeze. "We're holding up the show."

Darcy led the way down the stairs, and out to the arboretum of Nashville's Opryland Hotel.

This was a popular place for weddings, especially in June. Now, in March, it was far less crowded than normal, which influenced Hailey's decision to be married there. She had chosen to keep the wedding party small, with two attendants each.

Darcy stopped under the tall, ornate bower, leaving a place for Meredith to stand next to the bride. The groom and his party had already come in together, and were standing in their respective positions.

Meredith's eyes were so riveted on her husband's face, as she neared the bower, that Darcy found herself a little concerned about her possibly tripping, in her condition. Meredith, however, slipped beautifully into place and, even as the bride was announced by a subtle change in the music, she commanded Joel's gaze, as if it were *their* wedding.

Darcy was mesmerized by these two, so much so that she could scarcely pay attention to the ceremony, even though it was her brother who was getting married.

She had first met Joel and Meredith at their wedding at the Hermitage, almost a year ago when her brother, Ross, served as Joel's best man. She knew then that she never wanted to settle for anything less than the intense devotion they shared, which is why she wasn't too devastated when she and Bruce Spillers broke up. Whatever 'it' was, that wasn't it.

Meredith often teased Hailey about owing Joel "big time" for introducing her to Ross. Darcy reflected on that, as she complied with the minister's request that everyone's head bow in prayer. Ross was a police officer and Joel's closest friend. Joel had caught the look on his face, when

Hailey came out of his office and into the lobby, where Ross had been waiting to see him. He was quick to supply the impromptu exchange of names, and stood back and watched, as things just naturally clicked into place.

Ross had promptly driven over to his sister's apartment to ask if she believed in love at first sight. Having never experienced it, Darcy couldn't attest to it, but encouraged him to find out for himself. It didn't take long for him to report back that it really existed. This strengthened Darcy's resolve to save herself for the real thing, and not to settle for a counterfeit. She now believed that she would know God's man when he came.

She straightened and forced herself to concentrate on the wedding.

Gary Brenner, pastor of Covenant Fellowship where many in their circle of friends and family worshipped, presided over the service, as he had done for Joel and Meredith. His own fiancé, Joel's mother, Laura Etheridge, looked on with the customary happy tears. Hailey's parents, Dan and Gail Fisher, beamed their joy on one side of the aisle while Curtis and Edith Decker mirrored their expressions on the other.

She studied her brother's other attendant, Felix Brasseaux and smiled. Felix, who had brought along his girlfriend Polly, was the most extraordinary character she had ever met. He was a U.S. Marshal from New Orleans, and Ross's good friend. He was big, and burly, and a little gruff, but was absolutely harmless, unless you were on the wrong side of the law. He had saved Joel Etheridge's life a couple of Christmases ago, and Meredith loved him dearly.

Darcy allowed her eyes to rest on her brother's handsome face, and she silently thanked God for giving him someone as good for him as she was sure Hailey would be. Hailey loved the Lord with all her heart, and Darcy knew that her relationship with Him would carry over into her life with Ross.

This train of thought forced Darcy's mind back to its former meditation. At twenty-eight, she had often wondered if she was too particular about the man she was hoping to find, but today she realized that when it came to the man she would spend the rest of her life with, she couldn't be too particular. Today, she was stubbornly convinced that a Godly man, "Father's choice," as Meredith put it, was definitely worth holding out for.

She lifted her chin with renewed determination. Meredith was right. She would wait for Father to choose for her, and she wouldn't be sorry.

Darcy blinked in surprise, as she realized the wedding was over. Had she daydreamed through the entire thing? Apparently so! The groom had just kissed the bride, and now they were being mashed by hoards of people. After a while, everyone made their way upstairs to a banquet room for the reception.

Darcy had begged Hailey not to aim the bouquet at her, but just as soon as she released it, Meredith gave it an expert tap, and sent it sailing right into her arms, to the delight of the entire party. She gave Darcy a mischievous wink and grinned at her pink face.

Gradually, the crowd dwindled until there were only family members and a few close friends left. Darcy gave her brother a tight hug and planted a kiss on Hailey's glowing face.

"Are you going back to your job, Hailey, after the honeymoon?"

She made a face. "Probably not. Right now, I can't see myself missing having to fly all over the country, pointing out the emergency exits and passing out peanuts and ginger ale so... I kinda doubt it. Not anytime soon, anyway. But we'll see."

"Well, it was a beautiful wedding, and you guys are absolutely perfect together," she said sincerely. "Call me when you're back home, and tell me all about Canada."

"We'll bring you back a Mountie," Hailey offered. She smiled, simply because she couldn't stop it.

"A *picture* of a Mountie will do just fine," Darcy returned, ignoring Meredith's teasing, maniacal expression. "I've gotta take off. Love you guys!"

She made the perfunctory rounds, ending with her parents, then headed to her car.

She drove slowly back to her small apartment in Smyrna, a neighboring town just southeast of Nashville, and sat in the car a moment, before getting out. It had been a long day, starting at six that morning, and fatigue suddenly kicked in.

"Why're ya lookin' like a girl for?" The high-pitched voice of a disgusted eleven-year-old boy cut into Darcy's thoughts.

She smiled down at the picture little Wallace Greer made in his dad's big rubber boots, as she unlocked the trunk and retrieved her suitcase from her car.

"I went to a wedding, that's why."

Her landlord's son wrinkled his nose in annoyance. "I hate weddin's! You have to wear a suit, and you can't get nothin' on it and if you do, you either get a whippin' or lose a priv'lege. Dependin' on whether or not it comes out. Same thing for funerals."

Darcy rumpled his thick, blonde hair with a grin and marveled, as she often did, at how large and beautiful his deep, brown eyes were.

Wally was a great kid, one of hers, in a way, since she was the youth pastor at the church he and his family attended. Even though he was too young to be part of her group, she felt a bond with him, in spite of his not having hit the thirteen-year marker that would make him a teen-ager. Apparently, Wally felt it too, because he had become Darcy's constant shadow, when he wasn't found in the company of his next-door buddy, Foster Ames.

Wally grabbed Darcy's suitcase and followed her to her apartment in their backyard, dragging it through the dirt. She shook her head and held back reproof. He was trying to help, and she could always clean it off, after he left.

"Just leave it by the door, Wally," she suggested. "And thanks for lugging it for me."

"Whatcha got in here, anyway?" Wally was always curious.

"The things I changed out of. My jeans and tennis shoes."

"Well, put 'em back on, if you want *my* advice." He gave her a wise nod. "If you mess around and get somethin' on that dress, Mama'll go off like a rocket!"

"You think so?" Darcy tried to wear a serious face.

"I *know* so! She don't like dirt, and she *really* don't like it when you wear your good clothes to play in!" His warning was given with wide-eyed urgency.

"Well, I wasn't planning on doing any playing, but I guess I'll change into something I can relax in." Darcy unlocked her door and pulled her suitcase through. "Why don't you scoot so I can do that, and I'll see you in a little bit?"

She peered across the yard, at a little face poking through the hedge. "Anyway, there's Foster waiting for you."

He glanced over briefly. "We're gonna build a dam."

She could tell that he hadn't intended to let that slip out, by his late tinge of color.

"Are you? Where?"

Wally grinned and shrugged.

"Don't tell me, then," Darcy decided. "Just leave me out of it."

He clunked off in the huge boots, that struck him just below the seat. Darcy watched him lumber along for another moment, before she closed the door and headed for a hot shower.

She stopped as she caught her reflection in the full-length mirror. She had balked at first, when Hailey picked out gray dresses because, with her dark auburn hair, clashes were inevitable. She knew it would look extraordinary on Meredith, because Meredith would look great in a barrel, and besides, the color was an exact match for her beautiful eyes.

She was surprised to find that she actually liked it, after all. It was a dark gray tea-length lace dress, with a dropped vee-shaped waist, scooped neck and fitted sleeves. It dramatized her flaming, shoulder-length hair, and light-blue eyes, suited her slight athletic frame and, unlike most bridesmaid outfits, she really could wear it again.

"Not too shabby," she commented. She lifted up a pair of old cut-offs and an oversized tee-shirt, and sighed at the thought of shedding her pretty wrappings, and becoming ordinary again.

"Okay, Cinderella." Darcy gave her reflection a parting glance and submitted to the unavoidable. "It's midnight. The ball's over."

She pulled off her slippers and eyed them ruefully. "And the prince stood me up!"

Chapter Two

Bett Greer flashed Darcy an indulgent smile as she opened the back screened door and stuck her head in.

"You're up early, Darce." She wiped her plump hands on a dishtowel, and reached into the cabinet for an extra coffee mug.

"Good morning, Bett," Darcy returned sleepily. "I hope that's for me."

"It's got your name on it."

Actually, it did. Wally had made this particular mug at vacation bible school and painted on the names of everyone in his family, including Darcy, who had naturally grafted in.

She took it gratefully, and perched herself on the stool at the snack bar. "Whatcha got there, Bett?"

"Seeds." Wally's mom shuffled the colorful packets around absently. "Stan's going to till the far end of the yard up for the garden this evening, when he gets in. I'm afraid there's going to be a little noise for a little while, out behind the apartment."

"Oh, I don't mind." Darcy picked up a pack of seeds and waved it toward Bett in delight. "Watermelons!"

Bett laughed and pulled up a stool for herself. "You better know it! Wally's watermelons. He's always planted 'em himself, ever since he could walk."

"Does he share?"

"Not too well the first week, but after that, he practically force feeds them to you."

Darcy smiled and sorted through the rest of the pile. "Peas, potatoes..." She broke off with a grimace. "Don't invite me over when you have this! Spinach, ugh!"

"Let me see that." Bett took the envelope and frowned at it. "I didn't buy that." She tilted her head to one side, and gave it some thought. "Not that I don't like spinach, but no one else around here will touch it. I wouldn't have bought it just for me."

She gave up her study as the phone in the next room began to ring, and hurried to go snatch it up.

Darcy turned her mug around and idly read the names written in Wally's crooked script. "Daddy" was Stan Greer, a forty-seven-year-old construction worker. Stan was a good-natured, dark-complexioned man who, more often than not, was found in overalls and a green John Deere cap.

"Mama" was, of course, Bett or rather, Elizabeth. Bett was forty-one, short, plump, and blonde, like Wally. She usually padded around barefoot in baggy shorts and large comfortable tops, and had a fondness for romance novels, fudge, talk shows, and gossip. Nothing mean-spirited, just juicy, little tidbits to punch up life, a little.

"Audra" was Wally's big sister. Audra was seventeen and, with her father's olive skin and her mother's clear green eyes, she was exceptionally pretty. She was quiet and prone to moodiness, but Bett dismissed it as being such a weird age.

Wally's older brother was "Calvin". Calvin was fifteen, and even more quiet than Audra. He was serious and reflective, and the reason for all the Honor Student bumper stickers on Bett's Oldsmobile. He periodically begged her to remove them, but to no avail. Wally generously offered to take them off for a quarter apiece, with some steel wool and gasoline, but Bett overheard and negotiations were broken down.

Darcy laughed quietly at her own name, scribbled next to Wally's. If she ever had a son, she hoped he'd be just like him. Wally was a heart-full. She put down the mug and glanced up, as Bett came back in.

"That was Myra Ames, looking for Foster. The last time I saw him, he and Wally were creeping out across the back field, with a bucket and a couple of Stan's old trowels. Well," she corrected, "Foster was creeping. Wally was sort of wobbling. He's taken to wearing Stan's boots, for some reason."

Darcy opened her mouth to volunteer an explanation for the boots, then checked herself. She'd better just convince Wally to tell his mother what he was up to.

"I'm sure he'll show up for lunch," Bett continued, picking up the seed packets and laying them in a drawer.

Darcy sipped her coffee in silence for so long, that Bett regarded her curiously.

"So, tell me all about the wedding," she suggested, returning to her roost across the bar.

"Beautiful!" Darcy leaned her elbows on the counter and thought back on yesterday's ceremony. "Hailey looked like an angel. Having the wedding at the hotel's arboretum made things really convenient. Plus, that place is gorgeous."

"I wish we could have gotten back from Franklin in time for the service, but there was no way to make it work out," Bett said regretfully. "Did anyone videotape it?"

"I did see some guy running around with a camera, now that you mention it."

"Good! Maybe a copy of it will float this way." Bett leaned closer, in a manner that usually preceded a confidential moment. "The district has a new state youth director."

Darcy looked at her strangely. "Why wasn't I told?"

She shrugged lightly. "I just found out this morning, when I took Audra to catch the field trip bus to Gatlinburg. I stopped by a yard sale on the way back, and saw Pastor Todd's wife, Wanda. She said he had just gotten settled into the church rental, and is going to be the speaker at the next district rally."

Darcy kept her puzzled look. "But, I didn't get a letter or anything, mentioning a new state youth director. And what happened to Les Chapman?"

"He's going overseas, to one of those communist places." This didn't explain much to Darcy. Bett Greer thought that everything east of North Carolina was communist territory.

"Well, I still don't understand not being told. Pastor Frank never said a word. Strange, that I'd have to hear it through one of the neighboring churches."

She pushed her cup to one side and stood up to leave. "What's his name, anyway?"

"MacSomething... Scottish or Irish. Mac..." Bett frowned and concentrated. "Beats me! But his first name is Neil. I remember that, because I had an Uncle Neil."

She looked up at Darcy with a sly gleam of teasing in her eyes. "Oh, there was one other thing. Wanda Todd says he's single and gorgeous!"

"And probably knows it." Darcy shuffled out the door and threw a nonchalant wave to her laughing friend.

She climbed into her car and headed for their little church. She had a load of papers on her desk that needed clearing up, and she had several calls to make. Pastor Frank had left a message that he wanted a few minutes to talk with her. Maybe it was about Neil MacWhatever.

Darcy glanced down at her dashboard clock. She had to be at her other job at eleven. She wished, yet again, that she could devote all her time to pastoring the youth at her local church, but she could never survive on what the struggling little fellowship paid her. It took her position at The Last Word book and music store to balance things out. On the bright side, the church was beginning to show signs of steady growth, and if the trend continued, maybe she could afford to give more time to the kids.

Darcy whipped into the parking lot and sailed into her office, already in hyper-mode. Frank Lynwood heard her breezy entrance and came to the door, as she was settling in, to sort through her pile of correspondence.

"Got a minute, before you bury yourself?" His smile-creased, weather-beaten face broke into a friendly grin.

"For the boss? Oh, I guess I can juggle around you."

Darcy enjoyed kidding her pastor. He was a gentle man of quiet authority, who was neither "pedestal minded" nor religious. This made him very approachable for adults and children, alike.

Pastor Frank slid into a seat in front of the desk, and eyed his youth pastor speculatively. "Have you heard the rumblings, yet?""

"About the new youth director?" She waited for his slight nod. "Bett filled me in this morning. What I can't understand is why I never got some kind of notice from the state office."

"I believe that's forthcoming, after the fact."

Darcy noticed her pastor's approach to aging for the first time, as he picked up a pencil and rolled it back and forth, in heavily veined hands.

"Les Chapman left rather... abruptly."

She puckered her brow and waited.

"He's been wanting to work in missions for a long time. That's never been a secret. No one expected him to just up and vault, though." He chuckled quietly. "I guess it's true what they say. When you gotta go, you gotta go!"

Darcy smiled down at her desk. "How were they able to replace him so soon with whoever it is?"

"Neil McCallen," Pastor Frank supplied, leaning back into his chair. "Well, there's a mystery. He just showed up here last month. Here, meaning Murfreesboro. He was actually in Middle Tennessee before, but left for a while. Anyway, Barry Todd needed someone pronto, and the General Board told him about McCallen, and recommended him highly. No one seems to know too much about him which, let me tell you, is driving Sister Todd crazy, but I'm not worried. Between her and Bett Greer, we'll have his driver's license number and underwear size in a few days."

Darcy shrieked out a laugh that echoed down the hallway. Her pastor gave her a wink, and rose to leave. He paused in the doorway and turned back around.

"Oh yeah... that's not even what I came in here for. Softball. I knew it was something else. The churches are forming their teams now. It's boys and girls, mixed. Faron Waldrop says he's available to coach again this year, so give him a call, if you want to get these kids involved."

"Oh, I've already been informed by a committee of about twenty, that they fully intend to be involved," she replied. "I might as well put him down on the old call list."

"Right!" He gave her a mixed wave of agreement and dismissal, and sauntered back to his own office, her pencil riding behind one ear. Darcy wasn't concerned. Whenever she ran low, she just marched into the pastor's study, opened his top drawer, and ransomed one of her writing implements. So did Freida Kirkland, the church secretary, and Willis Sanders, the treasurer. Everyone knew about Pastor Lynwood's absent-minded kleptomania.

Darcy shook her head in amused resignation, and got ready to plow through her desk. She stole a peek at her watch. Meredith Etheridge had agreed to come to the store today for a couple of hours to do a CD-signing. Darcy didn't want to keep her waiting. She pulled her telephone over, and got down to business.

Meredith halted in her tracks and looked back at the telephone with annoyance. It was probably for Joel, who was in the shower, getting ready to go to the office. After the fourth ring, she realized the answering machine was turned off, and snatched it up abruptly.

"Hello!"

There was a brief pause, before a decidedly feminine voice chose to begin purring.

"Joel Etheridge, please!" The tone had an imperative edge that was irritating.

Meredith made a face, and tried to suppress a hostile response.

"Joel isn't available, just now. You may leave a message, if you wish."

The purr checked itself, momentarily. "When will he be available?"

"It depends on what you mean by *available*." She bit off her words, slipping a little in her resolve to be civil.

"I mean, of course, when may I speak with him?"

Meredith bristled. "What you may do is leave a message. If, or when, you speak to my husband, is entirely up to him."

The woman on the other end of the line halted only a second, before changing her tactics. "Oh, then this must be Meredith!"

"It must be," she asserted dryly. Who else did this idiot *think* it was? She scowled impatiently at her sarcastic self.

"Oh, how nice!" More purring.

"Would you like to leave a message?" Meredith repeated, in a frigid tone.

"Just tell him Janis called. He has the number," she added, with emphasis.

"Right. Don't let me keep you."

Meredith received no response to this impulsive jab. She shrugged and hung up, turning on the machine, as she did so.

"Sorry, Father," she mumbled as she slipped into some old sweat pants that still fit, and pulled on one of Joel's big tee shirts. "Guess I'd better meet You in the window seat after Joel leaves, and catch it for that, huh?"

Father smiled at her tenderly and watched her plod barefoot down the stairs. He always looked forward to their visits.

Meredith stopped to scoop up Hookline, the huge, gray cat who actually ruled the house, and graciously allowed boarders. She muttered abstract cat-talk into his twitching ears, before dumping a can of liver into his dish. Hook shivered in delight, and rammed his face into his stinky breakfast.

Joel wasn't long joining his wife in the kitchen. He had a towel around his shoulders, and was drying his thick curls vigorously.

"Was that the office already, baby?" He stopped and gave her a light kiss, before inspecting the refrigerator's contents.

Meredith watched him ferret around for whatever he was looking for.

"It was Janis." She waited.

Joel turned and looked at her questioningly. "One of your friends?"

"It was for you," she said quietly.

He gave her another searching glance, then resumed his quest to find the orange juice. He finally came up with it and turned, to find his wife looking at him oddly.

"What is it?" He shook the juice, and reached for a glass.

"*Who* is it?"

"Who is *who*?"

"Joel!" Meredith shot him a glare. "Who is this Janis chick, and how did she get our home number?"

"Beats me." His eyes backed up his claim, and Meredith relaxed. Pregnancy was making her a little touchy.

Joel rested a thoughtful gaze on her, before he set the juice down, and punched the speakerphone option on the kitchen telephone. He hit a speed-dial button and waited for his office to answer.

"Etheridge and Associates."

"It's Joel Etheridge. Get Delores for me."

A young intern hurried to comply with the boss's request, and Joel's secretary was connected immediately.

"Good morning, Joel." Delores McGee's pleasant voice filled the kitchen.

"Good morning," he responded briskly. "Listen, Dee, do we know a Janis?"

She hesitated and thought about it. "I don't know," she said slowly. "I don't believe so. We should, though, it's a common enough name. Let me think... "

"Someone named Janis called here this morning. She told Merry that I had her number. I have no idea who it is."

"Yes, but you know how you are, Joel," Delores chided gently. "Someone probably gave you a business card and you tucked it away, and never gave it another thought. Check your billfold."

"That doesn't explain how she got our home number," he grumbled, pulling his wallet out and filtering through various cards. He held one up and looked at it curiously.

"Here's something... Janis Sheridan. That's all. No company or anything. Just a name and number."

Delores repeated the name to herself. She couldn't place it, and it didn't sound even vaguely familiar.

"Sorry, can't help you. Maybe something will come to me later."

"Yeah, think about it. See you in a few." Joel snapped off the phone and further examined the card.

Meredith continued to watch him with less reserve. He felt her eyes on him, and glanced up to find a look in them that was much more like what he was hoping for. He flashed her a smile and opened his arms, like the gates to a place she loved, and she wasted no time hurrying in.

Joel took his time kissing her, then rested his forehead against hers and swayed with her in a gentle dance, so slow, they were almost standing still.

"What's your problem, Missy?" he asked, in a teasing whisper.

"I'm just fat and grumpy." She leaned into him and closed her eyes in quiet bliss.

"You're not fat, you're just packing my boy around." Her husband stroked her stomach softly, before giving her nose a tweak. "But I will accept Grumpy."

"Then you must be Dopey," she goaded.

"Hmmm..." Joel's eyes lingered on her lovely face. "You wanna fight?"

She touched his chin with a delicate fist, then grinned and pulled away. "As a matter of fact, I do. You might pass that along to Janis, when you speak to her."

"I have no intention of speaking to her," he informed her lightly. "I don't chat with women who call the house, and get my old lady all worked up. Delores can field this one."

He coaxed her back into his arms, with little effort. "Want to go out for dinner tonight?"

She twisted her lips in a little grimace that made him laugh.

"Oh, so I'm cooking tonight, then?" he asked.

"You love me, remember?" she countered.

"So I'm cooking tonight, then."

He gave her a kiss to match the last one, drained his juice glass, and headed off to find the rest of his clothes, as Meredith let out a relieved sigh, and decided to show up early in the window seat. This might take a while.

Chapter Three

Darcy pulled her visor down lower over her eyes, and lifted her damp hair up from her hot neck. It was unseasonably warm for April. She was sitting right out in the open, and the sun was blazing, but if she moved to a shade, she wouldn't be able to see the game properly.

She smiled, as Wally came lumbering up the bleachers with a diet soda aimed at her. *That kid is just eaten up with discernment,* she thought, gratefully reaching for the cold can, and holding it to her cheek for a moment.

"Thanks, little buddy! How'd you know I wanted this?"

"Mama said to ask you an' I said, 'Heck, all ya gotta do is look at her sweatin' like a racehorse! 'Course she wants it!' So I just went ahead and brung ya one."

"Pretty sharp, kiddo!" She gave him a fist bump and leaned back against the bleacher bench behind her. A shadow fell over them, and they both looked up to see Darla McIllwain lower herself down on Darcy's other side.

"Hey, girlie!" Darcy patted her leg with a smack. "Why aren't you in the dugout?"

Darla wrinkled her pretty sixteen-year-old nose and smiled sheepishly. "I'm grounded."

Wally gave her a look of frank admiration, and Darcy raised one eyebrow expressively. "What'd you do?"

Darla considered her sneakers contemplatively, as she idly swung her legs back and forth. "I stayed out past curfew."

"Really? How much past?" Darcy watched her face carefully and frowned at her careless shrug. "That's not an answer," she pointed out, in a flat tone.

"Forty-five minutes."

She continued to cover her with a relentless stare.

"Oh, okay," Darla gave in. "An hour and a half."

"And why did you do that?"

"I just got busy and forgot."

Darla received another silent probe. She sighed and flashed Darcy a guilty grin. "So you're not buying it."

"Nope. Peddle it somewhere else," her youth pastor advised blandly.

Wally suffered through this exchange with mounting impatience. "Ain't ya gonna say why ya really did it?"

Darcy gave him a benign smile, and Darla giggled.

"Don't have to," she informed him, with a shake of her blonde head. "Darcy knows, already."

"Well, *I* don't!" he informed her, absently swiping at something that buzzed by him.

"No, and you don't need to know, little one," Darcy murmured. Her eyes warned him to let it go, and he did so with great reluctance. She turned her attention to the field.

Darla sent numerous furtive glances toward her. After a little while, she ventured to lay her head on Darcy's shoulder.

Darcy pursed her lips and looked down at her repentant face. "You stink," she announced firmly, giving Darla another whack on the leg, and focusing once again on the game in progress.

"I know," Darla sighed. "But you love me, anyway."

Darcy hid a faint smile and kept her eyes on the rest of her brood's progress.

Wally calculated them with subtle envy. Before long, he claimed Darcy's other shoulder for himself.

It's only about a million degrees, she thought glumly. She kept hoping this would prove to be an uncomfortable position for her two bookends, but they seemed quite content to remain where they were. She relaxed and willed herself to focus on the game.

By the eighth inning, Wally was snoozing lightly. Darla was daydreaming about Cleston Reed. Darcy was glaring angrily at second base.

She leaped up in a fury, and Wally and Darla greeted each other with a surprise head-on collision. They blinked back and forth in painful confusion, then realized that their post had departed and was storming out onto the field, in heated opposition to the out called on Tommy Spence, one of their best runners.

"Oh, man!" Wally breathed under his breath.

Darla corrected him, sagely. "You mean, 'Take heed, oh man!' Decker's out for justice, and she means to have it!"

Wally hopped up and ran down to the fence in front of the bleachers, with Darla hot on his heels. They leaned into the meshed wire, and strained their ears to hear what was being said. In practically no time at all, straining was completely unnecessary. They could hear just fine.

"He was never tagged!" Darcy was gritting out savagely to the coach of the visiting team, who seemed very pleased with the call.

The man standing next to him, gazing down at her with his arms casually crossed, was next in line for her loud opinion. She didn't know who this yahoo thought he was, but as far as she was concerned, he wasn't much of an umpire!

"Nevertheless, that's the call," he informed her, struggling to keep a straight face, as Darcy nailed him with one assaulting look after another.

"He was never tagged!" she repeated, through clenched teeth. "What are you, deaf and blind? You need prayer, Jack?"

"My name's not Jack and yes, I think prayer might be in order, just now." He abandoned restraint, and grinned down lazily on her pretty face, while Darcy narrowed her eyes with cool hostility.

"Well, while you're at it, pray for intelligence and integrity, 'cause if you call *that* a tag, you're either an idiot, or a cheat!" She spun around on one heel and marched off the field, a heroine to be admired by one team, and an impressive force to be reckoned with, by the other.

The target of her disdain watched her make her exit, with an amused twinkle in his eyes. He clapped his hands with a single loud pop and moved off to the sidelines. "Play ball!"

Darcy stayed just inside the fence for the remainder of the game, a visible warning to the man still finding this funny to not make any more sloppy calls. Her face took on a stoic cast and lifted into only the faintest smile, when her kids won by two runs.

She passed her adversary on her way to the car and deliberately changed her course to avoid him, to his secret regret. He was hoping for another sparring match.

Darcy waited for Wally, who insisted on riding home with her. As she drove in that direction, a cool shower and a hot meal loomed hopefully at the helm of all things.

"Man, Deck, you sure hammered that wise-guy umpire!" Wally's face was wreathed in respect and affection.

Darcy hadn't reckoned on this! She hadn't reckoned on anything, she had just spilled out onto the field, with no thought as to what kind of example she was setting for her kids.

"Wally, what I did was dumb," she began, in an attempt to mop up her mess.

"No way!" her staunch supporter insisted.

"No, listen," she said. "I've always been too competitive in almost everything I've ever done. Tennis, basketball, track meet... no matter what. I've always gotten hung up on winning, and forgot to enjoy myself. This was just a game. It didn't really matter about the tag. I just got so caught up in winning, that I didn't stop to think, and I said a lot of things I'm sorry for."

Wally glanced up at her with a shrewd expression in his big brown eyes. "Would you be sorry you said 'em, if we didn't win?"

His wise question stung Darcy, and she flinched a little.

"Good one, Wally," she replied softly. "Probably not as sorry... but still sorry. Know why?"

He shook his head and waited.

"Holy Spirit. I might have ticked Him off, acting like that. Well," she corrected her theology, "maybe not ticked off, but I wasn't acting like Jesus. I can tell by this rock in my stomach."

She caught Wally's startled face and laughed. "Not a real rock, sweetie! Just a heavy, sad kind of feeling we all get, when we know we've done something God isn't particularly thrilled with."

Wally let out a loud, empathizing, burst of heavy air.

"Been there, done that?" Darcy shot him a knowing look. He grinned and stared out the window at the passing scenery, without comment.

Darcy studied his handsome little profile thoughtfully. She let him simmer in his own reflections, and they finished the trip home in mutual silence.

Stan and Bett pulled in just behind them. Calvin sent Darcy a teasing grin, as he retrieved his glove from the back floorboard and sauntered toward the house. She had put on quite an exhibition! So had he, for that matter. Not one ball got by him, and Sandy Mott had noticed. He would hear about it at church tomorrow, too. Life was good!

Darcy read his mind and laughed, as he flashed her a peace sign, and moved smoothly through the back door.

Audra strolled over and stood watching Wally signaling Foster Ames through the hedges.

"Darcy, do you know where Wally and Foster have been running off to, lately?" She turned inquisitive, green eyes up to Darcy.

"All I know is that they have some kind of project going on. I told him to leave me out of it." Darcy knew she was being evasive, but she felt uncomfortable saying too much, until she had interviewed Wally, herself. She just couldn't seem to remember to do it.

"Well..." Audra never seemed to speak above a murmur. "I only ask, because he came into the kitchen this morning, smelling like... never mind." She shook her head and headed indoors.

Darcy sent a puzzled look after her. Smelling like what? She shrugged and dismissed Audra's remarks, before wandering over to Stan and Bett, who were clearing out soda cans and chip bags from the car.

"Guys, I just wanna tell you that I'm sorry for blowing my stack at the game. I really am. I don't know what got into me. Well... that's not exactly true."

Stan raised up and furrowed his brow. "You call *that* blowing your stack? Besides, it was a lame call!" He reached back in for more trash.

"Yeah, but it was still a bad example for the kids. I need to be more careful."

Darcy broke off, as she noticed an odd little smile playing around the corners of Bett's mouth. Bett caught her scrutiny and hurried to mask her give-away expression.

"What is it?" Darcy knew it had something to do with her.

"What is what?"

How did she manage such an angelic facade? Darcy regarded her suspiciously. "Oh, come on, Bett, I can tell you're up to something!"

"No, I'm not!" She denied it most convincingly. "I'm really not, honest."

"Then why are you wearing that proverbial cat-dining-on-canary look?"

"I'm not!" She shut the rear car doors and left the rest for her husband. "I just thought you were funny today, that's all." She ambled off with another Mona Lisa smile.

Darcy knew it was more than that but, gossip that Bett was, when she wouldn't spill, she wouldn't spill. Whatever it was, it was obviously worth more to Bett if she sat on it for a while.

Darcy recognized defeat. She gave up and retreated to her apartment, for that cool shower she had been planning. Her scheme also involved a good book, hot chocolate and a grilled cheese sandwich, followed by dipping in and out of a series of catnaps on the living room sofa.

Laura Etheridge laid her bible down on the kitchen table and stared at it blankly. All morning, she had been having the strangest feeling that something just wasn't right. Now, in the late afternoon, she was still under the weight of it.

Try as she would, she couldn't pinpoint anything specific. At first, she thought it was just a mother thing. She called her son, Joel, and was assured that he and Meredith were fine.

Laura had no way of knowing that she might have received a different answer, if she had spoken to Meredith instead of Joel, because whatever it was, Meredith was feeling it, too.

She hung up and called her daughter Iris, in Kentucky. She and her husband, Jack, seemed to be doing well. That wasn't it.

She just couldn't figure it out, but she knew it was something important. Finally, she dialed her fiancé, Gary Brenner, at Covenant Fellowship church. She exchanged pleasantries with Marianne, the secretary, before being put through to Gary's office.

"Laura!" His delight was evident. "Could you tell I was sitting here, thinking about you?"

Laura dimpled at the obvious delight he took in hearing from her. "I've been thinking about you too, Gary. Only in a more practical sense than what you mean."

"Well, not what I was looking for, but I'll take what I can get." He leaned back with a little laugh, and planted his feet on his desk. "What's going on?"

"Have you been... well, feeling anything... I don't know... just anything out of the ordinary, today?"

"Not so much since lunch, but I've had a packed afternoon, with not much time to think about it. This morning was a little odd, though."

Laura caught hold of that. "Odd, how?"

"Oh, nothing really concrete. Just a sort of vague sense of things being a little bit off. I won't dignify the psychic community by calling it a premonition, but you get what I mean."

She sure did!

"Gary, something's going on. I don't mean to sound like some sort of thundercloud prophet, but I just know the enemy's up to something."

Gary reflected on her words soberly. Laura was an intercessor in the true sense. There was nothing flaky or spooky about her. She wasn't into sensationalism, or finding a demon behind every tree. The Holy Spirit was very definitely flagging her attention.

"Are you going to be in this evening?" he asked after a brief pause.

"Sure."

"Well, let's spend some time praying about it. I'll drop by... what time?"

"Come for dinner. Six."

"Okay. If you like, we'll call some of our friends, and invite them over to pray with us, after."

Laura felt a tremendous sense of relief wash over her. It was so good of God to put this man in her life! He never made fun of anything she thought was important, and he always rose to the challenge, when it was time to hit something in prayer.

"That sounds great, Gary."

"Good. I'll see you soon." His response was tender. "Call me, honey, if you need me before then."

"I will. Thanks." Laura rang off, and picked her bible up again. She knew she ought to be thinking about dinner, but this just seemed more important right now.

Chapter Four

Joel Etheridge leaned forward onto his desk, and studied the beautifully framed picture by his telephone. Actually, there was no frame lovely enough to grace the photo inside, but Meredith had finally come up with this one and today, as every day since then, he just could not stop staring at its trophy.

It was one of their wedding pictures. They had been married last April, on the grounds of Andrew Jackson's home, the Hermitage. Their first anniversary was coming up in two weeks, and Joel spent every free moment trying to think up ways to make it special.

He lifted the frame and smiled down at their happy faces. They were standing under one of those gnarled, ancient oaks. Meredith made him think of Shakespeare's Juliet, with her flowing, off-the-shoulder, white gown and the simple coronet of white blossoms in her long, dark hair. She had her hands resting on his lapels, and was gazing up at him, with the same adoring look in her deep gray eyes that she had given him the night she admitted she loved him. No woman had ever managed to arrest Joel's attention, let alone his heart, until this creature came into his life.

Joel silently called down yet another blessing on his associate, Marshall Edwards, and his wife Bobbie, for making that happen. Every moment he lived, he loved this woman a little more.

He would watch her stirring around their home in one of his tee shirts, caught in that awkward stage where their baby was too big for her own shirts, but not yet big enough for a full-blown maternity top, and marvel at his happiness.

They'd had several ultrasounds to check Meredith's progress, and were asked if they wanted to know their baby's gender, but they both felt they didn't need an ultrasound to tell them that Meredith was carrying their son. They were certain. After a few visits, Meredith finally agreed to be told, and the results simply confirmed what they already knew.

Joel put the photo back down, but not before brushing his lips delicately across his bride's breathtaking features. He studied it a moment longer, then sat back with a heavy sigh.

That sweet face had been clouded the past couple of weeks. Meredith claimed that she was feeling good and that nothing was wrong, but Joel knew better. He wished she would talk to him about whatever it was that was bothering her, but she continued to deny any worries and chided him for being too protective. He held back from pressuring her, in case it was a personal thing between her and Father, but if this kept on, he was going to get to the bottom of it.

Delores rapped lightly on his door and stuck her head in. "Joel, I need to take off. Remember, I have a dental appointment?"

He sat up and cleared his throat. "Sure, Dee, go ahead. Is the machine on, or are you going to let the interns field everything?"

"Machine. I have them filing and answering demo submissions." She turned to go, then stopped herself at the door. "Oh, I almost forgot. You remember asking me if I knew a Janis?"

Joel waited expectantly.

"I still can't place her, but one of the girls took a message from her during lunch. She left a different number from the one on that card you found. She called twice, so I called her back myself, and asked her if it was something I could help her with. She didn't seem to appreciate the offer."

Joel frowned impatiently. He didn't have time for people like that.

"She did schedule an appointment. I gave her thirty minutes next Thursday."

"How did that set with her?"

"Actually, she seemed fine with it. And the guys from Surrender are coming in right behind her, so she won't be able to milk the time."

Joel rubbed his temples and gave his secretary a bored look. "Are you coming back today, Dee?"

She grinned charmingly. "Not if my boss really has the big heart they're all talking about. I'm supposed to pick up my grandbabies when I'm done."

"Well, never let it be said that I would try to stand between a she-bear and her grandwhelps."

He laughed quietly, and stood up to stretch. "Go have a good time. In fact, I think I've had just about as much fun here, as I can stand, for one day. I'm going home to let my ornery little wife pick a fight with me. I might even let her win."

"When has she ever lost?" Delores let the door close on her hearty laugh, and Joel gathered up his coat and briefcase and followed her lead.

A long, slender hand stretched across the table for another cigarette, then paused, as if in conflict. Finally, its owner drew it back and chuckled softly to herself.

"I almost forgot," Janis Sheridan droned lazily. "Joel Etheridge is a man of particular tastes and convictions. He won't enjoy a woman who smells of nicotine. And I do so intend for him to enjoy me!"

She crossed over to her dresser mirror and speculated on her reflection. She knew she was a beautiful woman. She had heard that Meredith Etheridge was also a beauty, but she wasn't worried. She studied her ash blonde curls, and her brilliant green eyes with satisfaction.

Her figure had never produced anything but stares from desirous men and envious women, alike, and the low-cut dress she was wearing did little to conceal her curves. She felt quite confident that whatever she decided to have, she would have with no problem, and she had decided to have Joel Etheridge.

Janis moved coolly away from the mirror and picked up the telephone. She quickly punched in a familiar number and listened a moment, before hanging up and rippling with wicked laughter. She had been doing this fairly often, always with the desired effect.

"That's right, little wifey," she crooned. "Another call, another hang-up. Who could it be? Who, indeed?" She paused beside the window of her hotel suite, and looked down at the Nashville city streets, a strange light in her sultry eyes.

"Funny, how that never occurs when hubby happens to be home, isn't it? I'm sure that must seem a little odd."

Her voice took on a placid, hypnotic quality. "Pay attention, little wife. Keep a close eye on that handsome husband of yours, or someone might just spirit him away."

She continued to watch the scene below her window with fixed concentration, a strange smugness enveloping her, as she focused on the area of the city where she knew the offices of Etheridge and Associates were located.

She was more than a little put out, that his nosy secretary had the nerve to call, when she knew, good and well, it was Joel Etheridge, himself, that she wanted to speak to. It further galled her that the woman had given her a scant thirty minutes for a so-called appointment, but she would make good use of the time. That much was certain.

She turned at the sharp knock on her door, and strolled toward it with a fluid movement, not unlike a snake. Her eyes narrowed, as she opened it and admitted a large, bearded man and his older and smaller male companion.

"You're early," she observed, moving away and leaving them to close the door. "It's an annoying habit, Warren, sweetheart, that I do wish you'd overcome."

The portly, red-haired man smiled sardonically at her complaint. "And why, pray tell, is that? It certainly doesn't look as if we're interrupting anything."

Janis fixed him with an icy glare. "A situation that will soon be remedied."

He laughed outright and threw himself heavily into a chair, after first noting that the other man had seated himself. "Yes, well, not to underestimate your powers of persuasion, my dear, but you must admit that Joel Etheridge isn't exactly a playboy, with a bad marriage, and too much time on his hands."

"His moral fortitude and marital bliss are of no real consequence to me. He can drape himself in all the sanctimonious garb he wishes but, when everything is reduced to the lowest common denominator, all men are exactly the same."

She leaned seductively close and smiled at Warren Patrick's struggle to remain unaffected. "You're all after the same thing, aren't you, my love?"

Warren's taciturn colleague seemed to be not only oblivious to Janis's charms, but instead, regarded her with a bleak detachment that was unnerving. He had witnessed this gaudy display with little more than bored tolerance, and now cast a look at both of them, which commanded their silence.

"Is this some kind of game to you, Miss Sheridan?" he asked, with a quiet sneer in his voice.

She sat down on the sofa and gauged him cautiously, as he regarded her with subtle contempt.

"Because, if it is, let me assure you I will not tolerate losing. Every game has its rules and you'd better learn the rules for this one, and learn them well."

He gave her a mocking eye and noted her uneasiness. "So, morals and marriage are of no consequence to you, is that correct? Then you, Miss Sheridan, are a fool!"

"Oliver..." she began, in a placating tone.

He held up his hand to check whatever she had been about to say. "A fool, my dear Janis! Are you so enamored with yourself, that you think this man will simply turn his back on everything he has committed to, and come when you call? Is that what you believe?"

Janis found herself actually fidgeting with nervous self-consciousness, a sensation that was something foreign and distasteful to her. Sharp words of counterattack leapt to her tongue, but she choked them off with an effort.

It was never wise to anger Oliver Sullivan. He was a powerful warlock and the one to whom their coven made obeisance. She clenched her fingers together and waited mutely for him to finish.

Oliver gestured curtly toward the bar and Warren moved quickly to get him the drink he wanted. He leaned back into his chair and studied Janis Sheridan with a veiled expression, waiting to pursue the matter until he received his scotch. Janis shook her head at the one Warren held out to her, and he kept it for himself and settled back down.

"Allow me to enlighten you," Oliver resumed smoothly. "Joel Etheridge is one of these 'born agains'. Do you understand that expression? I know you are familiar with the terminology, but do you understand the full implications of it? It is apparent that you do not. Men like Joel Etheridge have been schooled to resist women like you. If you persist in approaching him with that Mae West thing you're trying, he will not only bolt like lightening, but you will have failed miserably. Janis, my little pet... " He leaned forward and eyed her menacingly. "Do not fail. That will not please me."

Janis licked her dry lips and tried to meet his eyes. "What do you suggest?"

"I suggest that the best way to fly with the ducks is to look like a duck, quack like a duck and, for all intents and purposes, be a duck. Do we understand each other?" he asked pointedly.

She nodded in wordless agreement.

"Fine." He drained his glass and stood up. "Warren!" Warren hurried to his feet and moved to open the door.

Oliver Sullivan paused and viewed Janis Sheridan through ominous slits, a dangerous smile on his lips. "Let me add this observation, that you will do well to heed. The way to insert yourself between Etheridge and his wife is not to make an enemy of her, not overtly, at least. That's not how these two operate. If you alienate one, the other quickly moves to defend and protect. Sweet, isn't it?" He gave a derisive smirk.

"You must somehow manage to make her seem to be overly emotional, an easy task in her condition. Meanwhile, you should appear to everyone else to be a decent, forthright woman with no hidden agenda, an innocent target of the wife's gestational hysteria."

He fastened her with a crude eye and appraised her slowly and deliberately. "I will continue to monitor your progress with interest. Goodnight, dear Miss Sheridan."

Janis sat staring at the door for quite some time, after the two men had taken their leave. She pushed back the rebellious thoughts that clamored to her brain, and made an effort to think clearly.

There was certainly no love lost between herself and Oliver Sullivan, but she was forced to admit that he was right. Perhaps calling the house and setting Meredith Etheridge off had not been too well thought out. It did seem that these Christian couples more or less fused more tightly together, when their relationships were openly threatened.

It could be that she had been too premature in creating enmity between herself and Joel Etheridge's wife. They were still essentially newlyweds and, if she complained, Joel would probably do whatever it took to pacify her, especially now that she was carrying his child.

Janis's eyes took on an ugly gleam. That was another issue. The last thing she wanted was for a baby to bond these two even closer. It would not suit her purposes at all for this child to be born.

Of course, that was not a major concern to Oliver. His focus was solely on shutting down Meredith Etheridge. She had long generated a stir, not just among the Christian community but out amid the secular ranks, as well. A diverse sector from street people to professionals adored her, and her music influenced a large populace who would never darken a church door. Oliver Sullivan had determined to put an end to that influence, but in order to take her down, the bond with her husband must be severed.

It was Janis who had been selected to enter the situation and maneuver things, in order to make that happen. Meredith's husband was of no interest to Oliver, once his guard was breached. She, however, considered Joel Etheridge the spoils of war and had determined that she should and would have him. He would fit her own private agenda just fine.

No, the initial phone call may have been unwise but still, since it was done, perhaps she could work with it.

She allowed herself a satisfied smile, as she crossed the room and opened a small box beside the bed. She fingered the amulet inside almost reverently, and lit the ornate candle beside it. It was time to enlist some outside help. Her eyes filled with ghoulish excitement, as she began to repeat the smothered words she was hearing inside her head.

Joel let himself in the front door and glanced around a moment, before looking over at the window seat, where his wife huddled in a little mound, her eyes closed, and the remains of now dried tears on her cheeks.

He waited a moment, unsure of whether or not to approach her. She prayed in the window seat often, and he didn't like to intrude on her time with Father. Yet, this looked different, somehow. His instinct told him that this was not a normal prayer time.

He hesitated only a second more, then put his things on the couch and quietly came over.

"Merry?"

She let out a breath, but didn't otherwise indicate that she'd heard him.

"Sweetheart." Joel frowned and sat down on the edge, reaching to lift her hair back so that he could see her face. She slowly opened her eyes and focused on him.

"Baby, what is it?"

She continued to stare at him for a moment, before looking away at nothing, outside the window.

He caught her chin with one finger and gently turned her face back to his.

"Can I do anything, Missy?" he whispered.

Meredith made a valiant effort, and came up with the semblance of a smile. "It's just a thing."

"Just a thing?" He'd been reading various books written for expectant parents, and this did seem right in line with the type of depression brought on by hormonal changes, that a few authors had touched on. Still, this felt less about depression and more about pure sadness. He smiled back and laid a kiss on her forehead. "Are you sure?"

"Yep. Just a thing." She sat up straight and shook off whatever it was, making more room for him on the cushion next to her. Joel took her up on her invitation and she leaned against him, just glad to be near him.

"I've missed you," she admitted quietly.

"That's why I'm not going to the office tomorrow," her husband answered, his gentle tone covering up the concern that creased his brow. "I've missed you, too."

Meredith turned and looked up at him with hungry eyes. "Really, Mister Man? You're staying home?"

"With my baby. My babies."

Meredith pulled his arms closer and rested for the first time that day. They sat that way for a long while, before she turned her face up to his and gave him a pleading look.

"What is it, honey?" He looked down, with his heart in his eyes.

"Could we... change our phone number?" She said it a little nervously, but there, she said it!

Joel took on a somber expression and his eyes became question marks. "Why?"

"Just... never mind."

"Does this have anything to do with that woman calling here?" He knew that it did. When he saw her next Thursday, he intended to let her have it!

Meredith looked down at her hands, something she always did when she was feeling helpless.

Joel cupped her face tenderly and searched it with loving eyes. "If that's what you want, that's what we'll do. I love you, and I want you happy."

"And can we move the answering machine downstairs?"

"We can do anything you want, little one. You're my sweetheart."

Two big tears slid past her long lashes and fell heavily onto his hands. He gathered her up protectively, and murmured quiet things into her ear.

He would have held her that way for hours, but his son had different ideas. He made a lunge that caught his dad neatly in the ribs. Joel drew back astonished.

Meredith's tears instantly changed to laughter, when she saw the look on his face. Joel had been spending an unusual amount of time at the office and, when he was home, their baby seemed to deliberately play 'possum. It was his first time to feel his child move, and her heart began to fill up with his joy.

Chapter Five

Darcy stood up on the church bus, and yelled for quiet. It took a while, but everyone eventually piped down low enough for her to be heard.

"You know how this works," she called loudly. "It's your basic roll call, so let's just do it and get it over with. I need a head count, in case someone loses theirs, before we get back!"

She held up a notebook and start belting out the usual roster.

"Ginger Ames! Kendall Black! Hayden Creed! Portia Glenn! Audra Greer! Calvin Greer! Michael Kirkland! Paul Kirkland!"

She looked up after each name, to make sure the kids weren't covering for anyone by answering to someone else's name. "Darla McIllwain!" Her face took on a disturbed expression as Darla failed to respond.

"Ethan Miller! Sandy Mott!" She grinned at the pleased smile on Calvin's face, and plowed ahead. "Sam Nethery! Cleston Reed!"

Her frown returned, as she received no response, other than muffled giggles throughout the bus. "Lonnie Sanders! Susan Spence! Tommy Spence! Jae Vincent! Todd Walker! Drew Watson! Randall Young!"

Darcy put down her list and fixed a probing eye on the group. "Does anyone..." She stopped herself. Better not get everybody started on why Darla and Cleston were both not here.

She turned and smiled at Faron Waldrop, who had volunteered to drive the bus to the district youth rally. "Guess that's all. Ready to roll?"

He grinned and slowly eased out onto the highway, as she took a seat just behind him. They drove along for several minutes before she looked up, surprised to see Audra settling down beside her.

"Can I talk to you a minute, Deck?" she asked timidly.

"Sure, honey. What's on your mind?" She still hadn't talked to Wally yet, so she hoped it wasn't about his secret enterprise.

"It's about Darla." Audra paused before adding unnecessarily, "And Cleston." She raised her pretty green eyes to Darcy's in silent entreaty .

"Are you keeping a secret?" Darcy asked quietly.

She nodded, obviously miserable. "It's getting harder to do, but I promised."

"And you don't want me to try and guess," she said knowingly.

"I wouldn't tell you if you did guess. You know that, Deck." Audra's demeanor was too old and tired, for such a beautiful seventeen-year-old.

"I know." She waited a moment, while Audra sorted out how she wanted to handle this.

"This is all I can say," she finally ventured. "Darce, you need to go see her. Say you can tell there's something wrong, and ask if you can help. Maybe she'll volunteer to tell you. She'll have to, sooner or later," she mumbled sadly. "She needs to talk to someone, and it should be you."

"She can't go to her parents?"

"She won't. Not with this."

Darcy studied Audra's troubled countenance, and reached over and squeezed her hand. "Okay, baby doll. I'll call her tomorrow, and see if we can get together. She'll never know we talked. How's that?"

Her face brightened instantly.

"That's great." She seemed genuinely relieved, as she rose to head back to her seat. "Thanks, Deck."

Darcy gave her a companionable wink. "No worries."

She settled down into her seat and pondered on Audra's words, for the remainder of the short trip to Murfreesboro, the neighboring town where the youth rally was being held. She started out of her deep reflections, as she noticed the church parking lot, ahead.

"Okay, hoodlums!" She stood up and turned around, blocking the exit with her small, but imposing form. "If you start acting like a bunch of deranged hicks, 'A', I don't know you and 'B', you're walking back to Smyrna. You got that?"

A wave of laughter spread through the group, even though not one of them doubted she would make good on her threat.

"There's food in the fellowship hall, after the service. Thirty minutes of that, and we're on the bus. All of us who plan to ride, that is!" Darcy gave them a last warning look, and stepped out to wait for them down on the ground.

They crowded into the building. and settled into a section of pews, just minutes before the service began, to wait impatiently for the main reason they came. Jae Vincent, one of their gang, was doing the special music. Every month's rally featured talent from the district's youth and Jae had been invited to sing tonight.

She stepped up to the microphone nervously, then caught the encouraging looks her buddies were sending her, and launched into her song, as confidently as if she were singing in the shower. Meredith Etheridge had spent several minutes one evening, praising her ability, and she had really pursued her singing with a vengeance after that. It paid off tonight. She simply floored everybody, then meekly took her seat, a shy smile playing around her mouth. She looked around for Darcy's mute validation and promptly received it, to her delight.

Darcy leaned back into her seat, and made a mental note to say something to her after the service. She looked up curiously, as she realized the guest speaker was being introduced. She had forgotten, until now, that it would be the new state youth director. She scanned the audience to see if she could detect Les Chapman's successor but her vision was limited, so she relaxed. She'd find out soon enough.

Pastor Todd finished his glowing introduction, and Neil McCallen rose and approached the podium. Darcy drew in her breath sharply and stared, as her group began softly gasping and snickering. It was the softball official she had blasted, a couple of weeks ago!

She closed her eyes in a quick, silent prayer. "God, You'd better go ahead and get started on forgiving me, 'cause I intend to kill Bett Greer, when I get home!"

She opened her eyes, unable to grasp a word the speaker said. All she could manage was a grim set to her jaw, and a smoldering look, that only briefly squelched her kids' glee. She wished her seat had one of those ejection buttons, like she had seen when she watched cartoons with Wally. She'd launch herself into another hemisphere.

Neil's eyes casually embraced his audience, as he chatted informally with the kids and their pastors. His gaze wandered past Darcy and quickly returned. A glimmer of amusement flickered just slightly over his face, as he managed to keep his composure and continue with ease.

Darcy scowled inwardly at what she perceived to be conceited gall. She hurriedly chastised herself. After all, she didn't know for sure if he was conceited, or not. He was probably a nice enough person. He just wouldn't know a softball, if it split his head open!

He seemed to have an endless supply of fascinating stories, and a quick wit that held his entire audience captive, or rather, everyone but Darcy.

Dear Lord in Heaven, how long was she gonna have to sit here? She looked up from checking her watch and stiffened, as he glanced her way with a provocative grin. He was deliberately goading her! Fine, then! Her first instinct had been to wait on the bus for the kids after the service, but she was never one to back down from a challenge, and he was definitely issuing one.

"Alright, buddy," she muttered under her breath. "Just wrap this thing up, and let's get it over with."

He must have read her mind, because he chose that moment to curtail his remarks and genially turned the pulpit back over to the pastor.

Pastor Todd came forward while leading the congregation in a round of applause, as Neil reclaimed his seat. He made several announcements, including a quick reminder about refreshments following the service, and called for a closing song, before giving the benediction.

Darcy was immediately surrounded by her entire troop, all talking at once. She hurried to quiet them down, then leaned into a sort of huddle with them.

"First, I want to say that you, Jae, were excellent! I've never heard you sound better. You're gonna go places with that voice, someday." The others echoed her sentiments but it was evident that this is not what any of them wanted to talk about, including Jae.

Darcy rolled her eyes, and dropped her voice even lower.

"Alright, listen good, because I'm only going to say this once. I've already told you guys that I'm not proud of what I did at the game. I said some stupid things and I'm sorry. I know you all think this is hilarious, having the same umpire I lit into, wind up being the state youth director. Ha, *ha!* Now, we've all had a good laugh. I'm sure I'll end up handing out apologies like Halloween candy tonight, so can you just make things a little easier by dropping it, and running off like good little boys and girls, for the next thirty minutes?"

She received some smothered giggles and a generous amount of hushed ribbing, as they made their way to the dining area.

"Thirty minutes!" she called after them, with a touch of 'don't make me come after you' in her voice. She bent down to pick up a forgotten jacket and her own belongings, and straightened up to find Neil McCallen grinning down at her.

"Which one of us goes first?" he asked, apparently getting a kick out of watching her fumble for poise.

She discarded insincere attempts at civility and leveled a look of pure annoyance at him. "Why don't we just sit here and pray for the rapture? That way, everybody goes first."

"Everybody, but us." He smiled in a way that would have been particularly attractive, if Darcy would have admitted it. "They won't let you and me go, until we patch up our differences. Come on, let's 'hiss' and make up."

She tried in vain not to smile. He lifted one brow in a comical fashion, and she actually gave way to a laugh.

"Oh goody, now we get to blend in with all the other sheep!" He gave her a flash of even white teeth, contrasted by a dark tan, and wheat-colored hair that came down in unruly curls, just past his collar. There was a hint of fun in his brown eyes, as he swiftly appraised her and liked what he saw.

"Tell me something. I'm sure I'm walking on thin ice here, but do you *play* softball, as well as you call it? And pull those claws in, I come in peace."

"I wouldn't pick out a place for my Nobel prize just yet, if I were you." Darcy advised him sweetly. "And my folks have a wall lined with trophies that say that, while I'm no threat to the St. Louis Cardinals, I'm also no slouch."

"Impressive! And these would be trophies for actually participating in the game, not... officiating?"

"He was never tagged!" Darcy shot him a look of open belligerence.

"No, let's don't go there, again." Neil chuckled at her irritated tinge of color. "Because I'd like to ask a favor, and I wouldn't feel comfortable asking you, if you're still miffed at me."

"Well, by all means, we want you *comfortable*, Mr. McCallen!"

"I hope we're still a little young for that Mister and Miss thing. I mean, if every kid in the state is calling me Neil, you'd sound a little funny grinding out 'Mr. McCallen' every time we run into each other. And I do believe you would grind it out like cornmeal!"

She smiled faintly and looked away. "What's the favor?"

"I want to meet with every youth pastor in this district before the end of the month. Since Smyrna is so close, I'd like to start with you. May I call you in a few days and see what your calendar looks like?"

Darcy hesitated then shrugged. "Guess so. As long as we don't talk about sports."

He shook his head and gravely presented a three-finger salute. "On my honor as a former scout!"

"I might have known," she replied dryly. "I'll be in the office every morning next week, from eight-thirty until around ten-forty, and then in the afternoon, from four until six."

Neil gave her a look of mild surprise. "Kind of odd hours."

"I have to work a part-time job, during the day and on Saturday. It'll probably be a little while, before I can afford to go on staff in a full-time position."

His eyes sobered. "Well, I hope that can happen soon. Those kids seem to depend heavily on you, and you can be much more effective if you can relax in one position, rather than struggle to keep up with two. I didn't mean anything derogatory by that," he added hastily, as he caught her defensive look. "I just think that maybe it would be to the state board's advantage to offer a little assistance in the area of finances. That's all."

She was a little taken aback by that last comment. "That... I wouldn't expect them to just dole out money to me. They don't even know me."

"That's their loss," he said lightly. "Besides, they don't have to know every one personally, within their denomination, to be of assistance when there's a real need, especially a need that they're quite capable of meeting."

His attention was distracted by someone motioning to him at the rear of the auditorium. He waved and nodded. "Pastor Wilkes," he explained, looking back down to catch her studying him closely.

He smiled as she dropped her eyes and pretended to look around for anything she might be leaving.

"Your name's Darcy, isn't it?"

She glanced up in sudden awareness that they had not formally introduced themselves. "Sorry about that. Yes. Darcy Decker."

"Darcy Decker. I like that. It's sort of musical."

"Well, *I'm* not," she declared. "Maybe my parents were hoping to inspire me, but it didn't work."

"Well, Darcy Decker, I'm afraid I promised Steve Wilkes I'd get with him after the service. He seems a little impatient to hold me to that, so I should probably make my way over to him, before he starts jogging in place." He rested eyes on her that still held a faint trace of teasing. "If we have to agree on that call, before we can be friends, then I concede completely, and beg your forgiveness."

Darcy said nothing and he stooped just a little, to get slightly below her eye level. and peered up at her in exaggerated pleading. She twisted her mouth in a reluctant smile and made him laugh.

"Fine." She shook her head. "You stand forgiven, so if you miss the Rapture, don't come whining to me."

"Oh, so you'll still be here!"

She tilted her head back and gazed at the ceiling in mock distress. "Probably, since you're the second person tonight I've considered murdering."

"Oh really, who's the first?" Neil was completely enjoying himself.

"You'll just have to read about it in tomorrow's paper, like everyone else," she returned sarcastically.

He chuckled, then looked at her quietly. "This is better. I've enjoyed meeting you, Darcy."

"Okay, I'll admit it. You're not as bad as I thought."

"I'll take it!" He gave her hand a quick squeeze and nodded toward the foyer. "Don't look now, but your passel of young 'uns is checking to see how we're doing. Try to look mad at me, that'll fix 'em!" He grinned at her peevish expression. "I'll give you a call, Darcy, sometime next week."

Darcy returned his wave and moved to gather her group. If all they had to do was spy on her, then they didn't deserve a full thirty minutes!

During the trip home, she was able to put a lid on their meddling questions and before long, they lapsed into texting, quiet conversations with each other, or else drifted off into little cat naps.

The bus finally pulled into the church parking lot and the kids either joined up with waiting parents, or began pulling out car keys and driving off in various directions.

Audra and Calvin piled in with Darcy, and were careful not to tease her, even though they swapped furtive smiles and knowing glances.

They didn't bother saying goodnight when she stopped in the driveway, because it went without saying that she fully intended to come in with them. They led the way in with a warning grin to their mother, who quickly busied herself looking for some imaginary thing she just had to have, that was supposedly in the lower cabinets.

"The jig's up, Bett!" Darcy planted herself on a barstool, then leaned way over the snack bar to glare down at her buried head. "Come on out of there, you blonde ostrich!"

Bett wrestled with herself not to laugh, and crawled out of her sanctuary with forced perplexity. "What?"

"Oh yeah, what! Like you don't know!"

She gave up the fight, and slipped into a happy little giggle. Darcy opened her eyes wide and stared at her, in a mixture of fun and frustration.

"That's why you were grinning, like a possum eating fire ants, after that game! You knew, the whole time, that I was out there yelling, like a stepmother, at the new state youth director, of all people, and you never said a word!"

Bett began laughing out loud and on purpose, wiping her eyes, as Wally came in to investigate all the commotion.

"I'm sorry, Darce!" She pulled up a stool and joined her. "I probably should have but... " She went off again, then gained some composure. "I just had to see your face! It was kinda bad to do, I know."

"*Kinda* bad, did you say? And what about the Grand Canyon, Bett? Would you say that's *kinda* deep? Would you say Niagara Falls is *kinda* wet?"

"What is it?" Wally demanded, eager to be in the middle of it.

"Nothing really, pet." Audra smiled and began foraging in the refrigerator for something to snack on.

"That was the new state youth director Deck was pouncing on, at the game," Calvin informed him, in spite of his sister's disparaging look. "You should've seen her face when they introduced the speaker tonight, and it was him!" He joined his mother's revived hooting, and Wally grinned in relish.

"Oh fine," Darcy mumbled, sliding off the stool and clomping toward the back door. She stopped and looked back at Bett with a pointed expression. "Should I call Wanda Todd, or did you want to do that, yourself?"

Her sarcastic query was met with a quartet of howls, as she rolled her eyes and headed for the comforts of an apartment full of inanimate objects, that probably wouldn't laugh at her.

Chapter Six

Neil McCallen waited until he was sure she was off the phone, then tapped lightly on the door.

Darcy raised her head in surprise. She thought she had the church all to herself today. Pastor Frank was in Nashville, and Freida had the day off.

"Come in," she called, quickly switching from curiosity to astonishment, as the door opened.

"Interrupting?" he asked, pausing with a pleasant smile.

"Uh... no," Darcy stammered. "I'm just... I thought you were going to call."

"Well, I was, and I probably should have, but I was headed to Antioch, and I thought I'd just pop in and see if I could catch you." Neil closed the door, and gestured toward a chair with a silent request.

"Oh, sure, grab a seat," she agreed quickly. "I'm sorry."

"No worries." He slid into the chair and gave her a friendly grin. "Darcy Decker, would you please explain to me why all these Tennessee towns are named right out of the Good Book? Antioch, Smyrna, Lebanon, Carthage, Calvary, Bethlehem... too many to be a coincidence, don't you think?"

She smiled and shrugged. "Maybe, but the scale is balanced by some pretty bizarre ones, as well. There's Yell, Bucksnort, Bitter End, Nameless..." She laughed at his surprised face. "And probably the most depressing name for a Tennessee town ever, Defeated."

"You've obviously applied yourself to this topic, before," he replied, with a sage nod.

Darcy inspected him with interest. "Are you not from Tennessee, then, Mr.... Neil?"

"Why, no, Miss... Darcy," he volleyed back. "No, I'm from Florida originally, then I became a long-time transplant in Illinois. I've lived in Tennessee before, but only sporadically, so far."

She nodded slowly. "I should have guessed."

"Why's that?"

"Well, your accent is... you really don't have one. Not one you'd expect from a Tennessee native, anyway."

"*You* have an attractive little twang, though," he observed. "You've kicked up Tennessee dust for quite a few years, haven't you?"

"Quite a few."

He ran a fingertip lightly around the chair arm with a little smile, and nodded. "So, tell me how things are going in the juvenile department."

Darcy looked down at her fingers and pretended to find a problem with a nail that needed immediate attention.

Neil watched her quietly." Is that not something we can talk about?"

She hesitated, then got up and reopened the door he had closed.

Understanding swept across his face. "I'm sorry, Darcy. I wasn't thinking."

"No, that's okay, I just don't want to create a breeding ground for gossip." She gestured carelessly at the door, as if to dismiss it, then raised her eyes and showed him a troubled countenance.

"Really, the truth is that I want to be able to see anyone who comes down the hall, while we're talking. About your question... well, Les Chapman and I never really got into what goes on here, in a little town like Smyrna, and I guess I'm just not used to having the state office take a real interest."

"Get used to it," he suggested softly.

She studied him for a moment, before returning to her seat and leaning across her desk to face him squarely.

"Neil, don't ask, unless you're willing to really listen. I do need to talk about something, so I'm not into rhetorical questions, just now."

"I didn't ask you one."

Darcy really did want to unburden herself, and having someone who was not part of this local body, and who was offering a listening ear, was just too tempting. Besides, she reasoned silently, it was part of his job.

She picked up a cassette tape and began to toy with it, turning one of the wheels with her fingertip as she mentally structured her remarks. Neil raised his brows in surprise, since he hadn't seen a cassette in quite some time, but made no comment.

"I don't have a large crew to oversee," Darcy began slowly. "Only about twenty or so. I should be able to keep a good eye on things, even with a second job."

"Someone fall through the cracks?" Neil asked, after a lengthy pause.

She looked away and nodded, her eyes bright and watery.

"One of my girls has been seeing a boy in our group for several months, now. It's not the first time she's liked a guy at church and at first, I wasn't too concerned. She's never given me any reason to be, before. The boy is a great guy, too. It's not as if he really doesn't love the Lord, and he's only here to check out the babes."

She indulged in a deep breath to steady herself. "Anyway, she started getting into trouble with her parents. She couldn't play in the game at Laverne a few weeks ago, because she was grounded for breaking curfew with him. Neither one of them showed up for the rally last Friday night. I finally cornered her yesterday at church, and made her talk to me."

She held Neil's eyes with a direct gaze. "She thinks she's pregnant."

He showed no reaction, other than to shift his position in the chair. Darcy lowered her eyes and stared blankly at the cassette she had managed to destroy with her nervous fingers.

"I hope that wasn't anything important," Neil said, eyeing it with faint amusement.

She blinked and looked up in consternation. "It was! It was a master copy of yesterday's sermon!"

She had to laugh out loud at his look of disbelief. "I'm afraid Pastor Frank is still not quite ready to move into this century. Cassettes are about all he can handle. Freida just burns them onto CDs. We've stopped trying to change him, for now, and we don't even dare bring up the subject of live-streaming but, sooner or later, he'll have to admit that computers and MP3s are not just fads."

He reached out and took the cassette from her with one hand, gathering up several feet of pulled out tape with the other. "Let me see what I can do," he said, giving her a teasing glance.

He took a pencil from her desktop and used it to begin methodically spooling the tape back onto the wheels, before returning to their conversation.

"Darcy, are you feeling like you should have somehow known that these kids were having a physical relationship? Are you taking on the responsibility for it?"

"Oh, I don't know," she mumbled, resting her chin in her hands. "I don't know what to think. I also don't know if she would have come to me on her own, if I hadn't approached her, and that bothers me."

He nodded. "I can understand that. And you may never know the answer for sure, so you just have to get away from it, and not let it do a number on you. As far as the girl is concerned, what happens next?"

"I've asked her to talk to her parents. She won't, of course. She says she's taking a home pregnancy test today at school, and that she'll call me with the results." Darcy leaned back, and fastened him with a look of uncertainty.

"Neil, I know something this serious about this girl, while her own parents have no clue. And it would absolutely floor them! How do I handle it? Do I talk to them about it and have her hate me, and never trust me again? Or do I just keep on encouraging her to go to them? And what about the boy's parents?"

Her genuine distress tugged at his heart. He weighed his answer carefully. "Darcy, these parents are entrusting you with their children's care and spiritual influence. One of the reasons there's a need for youth pastors, in the first place, is because society seems to dictate a natural chasm between teenagers and their parents, and a third party is often sought to fill it. In this case, that would be you. Yes, so far?"

She took the newly mended tape he offered without even looking at it, and slid it into her drawer, her eyes never leaving his face as she slowly nodded.

"You can't knowingly allow parents to remain in the dark, when an issue is this serious. These are not just moms and dads, they are suddenly prospective grandparents. They have a right to know."

He read her face and leaned forward to continue. "I'm not saying to go behind these kids' backs. I'm saying to call them in here, regardless of the test results, and inform them that you are giving them a chance to come clean with their parents about the nature of their relationship, or that you will assume it's okay with them if you do it, yourself. Knowing that these two are having sexual relations, and saying nothing about it is a breach of trust, not only to their parents, but to the kids."

Neil moved to the edge of his seat and riveted Darcy with somber eyes. "Those of us who work with youth can so easily fall into that trap where we want them to like us. But we don't gain their respect by going along with their bad decisions, and not rocking the boat, in order to be thought of as 'cool.' We do that by having a clear set of convictions that we maintain, regardless of the opinions of the media or society. Kids want a 'constant' in their lives, Darcy."

A light seemed to turn on in Darcy's eyes. "I know you're right."

"I know you do," he said simply.

She gave him a bright smile. "That's how it is, then. I don't look forward to it, but I know that's the way to go."

He returned her smile. "Good. And I wish you'd give me a call and let me know how this thing plays out.

"Touching on something else, let's go back to that guilt issue we talked about earlier. You mentioned feeling that you should have seen this coming, even holding down two jobs. I want to talk a little more about the possibility of getting some financial assistance to allow you to focus on this office more." He casually surveyed her. "That is, if this is your preference and priority."

"It really is, but this is a small church. It's full of potential, but potential doesn't pay the bills. It's also full of some great kids," she added, with feeling.

"I could see that Friday night. I could also see how these great kids feel about their youth pastor. Which is why I've decided to meet with the state office's financial board. I want to see about initiating funds to assist this church in providing you with a decent enough salary to keep you more visible, and available to these kids."

He grinned at the way she widened her blue eyes. "Do I have your permission to plunge ahead?"

"Well... sure, if you feel this is something you want to pursue."

"I most certainly do." Neil glanced down at his watch and stood up regretfully. "I wish we could just sit here and make a day out of it, Darcy, but I've got that Antioch thing, and then another appointment in Franklin."

"You're a man about town, aren't you?" She pushed her chair back and moved ahead of him through the door and down the hallway to the foyer.

"Well, I've never been one to just sit around," he admitted. "Sometimes, the best medicine is to stay busy."

"Medicine?" Darcy quizzed him with a quick glance.

Neil met her eyes steadily, as he reached inside his lapel pocket for a business card and an ink pen. "Scratch that last comment."

He flipped the card over and scrawled a set of numbers on the back. "My cell and home phone," he explained. "I really do want to know how this situation with the kids turns out. Give me a call?"

"Sure." She took the card and tucked it away in her jeans pocket. "Thanks."

"I'll be in after six. Remind me when you call, I had some other things I wanted to ask, or we can set up an appointment for that, later."

He pushed the heavy glass door open and turned to scan her briefly. "Are you sure you're okay, Darcy, with all this?"

"I'm fine. Really," she added, as he raised his brows in question.

"Okay. Then I'm off to impress a bunch of suits." He grinned at her laughter and tossed her a brief wave. "Call me!"

Darcy watched him drive away, before she remembered that she hadn't thanked him for fixing the sermon tape. She turned and wandered back to her office thoughtfully.

There was a new peace settling over her, just within the last few minutes. Maybe it was the fact that Neil McCallen had shared a lot of wisdom with her. Revelation has a way of clearing obstruction so rapidly when it comes, that it can leave a person in a tranquil, almost dream-like state. She sank back down at her desk, and pondered not only his words, but also the manner in which he shared them with her.

She tinged with renewed embarrassment at the way she had practically assaulted him a few weeks ago. Boy, had she ever pegged him wrong! Neil McCallen was turning out to be not only a pretty good sport, but a valued counselor, as well. Maybe even a good friend.

Delores yanked up her telephone a little clumsily, as the pile of papers she was balancing began to slide forward.

"Yes! Hang on, honey!" She cradled the receiver against her shoulder and raked her stack back into order. "Okay, Monica, I'm back."

Her mouth twitched with impatience, as she listened to the intern on the line. She let out a sigh. "Okay, honey, just have her come on in."

She laid the receiver back down and rested her mountain of correspondence on the corner of her desk, taking her seat just as the door opened to admit a tall, attractive woman, who might very easily grace the cover of any fashion magazine. She started to rise, then thought better of it. Perhaps she'd better retain her position of dominance that the desk of Joel Etheridge's personal assistant afforded. Delores was not a little surprised as that thought occurred to her.

She focused closely on the woman as she indicated the sofa to her right. "Hello, Miss Sheridan. I'm Delores, Mr. Etheridge's assistant. If you'll just take a seat, I'll let him know you're here."

Janis Sheridan bestowed a calculatedly warm smile on her and sat down. "Thank you so much, Delores," she murmured, in a low, throaty voice.

Delores rang her boss's office and advised him of his appointment's arrival. She shoved back from her desk and gestured to the woman to follow her. "He'll see you now," she remarked over her shoulder.

She opened the door and stood by to let Janis Sheridan pass, as Joel stood up and nodded briefly.

"Mr. Etheridge, you have those band members coming in about half an hour," she pointed out meaningfully, addressing Joel formally for the benefit of the woman who now sat in front of his desk.

"Thanks, Dee," he acknowledged. "Just let me know when they arrive, will you?"

"Of course." She eyed Janis Sheridan summarily before taking her leave.

Joel had shared with her about Meredith's apparent depression since that initial telephone call, and that's all it took for Delores to decide that she neither liked, nor trusted this woman.

She closed the door behind her, and immediately crossed over to her desk to begin to pray for her boss.

Chapter Seven

Janis Sheridan eased slowly into the chair Delores indicated and appraised Joel Etheridge with carnal approval, as he glanced at his secretary's retreating form, and sat back down at his desk.

He closed a folder he had been studying, and looked up at her with a cool, unimpressed air.

"Miss... Sheridan, is that right?"

"Janis," she corrected demurely.

"It is my understanding," Joel proceeded, in a tone that revealed his displeasure, "that you have been quite insistent that we speak. In fact, my wife mentioned that you even called our home, one morning."

Janis bit off any sharp retort she was tempted to make regarding his wife, and hurried to don the cloak of false humility she had been weaving for the past few nights, in her hotel room. "Mr. Etheridge, please allow me to apologize for being so insensitive!"

"What I'm more interested in hearing," he cut in dryly, "is how you found yourself in possession of our home number, to begin with."

"Underhanded means, I'm afraid," she confessed with a meek cast of green eyes. "You see, my company supplied me with both your office and home numbers. I'm not sure how they managed to obtain your personal information, but Barry, in Mr. Crenshaw's office, has a most uncanny ability to circumvent practically any obstacle. I've learned, over the years, to just take whatever assignment I'm given, and not ask any questions."

She swept her lashes up in helpless appeal. "I hadn't intended to use your home number, Mr. Etheridge, at all. I really thought I was dialing your office. I just assumed your wife was your secretary.

"In fact," she continued, lying with unbelievable precision, "I was expecting to get an answering machine, and was planning on just leaving a message and hoping someone would call me."

Joel narrowed his eyes and leaned back, crossing muscular arms over his broad chest, additional physical attributes that appealed to Janis Sheridan's sensual nature.

"Let's leave all of that, for the moment," he decided abruptly. "Why are you here?"

She forced a bright laugh. "Right to the point! Alright, I'll try to accommodate you, the best I can. We... that is, the company I work for... we are a private production company that is conducting research for an upcoming documentary on music across this country. We're developing the idea in conjunction with public broadcasting, and are hoping to begin actually filming before the end of the year. But a lot of front work goes into a project of this size.

"I'm only part of an extensive research team that is camping out in cities across America. We have people in Memphis and New Orleans working on the influences of blues and jazz. There is a team in Detroit studying some of the contributing forces behind the Motown sound. We have representatives in L.A., Seattle, the Mississippi Delta, all along the Bible belt, across Appalachia. You get the idea. And of course, there's Music City to be heard from. Two of my colleagues are here with me, investigating the roots of country music. I, myself, am handling the aspects of not only gospel music's heritage but also contemporary Christian music, which, of course, brings me to the reason for my being such a nuisance to you and your office."

Janis smiled disarmingly, and resisted the urge to cross her legs seductively and lean forward, to reveal her feminine charms. There was time for that later.

Joel remained impassive, and simply waited for her to get on with it.

"I fully intend to interview others in this field, but you just seemed such a natural choice, when strictly focusing on the contemporary category. I mean, not only are you highly visible as an award-winning executive in this area, but your wife is one of the most sought after artists to come along in years!" She managed a look of innocent entreaty.

"What I am hoping for, Mr. Etheridge, is that I may schedule some time in the near future to maybe pick your brain. You see, I don't claim any religious affiliation, myself, and to be quite honest, I'm not even sure how to intelligently interview people from the Christian community. I'm sure all of you have your own protocol and a readily anticipated line of inquiry and, well... jargon, for lack of a better word. I'm afraid I'm your basic heathen, and you might as well know that this assignment makes me a little nervous."

Janis provided such a convincing display of insecurity, that Joel relented in his aloof carriage. When possible, he believed in extending himself to unbelievers, as a witness of God's love.

"Well, Miss Sheridan, let me first say that, upon your arrival, I had every intention of taking you to task for upsetting my wife. I see now, that it was a simple error and one that I'm sure will not be repeated, especially since we've had that number changed."

He smiled, almost amiably. "You see, my wife is pregnant, and I don't want anything upsetting her. She had a bad experience with a pregnancy years ago, and I do all I can to insure that this is a safe and enjoyable time for her."

"Of course!" Janis laid her hand on her throat in feigned concern. "I wish you knew how very sorry I am. I've only recently become acquainted with your wife's music, and I'm already a big fan. I'm so sorry to have upset her to the point that you had to get a new number."

"Actually, it's slowly leaked out over the years and needed changing anyway. Maybe you did us a favor."

"I hope so!" She sat up straighter in her chair. "Mr. Etheridge, do you think there's any chance at all that we could meet again within the next week or two? I only have a short amount of time allotted for this assignment, before I have to move on to something else."

"I think that could be arranged. Do you have to know when today, or can I just have Delores call you and set something up?"

"Oh, that would be fine, really." She glanced down at her watch. "We seem to be running out of time here, and I know you have another appointment coming in."

"We have another fifteen minutes," Joel pointed out reasonably. "Unless nothing else needs to be said until our next meeting?"

"Our next meeting will be fine." She smiled brilliantly. "I really only came to apologize for my actions, and to ask if you would consider my interviewing you for this project." She rose and collected her empty briefcase. "Thank you so much for seeing me, Mr. Etheridge."

He stood up and shook her extended hand briefly, then reclaimed his chair.

"Certainly. Just arrange something with Delores on the way out, or she'll call you. Good day, Miss Sheridan."

"Good day." She concentrated all of her beauty into her parting smile and let herself out, after realizing that he was not going to escort her to the door.

Joel watched her leave thoughtfully.

"You're not eating." Hailey studied her friend's lovely but pale face, closely. "Are you not feeling well, honey?"

Meredith pushed her fork listlessly around in her salad with a distracted smile. "Do you realize how many times a day I get asked how I feel, Hay?"

"How many times a day do you tell the truth?" she countered shrewdly, not being taken in by diversionary tactics.

Meredith laid her fork down, and lifted her beautiful gray eyes to the perceptive brown ones of her best friend. "Please don't do inventory on me, Sissy."

"If you'll just knock off the artful dodging, I won't have to," she retorted. "When I ask you a question, just give me a straight answer, and cut the crap."

Meredith picked up her fork again and pretended to take a half-hearted interest in a piece of tomato. "When I already know what someone's gonna say, and it's not what I wanna hear, I just save myself a trip and don't go there."

"So you've picked up a tenth spiritual gift, have you? You hear things before they're even said?" Hailey took the fork from her and laid it on her own plate. "Why do we have to begin every talk with a huge discussion about whether or not we're gonna *have* the talk? We both know we are, so let's just have it."

She dodged a tomato wedge and favored its launcher with a fed up expression. "Knock it off!"

Meredith grinned and held out her hand for her fork. Hailey hesitated too long, and received another attack of killer tomatoes.

"Here! Take the stupid thing! But stop using it as a prop to ignore me with!" She slapped it into Meredith's hand with the skill of a surgical nurse, then speared her with a probing eye. "Now, out with it."

"Leave me alone, psycho-chick."

"At least you didn't call me psycho-*slut*." Hailey grumbled.

Meredith giggled softly. "I've already apologized for that. Besides, I got convicted over it."

"You got *convicted* over something?" she teased in mock disbelief. "There may be hope for you, yet!"

She kept a gentle smile, but touched her friend's hand in all seriousness. "Tell me what it is. I've been watching you carefully for weeks now, and I know it's not just the pregnancy. It's something else.

"If you and Joel are going through something, then I'll stop asking questions, because that's none of my business. But if something else is upsetting you, sweetie, maybe it'll help just to talk to your friend who, believe it or not, loves you."

Meredith put away her culinary toys and looked directly into her eyes. "Hailey, don't keep on until you finally get me to open up, and then spend the next thirty minutes telling me why I'm wrong. I can get that anywhere."

"I won't do that, I promise. I'll just listen."

"Okay." She leaned back in her chair and crossed her arms almost defensively, before continuing. "You remember a while back, when I told you about that woman who called the house and asked for Joel? Janis Sheridan?"

Hailey nodded but said nothing.

"I know you'll think I'm overreacting, but someone has been calling the house everyday since then, and hanging up when they hear me answer. Several times a day, in fact," she added darkly.

"That's why you changed your number? Why didn't you say something, honey?"

She shrugged and looked away.

Hailey watched her facial expressions contort, as if she were trying to suppress tears. She got up and grabbed a box of tissues from her kitchen counter. "Here, baby."

She tucked one into Meredith's hand, and sat back down at the table. "Meredith, does Joel know that's why you wanted the number changed?"

She shook her head and wiped at the corner of her eyes. "He thinks I just really got ticked off by that one call, and that I wanted to make sure it didn't happen again. And he thinks..." She faltered.

"What does he think?" Hailey asked softly.

"He thinks I'm overly emotional, because of the baby. He thinks I'm jealous all of a sudden, and he talks to me like I'm a little girl."

"How do you mean?"

"Like trying to lay all this drugstore psychology on me, that he picked up from some kind of 'So Your Ol' Lady's Rabbit Died' book. He tells me it's normal for pregnant women to get really insecure, because they're going through so many changes, and gaining weight, and they feel ugly."

She wadded the tissue into a tight ball and sniffed. "Just pregnancy logic, you know. He thinks I let that Janis woman get to me, for no reason at all, and that I'm allowing the enemy to hit me with jealousy, while I'm vulnerable."

She intercepted Hailey's next question. "No, I'm *not*, Hailey. I admit all of my other faults, so why wouldn't I admit to being jealous?"

"No reason."

"Exactly." She looked down at the tissue she had begun shredding into little bits. "Anyway, I know he was trying to be helpful, and I know he loves me, but after all of that, I just decided not to mention the other phone calls. But I know it's her, Sis. I can't explain it and I can't prove it, but I do know it."

"Well, let me ask you something," Hailey said, after a quiet moment. "Say it *is* her. What do you think she's after? Do you think she's making a play for your husband? Because if she is, Meredith, Joel doesn't even know that there *are* any other women in the world, besides you. You know that!"

"I know," she admitted. "It's not that I'm afraid Joel is going to be attracted to someone else. I'm not afraid of losing my husband." She looked up from the mess she'd made of the tissue and gave her friend a look of appeal. "See, I don't know how to make anyone understand that. It just sounds like I'm in denial, and I'm not. I mean, she might try to go after Joel, but there's no way in the world she'll get anywhere. That's the last thing in the world that bothers me. Joel's too much like Father, for that to happen."

"Then what is it?"

"That's just it, I don't know." Meredith rested troubled eyes on Hailey's face. "I don't know, Hailey. Some kind of... foreboding, I guess. I just keep getting this sense that something bad is going to happen. Maybe this Janis person has nothing to do with it. Maybe she just happened to coincide with something else that I'm picking up on."

Hailey rolled her eyes, and looked over at her clanging telephone with exasperation. "I ought to just let it ring. It's probably someone urgently warning me that my warranty

has expired on a car I haven't owned for over twelve years."
She hopped up and grabbed it in mid-ring.

"Hello?" She motioned to Meredith. "Yep. Right here, hang on."

Meredith quickly pushed back her chair and took the receiver. "Yes?"

"Baby, I miss you!"

"Hey, Mister Man!" Her face immediately reflected what was going on in her heart. "Are you still at the office?"

"I'm at the end of Hailey's street and heading for her driveway. Did she pick you up, or is the Jeep there?"

"She picked me up and we went to the mall, then came back here for lunch."

"Good. Going my way?"

"I am!" She couldn't see him fast enough.

"Well, I'm whipping in now. If Hailey won't be offended, I'll just wait for you out here."

"No, she'll be fine with it. I'm on my way." She hung up and smiled at her friend.

"Joel's out in the driveway. Will I seem like an ungrateful lunch guest, if I bolt?"

Hailey laughed. "To the man you love? You said it yourself, I'm fine with it. Bolt away, girlie." She walked her to the door.

"Hey, listen... we're not done with this, okay? I'm taking you very seriously and I'm praying for you. Scoot!" She gave her a hug and watched her practically run to her husband, who had gone around to the passenger side to see her safely into the car.

Hailey felt like an intruder, but she couldn't resist watching the way Joel's face lit up, as he pulled Meredith into his arms and covered her face with his kisses. She knew he was telling her how much he loved her, and she knew Meredith was hungrily drinking it in.

"Well, God," Hailey said, as she closed her door and started back to the kitchen. "I think Meredith's right about one thing. If that woman does set her sights on Joel, she's gonna miss, and miss big!"

Joel backed his Cadillac smoothly out of the drive and gave his wife's hand a warm squeeze, as he drove toward their home. "How's my son today?"

Meredith looked down and smiled. "Kinda quiet for a change. Good thing, too, he's been trying to break my ribs. I could use a rest." She leaned her head on his strong shoulder and closed her eyes.

"Merry?"

"Hmmm?"

"You remember I told you Janis Sheridan had made an appointment to come to the office?"

She opened her eyes and looked up at him. "Was that today?"

Joel nodded. "She only stayed a few minutes."

"Well, what did she want?"

He glanced down at her and dropped a light kiss on her hair.

"To begin with, she wanted to apologize for calling our house last month. She said the production company she works for gave her both my home and office number, and that she accidentally called the wrong number. She thought you were my secretary, at first."

"I'll just bet," Meredith muttered, under her breath.

Joel didn't seem to hear her. "She explained why she's in Nashville and why she wanted to meet with me. Her company is researching various types of music in America for a public television special. She was sent here to cover the gospel end of the spectrum. They hope to begin filming before the end of the year, provided they can finish their preliminary work."

Meredith listened to all of this with reservations she couldn't understand. Both she and Joel were interviewed all the time for things along these lines. Why should this time be any different? And why couldn't that call have been a mistake? A sudden thought brought a scowl to her face.

"Joel, since when does a business answer a phone by just saying 'hello'? I certainly didn't say, 'Etheridge and Associates'."

He lifted his brow and pondered that one for a moment. "Well, maybe she just didn't pay any attention to how you answered the phone, one way or the other."

Meredith let her eyes wander out the window, to the passing world, not even realizing that she had released his hand and shifted away from him.

He watched her quietly. "Are you mad at me about something, Merry?"

"Why?"

He glanced down at the space between them then looked around at traffic, tension rippling faintly across his jaw. "No reason. Never mind."

Meredith followed his eyes and wondered what had made her do that. Was she secretly mad at Joel? She looked back up and caught a hint of sadness on his handsome face, as he stared straight ahead. Her heart rebuked her.

"Joel, pull over."

Joel immediately swerved to the right and stopped the car against the curb, thinking she was going to be sick. Instead of throwing open the door, as he expected her to, his wife startled him, by practically climbing onto his lap.

"I'm not mad at you. I'm only mad about you." She took his face between her hands and laid a long deliberate kiss on his lips.

When she finally pulled away, Joel flashed her a happy grin before reclaiming her hand and easing the car back into traffic and toward their home.

"I bet you could manage *both*, if you put your mind to it."

Chapter Eight

Darcy blinked back quick tears, and stared at Neil McCallen in wonder.

He laughed at her reaction and leaned closer to her desk, in a kind of playful inspection.

"Well, Darcy, if I'd known you were going to cry over this, I'd have left well enough alone."

Her watery eyes instantly crinkled into a brilliant smile that almost took his breath away. She was incredibly pretty! He mentally frowned, and put that thought firmly away.

"Is this good news to you, or did I lock you into something you may not be ready for?"

Darcy opened her eyes wide and sailed a harmless wad of paper at him. "What, are you, *kidding*? This is great news! I'm just having trouble taking it in."

He grinned, apparently pleased with her response. "I'm glad to hear that. For a minute, I thought I blew it."

"Neil, what made them go for it?"

"They're all afraid of me," he assured her airily.

She puckered her brow, then broke into another one of those radiant smiles. "Goof!"

Neil chuckled and sat back. "It just must have been God, Darcy. I'm sure you prayed about it and I certainly did. I just happened to meet with the board at a time when they were able to hear from God. You're now a full-time youth pastor."

She retained a look of bliss that was almost comical, and he indulged in a hearty laugh. "Darcy, you look as if I'd just told you that you are now a full-time millionaire. You're not, by any chance, glamorizing this position, are you?"

"No chance of that," she returned dryly. She rested a gaze on him that she had no way of knowing was disturbing. "I'm sorry I didn't call you the other night, the way you asked me to."

"And you should be. I sat right there and stared sorrowfully at the phone, until I fell asleep. I even made the operator call me and prove that it was working."

"Do you pray with the same mouth you lie out of?" she asked, sarcastically. "You were probably in your office holding auditions for Mrs. State Youth Director."

This line of ribbing took him by surprise, but he recovered smoothly. "No, I was done with that by six. It turned out that none of the finalists could fry chicken, and I can't accept that. I have high standards."

"Well, if you were camped out by your phone all night, waiting for *me* to call, they can't be too high." She tilted her head back and looked at him through half-closed lids. "You lie, Sitting Bull. Make that *Spreading* Bull!"

Neil had a quick wit himself, and was always glad when someone could spar competently with him. He was going to have to stay on his toes with this one! He relaxed with a happy grin and flung one leg over the arm of the chair.

"Well, tell me this, Custer. All kidding aside, how did things go with the girl we talked about?"

Darcy glanced up over his shoulder to make sure no one was in the hallway, then back at his face with a relieved smile.

"The test was negative, but I didn't want to trust it, so I made her let me take her to a clinic."

"No baby?"

"No baby."

"And the rest of it?"

"Well, I took your advice and called them both in here. I told them they could either come clean with their parents, or I would. They didn't have much of a choice, so they agreed."

"Has that already happened?"

She nodded. "Big reaction, too, like you'd imagine. But both sets of parents got together and talked it over, instead of getting into an uproar over it. The kids can't see each other outside of church functions for a long time, meaning just that. And, of course, being alone together is absolutely out of the question."

She pushed a lock of hair away from her tanned face. "This is what I'm glad about. When some parents find out their kids are sexually active, they blow up and all of that, but they don't put an immediate stop to it. I guess they figure that once it happens, then that's it, that the kids magically become adults, or whatever. These parents were quick to point out to their kids that rushing into adult behavior didn't make them grown at all, and that, as far as they were concerned, they were still children, and were not going to be allowed to simply go their own way. I think the kids were actually kinda glad, if you can believe that."

"I can. It's like I said, kids actually do want limits." He compressed his fingertips together and viewed her closely. "How did that leave your relationship with them?"

"If there's any animosity, I haven't been able to detect it."

He smiled and nodded. "Not surprised. Plus, I told you so."

"Did you?" She grinned lazily. "I don't remember that."

"How convenient."

Neil had been suppressing something for several minutes and was feeling successful, until he heard himself blurt out, to his dismay, "Darcy, let's go grab lunch somewhere!"

She blinked at him, as if unsure she had heard correctly. "Sure, okay."

Neil silently fumed at himself. Why had he done such a stupid thing? This was completely unwise, and there was no way now to take back the invitation, without making things awkward. *Nice work, McCallen,* he reprimanded himself grimly.

He covered his misgivings well, and stood up and stretched. "You might want to grab a jacket. It's really windy out there. Come along, Custer!"

"Where to, my last stand?"

Neil wished he wasn't going to enjoy this so much.

"The thing you want to remember," he finished, as he turned his car into the church's parking lot, "is that once you establish a policy, it's not up for debate."

Neil killed the engine and looked over at Darcy, who had been gratefully soaking up his advice, all the way back from lunch.

"Teens are notorious for finding out where you draw the line, and then trying to re-negotiate the boundaries. You were a teenager not so long ago. You remember how you were."

"Thanks for trying, but we both know that's a distant memory." She grinned up at him. "I'm nudging thirty, and it's a fact that they don't trust us, after that."

"You're just a babe," he commented lightly.

"Compared to you? Trying to convince me you're old?"

"Haven't you heard my knees crack, when I sit down?" Neil asked, smiling at her wry expression. He tried for a serious face. "Really, you haven't heard the rumors the kids have flying around the district, that I take my teeth out at night?"

Darcy held out her hand and baited him with her blue eyes. "Let's have 'em."

He indulged in a quiet laugh, then stopped and looked at her curiously. "Darcy, what are you doing here?"

"Here, as in your car? Sopping up wisdom, I reckon."

His eyes flickered with something... she didn't know what.

"Here, in a small town like this, working in an obscure setting, with a bunch of kids. Why aren't you out and about with your friends, meeting people, getting married, having kids of your own? Or piloting jet fighters, if my remarks seem a little sexist to you. I'm never sure how to talk to women these days." He grinned in a way that set off the slight cleft in his chin.

"It's okay, I'm not a feminist. Besides, being a female is my best weapon."

Neil raised his brows. "Oh, how so, woman?"

Darcy shrugged slightly. "It has its advantages."

"And those would be..."

She leaned back slightly and regarded him with playful smugness. "I'm not telling."

He smiled then studied her for a few seconds longer than necessary.

She became a little self-conscious.

"So, what are *you* doing here?" she finally asked.

"Trying to figure you out," he returned quietly.

"It'll never happen." Darcy couldn't decide if he was really listening to her. He was looking at her, but he seemed to be deep in thought. "Anyway, same question, backatcha.

What are *you* doing in a small town, obscure setting... that whole thing."

"You didn't like my answer?" He continued to gaze at her intently and she struggled to appear unaffected.

"I was hoping for an honest one."

"You wound me. The very idea that I would ever be anything less than completely honest, with someone as discerning as you, is appalling."

She gave him an expression of irritation and he leaned forward and investigated the glint in her eyes. "Oops, made you mad."

"Nah... I'd have to care, one way or the other, for you to make me mad," she returned with comical aloofness. She slipped her purse strap over her shoulder and reached for the door handle. "This was nice. Thanks, Neil."

"Leaving so soon?"

"Well, now that I'm officially on the payroll, I'd better show up for my job, don't you think?"

"I won't fire you."

"You wouldn't dare!" She held up what was intended to be a menacing fist.

Neil caught it in his own large hand, threatening with a mischievous grin to bend it backwards.

"I wouldn't," she warned. "I just might crumple you like a paper cup."

"I doubt it. I'm bigger than you."

"Oh yeah?"

Neil burst forth with an incredulous laugh. "What do you mean, 'oh yeah'? Seriously?"

He unfolded her hand and laid it against his own to measure the difference. "See that? Don't mess with me, little bit!"

She looked down at their compressed hands, and then back up at his face, with a puzzled smile. He held her eyes for a moment, then released her hand as suddenly as he had taken it.

"Remember, I mentioned youth camp to you, a couple of weeks ago?"

Darcy was taken aback by this abrupt change of pace, but managed to make the adjustment, albeit awkwardly. "Yeah, sure."

"Have you given any thought to being a counselor?"

"Since I'm giving my notice at the bookstore, it's no longer a problem. That was my only concern."

"See how uncomplicated your life is, now that you get to devote all your time to this profession?"

She smiled and opened the door. "Uncomplicated, huh? I guess I'll have to take your word for that. I guess we'll see." She moved to get out of the car.

"Darcy ..."

"Yes?" She turned to look back at him and found him staring at her with such an unsettling urgency, that her heart seemed to misfire.

"What is it, Neil?" she asked gently, when he just kept sitting there looking at her.

Something hungry leaped into his brown eyes. His facial expressions wavered between tenderness and distress.

"Nothing, I just... thanks for going to lunch with me."

She didn't try to hide the perplexity she was feeling. "Well... thanks for asking me. I had a good time."

Another silent lingering look.

What was this? Why couldn't she just bring herself to fling some humorous barb at him, and hop out of the car?

"Neil, is something wrong?"

He glanced away. "No."

"It seems like it."

With a great effort, he whipped out a sunny grin and cranked the motor. "Just too much soda."

The remark was so unexpected, that Darcy blinked in surprise, then hopped out of the car with a laugh and a little wave.

"Well, you go take care of that. See ya 'round, S. Bull!"

"Later, Custer."

She watched him drive away with a strange concoction of confusion and delight brewing inside her.

Maybe she was just reading too much into it, but... no. She wasn't a connoisseur of men, but she was also not immune to knowing when someone was attracted to her. It was what it was. She and Neil had just finished searching each other's feelings.

Darcy had never been a girl who indulged in self-delusion. As a rule, she was forevermore brutally honest with herself, to the point of being harsh, but there was no point in siding with caution on this one. There was definitely something happening between them.

She wandered slowly back to her office, an odd little smile playing quietly around her mouth. She meditated on the lightness of her heart, but wasn't surprised to find it there. She had already forced herself to admit, some time ago, that she was beginning to care for this man.

Neil sped away from Grace Chapel with a mixture of anger and shame warming his face.

"You're an ignorant fool, McCallen!" He took himself to task out loud, his hands gripping the wheel tightly. "You have absolutely no business, and no right, involving yourself with that girl. She deserves way better than you!"

Not allowing himself to reflect on those intimate moments with Darcy was going to be a battle, but it was a battle that he had to win. He couldn't let himself care for Darcy or for any other woman. Happily-ever-after was never going to work out for him.

He let out a long sigh. "Help me, God," he prayed. "Don't let me give in to what I'm feeling for Darcy. I don't want to hurt that girl."

Chapter Nine

Marshall Edwards laid his arm around his wife's shoulders, and listened carefully to what Joel's mother was telling them.

"I wish I could be more specific." Laura glanced up to Gary for the understanding look she knew she would receive. "I keep telling myself that I'm probably imagining things, but I don't think I'm a person who's given to that sort of thing. At least, I hope not."

"If you are, then you and Bobbie are *both* imagining things," Marshall commented, giving his wife a knowing glance. "She's been feeling it, too."

"I have, Laura!" Bobbie said fervently. "For the past... oh, I guess four or five weeks. I wish we could have come over, the first time you called us about it. Whatever it is, I can't seem to shake it. I keep getting this sort of warning in my spirit."

"That's what it is, a warning," Laura agreed quickly. "I've called and checked on the kids, and they insist they're fine. I've done days and days of self-analysis in case it's something going on with me. I just can't peg it, and it won't go away."

Gary leaned forward in characteristic intensity. "I don't know that we necessarily need to identify the problem, before we begin to move forward in prayer. When Laura first called me about this, I was aware of a vague something, but it seemed more like a passing thing, rather than an urgent need, at the time. Lately, it's back and it's been more pressing and kind of... ominous."

"That's a good word for it," Bobbie agreed. "Like the feeling you get when they break into the show you're watching with a tornado watch, then you look out, and the sky in your back yard looks creepy."

"Well, there's a feeling we can all relate to!" Laura laughed at her friend's sheepish grin.

"Bobbie's a tough little cookie, until the big T gets mentioned," Marshall informed them, giving his wife's shoulder an affectionate squeeze. "I guess everybody has that one thing that unnerves them, and that's Bobbie's thing. Can't say I'm too fond of 'em, myself."

"Well, you get my point," she replied, "and that's how I've been feeling, lately. Like we need to be watching out for something."

"Well, if I know the enemy at all," Gary contributed, "it won't be something obvious. One of his greatest tactics is to create a blatant disturbance, off to the side, so that we'll focus on that, and miss what he's really up to, behind the curtain. I would advise us to really get in tune with what the Holy Spirit is saying to us in our private prayer times, and whenever we open the scriptures. It pays to stay close to the One who knows the enemy's agenda, before *he* even does, and Who's always miles ahead of him."

"Just to be on the safe side, I've made a list of those who are particularly close to us, who might be potential targets, including our children," Laura declared, pulling a sheet of paper out from between the pages of her bible. "We need to cover them in prayer tonight."

"Yeah, that's a good idea," Marshall commented, as he leaned forward, pressing his fingertips together in anticipation, "because I was about to mention Meredith."

Laura looked at him sharply. "What *about* Meredith?"

"Probably nothing. Joel just happened to comment at the office today, that this pregnancy is making her a little moody."

Bobbie hooted at that. "What woman doesn't get a little moody when she's pregnant?"

"That's true enough," Laura concurred. "Well, little Merry's right here with all the rest, so let's get crackin'."

She grinned up at Gary. "Or was that your line?"

Hook leaped down from Meredith's lap and sauntered away from their window seat, in search of anything edible. She watched him waddle along with a faint smile, then cast a parting glance back up through the big oak outside.

She felt bad about not talking to Father today, but she just hadn't been feeling that chatty, lately. She pulled herself up with an effort and sat up straight, her mind churning with a thousand things at once, just as it had been doing all day.

Their phone number had been changed for almost two weeks, now. Two quiet, reassuring weeks... until today. All at once, out of the blue, it had started again. Four calls, four hang-ups. Once, though, she could have sworn she had heard a stifled laugh.

She leaned her head wearily against the windowsill and let out a deep sigh.

Hailey had insisted that she tell Joel, but what would she say? That Janis Sheridan was calling their house, over and over again, and hanging up?

I'd sound like an idiot, she thought. *Joel's already been hinting that I'm too sensitive lately, and that I need to stop letting my*

She blinked back hopeless tears, and roused herself
from her troubling speculation, then began manipulating the
side of her head with her fingertips. She'd had a dull
headache all day. She knew she needed to climb upstairs and
get a shower. Joel was taking her out tonight, to celebrate
their first anniversary. She smiled to herself, but it was
tinged with bittersweet regret.

They'd originally planned to go to their cabin in the
Smokey Mountains, but Meredith had long ago promised a
close friend that she would sing a duet with her on her
debut project, and the studio dates were locked in. It would
cut their trip short, and she didn't feel she'd be physically up
to a long, grueling session on the heels of traveling. She'd
asked if they could save the cabin for another time.

Joel was disappointed, because he'd wanted this first
celebration to be one that his wife would always remember,
but he agreed. He'd suggested instead, reserving a private
venue and inviting their close family and friends to share the
occasion with them, but Meredith managed to convince him
that she would prefer an intimate evening alone.

Wanting to please her, he booked a private dining
room at one of Nashville's finer restaurants, and arranged
for a carriage ride afterward, although it was far from what
he'd hoped to give her.

Tonight, she felt a bit of remorse for letting him down
because, after all, it was his anniversary, as well as hers, but
she just couldn't face a lot of commotion, or social
interaction, right now. What she really needed was some
uninterrupted time alone with her husband.

I'm selfish, I know. She directed her thoughts to her dark
reflection in the window pane. *I should have just gone along with
whatever he wanted.*

She thought of her passionate Joel, with a sweet blush of happiness lighting up her eyes, and allowed herself to put away her earlier anxiety. He'd be home soon, and that was all she needed or wanted. Suddenly, it was all she could think about.

Meredith laid a protective hand on her baby, and rallied herself in preparation for the trek up the stairs, then stood up.

"Whoa, there!" She sat back down quickly and grabbed her head, which was swimming laps. "Back her down, girl. I guess I just got up too quickly."

She rested on the window seat for a moment until she felt a little more confident, then tried her feet again. "Steady as she goes," she cautioned herself, timidly altering her course toward the couch.

She stopped halfway there and reeled, clutching for anything to break her fall. All her hand could find was the lamp, and she sent it smashing to the floor with a loud crash, as she followed it. She rolled over and inspected her legs and hands that had met with the shards of glass upon her impact.

"Oh, Father," she breathed, as she pulled a sliver of the broken lamp out of her knee. Blood began to stream from the many places that had been pierced by the glass, and she looked around for something to wipe herself with. She spied a wadded up tissue on the end table and reached up for it, just as the room whirled and darkness enveloped her.

It was quite a few moments later, before the lock on the front door yielded to Joel's house key. He pushed it forward, wrestling with his briefcase, jacket and the flowers he had stopped to pick up for his wife. He saw her at once, and immediately let everything drop to the floor, rushing over with her name on his lips.

"Merry!" He stared in horror at the blood that streaked her legs, and covered one hand. "Meredith!"

She moaned from somewhere far away, but it was enough to stop his tears and jolt him into action.

"Talk to me, baby," he urged, in hushed tones, raking the glass out of his way and lifting her head just slightly. "Please, Merry, say something!"

She fought to open her eyes. "Joel." It was a whisper.

"I'm here, baby! I'm right here." His chest began to hurt him, as he grappled with sheer panic. "Look at me, sweetheart. Can you do that?"

She opened her eyes at last, and stared up at him in bewilderment.

"Am I on the floor?" She looked around at all the glass and suddenly began to cry. "I broke the lamp!"

Joel let fly a muted oath, damning the lamp, and laid his hand on her, to cover their unborn child. "Baby, what about your stomach? Are you cramping, at all?"

"I... no."

"Are you sure? Any pain anywhere? Anywhere at all?"

She took a quiet assessment, then shook her head. "Just where I got cut." She wiped a bloody hand across her face. "I guess my head hurts a little."

He tried to think clearly and checked her pupils, then leaned down to gather her up.

"Honey, I'm going to begin lifting you, but if you feel any pain... I mean even the slightest twinge, you stop me. Are you ready?"

She nodded, then moaned something unintelligible, as more tears hurried down her cheeks.

Joel stopped immediately, and tried to interpret her distress. "Say that again, sweetie. What is it, what's wrong?"

She raised her wet eyes to his and held up her gashed hands. "I'll get blood all over you."

Joel bit back an angry, frustrated snarl and instead, hurriedly devised a soft smile to calm her.

"Silly girl. The last thing I care about is whether or not my clothes get blood on them. Hang on the best you can, and up we go."

He lifted her slowly and easily, and laid her on the couch, kneeling down beside it to lean over her, with brooding anxiety darkening his eyes.

"Tell me, little one, how you're feeling right now". He pulled a few tissues from the box on the coffee table, and carefully touched them to the worst of her wounds, in order to determine how deep they were.

He stopped, when a flinch of pain swept across her face, and decided that there was enough coagulation to · safely wait, for the time being. "Other than these cuts, try to describe exactly what hurts, and what the pain is like."

She laid one arm across her forehead, and looked up at the ceiling, unable to process for a moment. Finally, she offered in a small, weak voice, "My ears are ringing like fire alarms." She pressed her lips together, as a single tear rested on her cheek, then looked over at him and tried to smile. "Or remember the cicada outbreak last summer? That, times a thousand."

Concern drew his brow, as he stroked her head with a fingertip. He stood to his feet and snatched up the phone. "I'm calling Lynch to meet us at the ER."

Meredith made no argument. She simply laid there, meek and still, while her husband verbally forced his way through an unsympathetic and robotic answering service, in the habit of running interference for the busy doctor.

Joel wasn't having any nonsense, or answering any questions from their script. He made this known, rather loudly and threateningly, and had Meredith's obstetrician on the line, within minutes.

He hung up after a brief exchange, and searched the room wildly for a blanket. He saw the one in the window seat Meredith had been nesting in, and quickly wrapped her in it, cradling her up into his arms.

"Stop worrying about blood on the blanket!" he barked, squelching her feeble protest a little sharply, due to his distraught state.

He knew he could get his wife to the hospital himself, much faster than waiting around for an ambulance. He carried her briskly through the door, stopping to grab his keys out of the lock, and hurried out to his car. His eyes burned with a blend of overwrought dismay, and tears, at the sight of his wife's wounds and her stark, white face. He shot down the driveway and out onto the boulevard, aiming his car at the hospital.

Janis Sheridan crossed her legs languidly, and favored her two companions with a satisfied smile.

"At the risk of your calling me on the carpet, Oliver," she said in a pleased manner, "I have to say that things are progressing beautifully ."

"Oh, do please elaborate, Miss Sheridan," the small, wizened man insisted, with an unmistakable taunt in his voice. "Impress me."

She peered at him through green slits. "Gladly. Let me begin by telling you that I have scored three separate appointments with Joel Etheridge, two of those just last week. I have another one coming up. We are becoming... how shall I put this... comfortable with one another. He talks to me about his little wife's pregnancy, and I ooze with concern and goodwill. I even offered to try saying a prayer for her, if you can believe that!"

Her eyes flashed scornfully. "I'll say a prayer, alright. I'll even light a candle for the dear girl."

"Is that it?" Oliver Sullivan asked dryly.

"Not quite." She knew it was foolish to exhibit too much assurance in front of him, but she didn't care. She was confident.

"I've slowly, but surely, been unraveling poor little Meredith's knitting. She's been making all kinds of wild accusations about me, I'm sure, but her husband's not taking her seriously, at all. In fact, he implied that she seems a little paranoid, lately. He's planning to take her to her doctor to see if he can talk some sense into her. Poor twitchy, little lamb."

"Meanwhile?" Sullivan pressed, seemingly unaffected.

She opened her eyes wide in question.

"Oh, come *on*, Miss Sheridan, surely there's more!" His eyes glimmered with evil.

"These things take time. But, since you ask, I did manage to see them at the food court, in a mall last weekend, and slipped behind a directory sign to listen to them. She was doing her best to malign me, but her husband laughed at her and told her she was just imagining things. He insisted that I was nothing more than a professional who was here to do a job, and that she was just borrowing trouble. He even went as far as to say that he had been finding me quite sincere and likable!"

"I suggest that he find you much more than that, Janis dear. It would be to your advantage."

"Oliver, I do wish you'd make up your mind," she dared to complain. "First you warn me not to try appealing to him physically, and now you say our companionable situation is not enough."

"When we discussed this before, you hadn't even baited your line, let alone hooked your fish. Now that you have him nibbling, set the hook and reel him in!" He blew out a cloud of smoke and laid his cigarette in the ashtray beside him. "Does this analogy get by you, Miss Sheridan?"

Warren Patrick emitted a derisive snort and drained his whiskey glass. "It just might, Oliver. Janis has never been one for the great outdoors!"

She shot him a look of pure hatred and settled her gaze back on Oliver's cold face.

"I'm not stupid. I get the point. What do you want me to do next? An all-out play for him, or something a little more subtle?"

"Only subtle enough to keep him from knowing what you're up to. Not so subtle that his male inclinations aren't stirred."

She set her own glass down and smiled slowly at Oliver Sullivan, as understanding passed between them.

Bett Greer fished a clump of wet tea bags out of her favorite pitcher, and shot a teasing grin at Darcy, who was perched on a stool, her entire upper body laid out across the counter like a rag doll.

"Well," she began as she squeezed the excess tea from the bags, and dumped them in the garbage under the sink, "that new state youth director certainly has things buzzin' around here."

"Is that a fact?" Darcy rested her chin on her folded arms, and looked up at Bett with a suppressed smile.

"Oh, yes ma'am!" She emptied a large cup of sugar into the pitcher and held it under the tap until she seemed satisfied with the color. "Freida Kirkland seems to think he spends way more time at our little church lately, than any other church in the district."

"What would Freida Kirkland know about it? She's hardly there lately, and when she is, she never pops her head outside her office door."

"She knows things," Bett assured her with a wink. She pulled out an ice tray from the freezer and glared at it.

"These kids are going to get farmed out to an orphanage, if they don't stop taking ice and not refilling the trays! I hate that! Stan's springing for a new ice maker, and that's all there is to it!" She pulled out another tray and headed to the sink to remedy things.

"Anyway," she ventured slyly, cutting a glance in Darcy's direction, "I don't need Freida to tell me what I already know. I'm not blind, for crying out loud!"

Darcy raised up onto her elbows and took the bait. "What exactly is it you're not blind to, Bett?"

"I've seen the way he looks at you." She handed Darcy a glass of tea and set about clearing up her mess.

"I don't know that he looks at me any differently than he looks at anybody else," Darcy protested, coloring slightly.

Bett snorted. "Honey, every woman in the world wants to be looked at like that! Besides," she added knowingly, "you're wasting your time, arguin'. Facts are facts!"

"Okay, maybe." Darcy looked down at her tea with a self-conscious grin. "I guess I've noticed it, too. I just didn't want to read more into it, than I should."

"Well, let's speculate for a minute, here," Bett suggested happily. "Let's just say, for the sake of an argument, that you are reading all this correctly, and that he really does have feelings for you." She caught Darcy's increased tinge of pink. "How about it? You think you might be interested?"

Darcy shrugged, and Bett gave the countertop an impatient slap. "You can't shrug your way out of this one. 'Fess up, kiddo!"

She screwed her mouth up in embarrassment, enjoying this interrogation, in spite of her resolutions to stay clear of Bett when she was on the gossip trail.

She knew this information was not only going to leave this kitchen, it would travel by express, but she allowed herself to be roped in, anyway. Maybe it was because she liked hearing what she already suspected... that Neil McCallen was attracted to her.

"I'm waiting." Bett cut into her thoughts.

"For what?" she countered.

"You *know* for what! Do you like the guy or not?"

"Okay, I like him! But we don't know that the feeling's mutual, so can we please not put it in the paper, just yet?"

"*Like* like, or something stronger?" Bett bore her green eyes probingly into Darcy's. "Never mind," she laughed, when her prey suddenly looked like the dark end of a lipstick chart. "I just found out what I wanted to know."

She broke off at the sudden look of utter repulsion on Darcy's face, and then replicated the expression exactly. "What, for the love of Mike, is that *smell?*"

"Ugh," Darcy responded, grabbing her nose and looking around, as if she expected to see the odor standing in the corner, waving at her. "Smells like you know what!"

"CALVIN! AUDRA! WALLY!"

Bett bellowed her kids' names in a way that alerted them to drop whatever they were doing, and get downstairs. "I thought I smelled something last night, but it sure wasn't as bad as this!"

"What?" Calvin appeared in the doorway with his sister on his heels.

"*Smell* that!" their mother demanded. "What *is* that?"

"Phew!" he said with feeling. "Smells like something crawled up under the house and died!"

"I've smelled it before," Audra volunteered in her quiet way.

"In the house?" Bett certainly hadn't, not *this* stench!

"No, I smelled it on... " she hesitated, then finished in a rush. "I smelled it on Wally, a few weeks ago, when he came in from playing with Foster."

Darcy remembered her mentioning something about a smell, when they were standing in the backyard, after the Laverne game. *This* is what she was talking about?

"I've got to get some air," she declared, leading the way to the back door.

"It's not as bad out here," Bett observed, as they stood around on the porch, "but I can still smell it." She waved through the air with one hand. "Wait 'til Stan gets home, he's gonna have a fit! Where's Wally?"

She looked around the yard, and over the hedges, that separated their property from the Ames, next door. "Calvin, you and Audra go find your brother! We've got to leave soon, anyway, if we're going to Franklin to see your grandma. Hurry up, and tell him to get in that tub, regardless of what he smells like!"

"Don't mind me, Bett, if I just mosey on over to my crash-site," Darcy said. "Anyway, it smells like it might be a sewer thing, and I want to see if it's found its way into the apartment."

She left them searching for Wally and hurried over to investigate her living quarters.

It was faint, but not nearly as noticeable inside and she breathed a sigh of relief and closed her door firmly. She didn't want smells from the outside finding their way in.

"Man, Wally, what have you been up to?" she muttered under her breath. "I'll bet it has something to do with that dam you and Foster have been building."

Her eyes opened wide in sudden realization, and she made a mad dash back over to the Greer's house. Bett was still standing out in the yard, trying to figure out where the odor was coming from.

"Bett, if it's what I think it is, you'd better see if you can get hold of Stan!"

Wally's mom looked at her curiously. "Why, what do you think it is?"

"I guess I should have said something about it before, but I didn't think it was a big deal at the time."

"About *what*, Darcy?"

"Wally told me the day of Ross's wedding, that he and Foster were building a dam."

She still didn't get it.

"Bett, you said yourself that you saw them heading across the field with an old bucket, and some trowels. Across the field," she repeated slowly and with emphasis. "The *field...* "

Bett's mouth dropped open in dismay.

"The leach pipe! Oh, my good Lord! Those boys have dammed up the leach pipe to the sewer! Stan's gonna blow a gasket! Although, he shouldn't. I told him when he backhoed out there, to cover all that back over, but he said he'd have to get to it later." She stared at Darcy in horror, before her expression morphed into a wide grin that immediately turned into spasms of laughter.

"What's so funny?" Whatever Darcy had expected from Bett, this wasn't it!

"Oh, Darcy!" Bett wiped her eyes and shook with an effort to curb herself. "My poor baby has been playing in..."

She couldn't finish, but she didn't need to. Darcy knew exactly what leach pipes were all about, and couldn't stop herself from joining in.

"Oh, God, help!" Bett gasped and pointed to a distant, approaching figure, then collapsed into convulsions.

The small, forlorn image of Wally was looming up, comically pathetic in his dad's huge rubber boots, and wet shorts that clung to his little bottom like slimy seaweed. Audra and Calvin accompanied him in the sympathetic manner of a priest and the warden, escorting their charge all the way to his execution.

"Wallace Aaron Greer, you get your butt in this house, and into that bathtub, before I blister you!" Bett did an incredible job of whipping off her grin, and replacing it with a dark, foreboding scowl.

Wally clomped noisily up to the back door and climbed out of Stan's boots.

"Whew!" Darcy pinched her nose and fanned herself. "That's it, alright! I'm outta here!" She scooted back to the lesser of two evils, her own apartment.

It was some time before she glanced out the window, and noticed Bett loading her brood into the Oldsmobile. She returned her wave, and grinned at Wally's disgruntled face, clearly visible through the windshield. Apparently, his siblings had taken pity on him, and magnanimously allowed him the privilege of riding 'shot-gun'. She watched them drive off, then pulled herself away from the window and over to the desk beside her bed.

She had a ton of correspondence to answer that had been piling up, since the first of the year. She smiled warmly at the realization that, thanks to Neil, she would soon be on top of everything, and have time to begin focusing on some new areas.

She put him firmly out of her mind, and forced herself to concentrate on the job at hand. She had been plugging away for over an hour, when the sharp rap on her door startled her.

"That'll be Stan," she alerted herself, pushing her work over to one side. Boy, she didn't want to be Wally, when he got back from Franklin!

Darcy got up and mentally prepared herself for Stan's interrogation as to why she hadn't said anything earlier about Wally's enterprise, and opened the door. She blinked in surprised confusion when Neil, instead, stood smiling down at her.

"Is it okay to just drop by?" he asked simply.

"Well... sure!" She shook herself and smiled back. "I'm sorry, I thought you were the landlord and... " She stopped and looked at him with wonder. "How did you know where I live?"

"Mrs. Greer told me, when I ran into her at Barry and Wanda Todd's a couple of days ago. I mentioned that I had your jacket, and she gave me the address."

Oh, she did, did she? Darcy was sure she'd just said this out loud, but was relieved to find that she had managed to restrain herself. She made a mental note to rake Bett over the coals later. She quickly veiled her annoyed expression, and exchanged it for a blank one. "My jacket?"

He handed her black windbreaker to her, with a little smile. "You left it in my car, when we went to lunch last week."

"But you didn't have to bring it all the way out here to the sticks, Neil," she protested faintly. "Bett could have brought it."

"I'd taken it out of the car by then." He gave a light shrug.

She began to realize that she was making him stand in the doorway. "I'm sorry, Neil, wanna come in?"

"Am I interrupting anything?"

"No, in fact, I could use a break," she declared, moving to one side and admitting him. She tossed the jacket onto the sofa, and caught the odd look on his face.

"You smell that, huh? I'm afraid little Wally Greer is in for a rough time, when his father gets home." She gestured to a chair, but he remained standing. "He and his pal next door have been industriously building a dam."

"Impressive," Neil commented.

"Yeah, well, Stan's not gonna be too impressed, when he gets home, and finds out they built it by closing up the leach pipe to the sewer."

He raised his brows and laughed. "Man, I never did anything half that creative, when I was a kid!"

"Me, either. But then, we didn't have Wally Greer to play with."

"He's that little fellow that sat by you at the game, isn't he?" Neil asked casually.

"As a matter of fact, he is." Her eyes reflected obvious pleasure. "I thought you didn't notice me, until I showed up in your face."

"I noticed." He cleared his throat suddenly and stepped closer to the door. "Actually, Darcy, I'm not staying. I just wanted to give your jacket back, and to tell you that if you want to be a counselor at camp, you have to register by Friday."

"I never received a form," she answered, in a quiet voice, disappointed at his retreat into formality.

"You didn't?" He looked down at her steadily. "Well, I'll try to get one to you Monday or Tuesday. You can wait as late as Thursday to mail it, since it's only going to Murfreesboro, or you can drop it by the office, if you're in the area."

"Okay. Thanks," she added after an awkward silence fell between them.

There it was again, that same searching expression she had seen before. He seemed to be finished, but he made no move to leave. He just kept looking down at her, one emotion after another, fighting for dominance.

"Neil," she dared, her heart banging against her ribs. "What is it? Why are you looking at me like that?"

He muttered something under his breath, and turned to go, whipping back around in the same motion, and jerking her roughly up against himself. He snared the back of her head in both hands and raised her lips to his.

Darcy yielded so completely to his kiss that, when he suddenly released her, she almost fell.

"I'm sorry!" He opened the door and stood in its frame, looking out at nothing, trying, but failing, to regain his composure. "I'm sorry, Darcy. I shouldn't have done that. I had no right to do that."

He suddenly sprang from the doorway and to his car, then drove off, throwing a small wave of loose stones and dirt, as Darcy stared after him in shock.

She laid trembling fingers on her throat and sank down onto a chair, with a painful mixture of ecstasy and shock. That was the kiss she'd waited all her life for! She had been telling herself that she would know it, when it came... that she would know the man she was created to love, and who was chosen for her. This was the man! She knew that, with all her heart.

Tears pushed through her lashes and made a hot wet path down her cheeks. Then why did he just tear out of here, the way he did? What did he mean by saying he had no right?

She lifted her fingertips to her raw, burning lips, and closed her eyes tightly, to keep her heart from leaking all over the floor.

"Stop it right now," she whispered savagely to herself.

She rocked gently back and forth, alternately reveling in the depths of what he had just made her feel, and recoiling from the regret she had clearly seen all over his face, when he pushed her away.

She lifted her head, as she heard the gravel crunch outside, and hastily mopped her face. She didn't want Stan, or anyone else to see her like this.

Her door flew open, and Neil charged back through it, a dark and turbulent anger lining his face and setting his jaw. He purposefully came to her and caught her wrists, pulling her to her feet. She held her breath, as the man who had just kissed her as if his life depended on it, now lashed out at her in fury.

"Let's get this straight," he demanded, tightening his hold on her. "I'm not a man who chases after women! I haven't intentionally pursued you, and I didn't mean for this to happen! Do you understand that, Darcy?"

She stared up at him wordlessly, and he gave her an impatient shake. "This can't happen, do you hear me? We can't do this!"

She continued to pelt him with everything that her heart loaded into her eyes. He closed his own to ward off what she was doing to him.

"Don't!" he said sharply. "Don't look at me like that."

"I can't help it," she answered meekly.

"Darcy!" His eyes pleaded with her. "I can't love you. I can't do it."

"But *do* you?" She pressed closer and made him return her gaze. "Do you love me, anyway?"

He gently but firmly put her away from him.

"Neil!" Her voice shook, with the force of her emotions.

"Stop!" he ordered, grasping her shoulders, almost crushing them with his frantic grip. He forced himself to loosen his hold on her, and continued in a voice rough with feeling. "You don't understand, so please just stop. It doesn't matter if I love you, or not. It can't happen for us, Darcy."

Bitter tears rushed onto Darcy's cheeks. "Why not?" she demanded angrily.

He made no reply and she pushed him in the chest in stormy defiance. "You owe me that much, Neil! I want to know why not!"

"Because!" he yelled at her, in distress. "I'm married!"

Chapter Ten

Darcy sank back down into her chair with a look of horrified stupor in her eyes. She slowly raised them to Neil, in a mute plea for him to tell her that he was joking.

He threw his head back, and stared at the ceiling in anguish.

The room was reverberating with a deafening silence, that grew in intensity, as the moments dragged by.

"Darcy..." He knelt down in front of her and tried to take her hands, but she snatched them back fiercely, and fastened him with a cold stare.

"Please let me explain," he began again.

"Explain!" She was outraged. "Explain *what?* How, all the while we've talked and spent time together, you just forgot to mention an insignificant little thing, like a wife?"

He touched her hand again and she jerked it up, as if she would slap him. A tiny vein began to pulsate in his temple. He stood up and clamped his hand firmly around her wrist, pulling her to her feet.

"You are going to listen to this!" he rasped. "I didn't come back here for nothing! You are *not* going to be left thinking that I'm the kind of man who would come on to you, and then drive back home to a wife!"

"Which is exactly what you've been doing!" she shouted back, trying in vain to wrestle free from his grasp.

"No, I have not!"

"Oh, so now you're telling me that you *don't* have a wife at home!"

"That's right, I don't!"

She narrowed her eyes in cold resentment. "What kind of a fool do you take me for, Neil?"

"I don't take you for a fool at all. If anybody's a fool, it's me, for thinking I could spend any amount of time around you at all, and not fall in love with you."

"Don't say that!" She tried again to pull away. "Don't you dare say you love me!"

"I *do* love you!"

"And your wife doesn't understand you, and the only reason you've stayed together is because of the children, but as soon as they're out of the house, you're gonna leave her!" Intensity surged throughout her body. "Well, don't leave her for me! Go home and *stay* home!"

"Just shut up and listen to me!" he commanded savagely. "I'm gonna make you hear this, if I have to stay here all night! I'm not telling you so that you'll just accept things, and we can be together. That's not gonna happen. I'm telling you so you'll understand that I'm not a decrepit, conniving excuse for a man who selfishly set out to have you!"

"Oh, well, gee, that's comforting," she returned bitingly. "It just happened. Neither one of us planned it, it was just bigger than the both of us!"

"Will you just shut up and listen?"

"What if I say no?"

They locked their eyes into a tight clench, which only served to heighten their rampant emotions. Neil slowly tightened his hold on her arm and pulled her forward until their faces were almost touching.

"You will listen to everything I have to say," he grated, in a strained, hoarse tone, leading her over to the sofa, despite her efforts to make him let her go. He drew her firmly down to sit beside him, and made her face him.

She raked him over with scornful eyes. "Fine! Get your little sob story over with, and then get out!"

Neil winced at the venom in her voice and made no effort to hide its effect on him.

"Please, Darcy. I promise never to bother you again, but please listen to what I have to say. I need you to really hear me."

Something in his tone got past her guard and she dropped her gaze to the floor.

"Fine," she repeated, coldly, but more subdued.

"I told you, some time ago, that I've lived here in Tennessee before, for about eight years. Some of that time was broken up with extended mission trips." He paused to stop himself from nervously rambling, and to force himself to focus on the task at hand.

He sent a silent plea for help from God, then took a deep breath. "Not long after I got here, I met someone and we began seeing each other pretty regularly. Her name was Madeline Holt. She was a singer, and did a lot of studio work in Nashville. I was crazy about her, and spent the next two years campaigning my brains out to get her to marry me."

Darcy blinked back fresh tears, then closed her eyes tightly.

He lifted his hand as if to touch her face, but drew it back. "I sort of knew, even back then, that she wasn't really in love with me. I kept putting that knowledge aside and persisted, thinking that I had enough love for the both of us. I guess I thought she'd grow to care for me. I must have proposed a million times and every time, she'd just laugh at me, and make some sort of joke. She never actually said no, she just didn't say yes.

"One day, after almost two years of making a complete idiot out of myself, she brought the subject of marriage up, herself, and wanted me to ask her, again. This time, she just up and said yes. Right out of the blue. She not only said yes, but she wanted to marry me right away. I didn't understand it, but I didn't ask any questions. I just bought the ring, got the license, and hired the minister. That was about six years ago. Darcy, please don't do that."

He saw her stiffen and look away, as if she wouldn't listen to anymore, and caught her other hand, pulling them both up to his heart in a pleading fashion.

"Please, hear me. I'm begging you."

She slowly looked up and relented, when she saw tears glistening in his eyes.

He hesitated, as if unsure of how to begin again, then plunged back in.

"On our wedding night, Madeline began crying. She kept on, for what seemed like hours. I gave up trying to make her talk to me and just sat there, watching her. Finally, she said she had to tell me something. I told her that whatever it was, we could work it out. I was completely unprepared though, when she blurted out that she was pregnant! I remember just sitting there, feeling nothing, like a dead man. All I could think about was the fact that she and I had never slept together, ever."

He smiled sadly down at the carpet and shook his head. "I mean, you'd think it would have occurred to me to wonder who *did* sleep with her, but I just kept telling myself that *I* hadn't... as if that meant it couldn't be true, then.

"She said she knew that a scandal would ruin her in the Christian music industry. She wasn't a signed artist, but she was in demand more and more, for studio work, and was in the middle of recording a demo that everyone was sure would get her a contract.

"When she found out she was pregnant, she just panicked. It turned out that the baby's father was a married record producer. Madeline didn't love me, but she also didn't love the thought of being finished in Music City, once the truth got out. She said she'd considered aborting the baby, but she was afraid someone would find out about it and that marrying me seemed to be the perfect solution, especially since the baby's father had no intention of stepping up. Since I had been ignorant of everything, I had just gone around feeling stupidly happy and lucky... until our wedding night."

He saw something like compassion in Darcy's eyes and continued, a glimmer of hope flickering in his heart.

"Anyway, when she told me, I pretty much fell apart. I don't know why. I mean, I had never kidded myself that she was in love with me. I just didn't think she was seeing someone else. I prayed about it long and hard, and finally decided that I would stay with her and we'd try to make a go of it. Here's a bit of trivia for you..."

He studied her hands in his for a moment, before he finished. "Not only did I not sleep with her before our wedding, I never slept with her after."

Darcy's eyes widened in disbelief. Without realizing it, she turned her palms up and laced her fingers into his, as he breathed a heavy sigh.

"Madeline seemed almost happy for a while, but I guess it was just gratitude, and the relief of dodging a bullet. Then, three months into the marriage, she miscarried. I had actually allowed myself to begin thinking of the baby as mine, so I was pretty upset, but she seemed pleased.

"Immediately on the heels of that, all the gratitude went the way of the child. She became indifferent to me, and then openly hostile. I guess she felt she had been cheated, and was trapped with me for life. We continued in that vein for another year and a half, before I was asked to lead a group of teens on a mission trip to Mexico. I balked at first, but she was insistent that I go. I thought about it, and decided that maybe what we needed was some time apart. I guess I was hoping for that 'absence makes the heart grow fonder' thing to kick in."

He stopped and studied Darcy's lovely face, that was softening by the moment.

"You're not doing your part," he accused gently, with the faintest ghost of a smile. "You're supposed to keep yelling at me, and not let me finish."

She drew her brow in a way that revealed the war going on inside her. "Go on," she finally whispered, unconsciously rubbing his fingertips.

Neil held her gaze with sorrowful, dark eyes, before resuming. "I was a little worried about being gone for so long. It would be for a few months. That's not good for most marriages, but staying around didn't seem to be helping. Besides, Madeline was going to be in the studio for two different projects, so I made up my mind to go.

"I had become more sensitive to God's presence and leading in my life, while I was in Mexico. One of the things Madeline resented the most was being the wife of a minister. I had been caving in to her, by not getting too involved in extra venues, but I came back from Mexico sure of my calling and at peace. I hoped we might be able to somehow start over again. So, you can imagine my childish surprise, when I bounded through the door with that whole 'honey, I'm home' thing, only to find that honey, herself, wasn't home."

He interpreted the question in Darcy's eyes. "She was just gone. I thought, at first, she was at a session, until I began to realize that all her things were gone. Everything. There wasn't one shred of her left in the house. I called everyone I could think of, her family members, the scant few I knew about, anyway... her friends, the studio. I even called the police, but they couldn't do anything about it. She was a grown woman and since all her things were gone, no foul play was suspected. They did locate her car a few days later at the Nashville airport, so it became obvious to them that she did hop a plane, but she didn't use her real name."

He stared down at the floor, mesmerized by something invisible. "That was four years ago," he mumbled, in a tired voice. "No one around here ever heard from her again or, if they have, no one's saying anything."

He pulled his hands from hers and leaned forward, resting his arms on his knees and closing his eyes, as if reliving his past all over again.

Darcy watched him, her heart beginning to ache with what she was feeling for him, in this moment. She tentatively laid her hand on his bowed head, and he looked up at her helplessly.

"I'm so sorry," she whispered.

"No, Darcy, don't be. I'm the one who's sorry. It doesn't change anything. I guess we both know that," he added, despondently.

He straightened up and let out a deep breath. "But I just needed for you to know. I'm so sorry that I didn't put away my feelings for you. I have no rights, here. I'm a married man, as far as I know. I mean, how do you serve divorce papers to someone you can't even find? Or *do* you serve divorce papers, especially if you're a minister?" He shook his head. "I just don't have any answers."

"But, Neil." Darcy touched his chin with her fingertip and made him look at her. "You can't just live the rest of your life in limbo, not knowing if you're married or not."

"Well, I guess I *am* married. She certainly never served *me* with papers."

"What about an annulment?" she asked quietly. "If the marriage was never consummated..."

"Oh, Darcy, I've asked myself those questions every day of my life, for the past four years. I even went as far as to see a lawyer about it, but I couldn't go through with anything. I don't know, I guess it was a combination of wanting to do the right thing as a man of God, and thinking that I still loved her, and that maybe someday she'd come back.

"What if there *had* been some kind of foul play? What if she hadn't been unfaithful once we were married, but just left impulsively, for whatever crazy reason? What if she *did* come back? There's so much controversy flying around about Christian divorce. Maybe I could slip through the cracks, if I were just a quiet member in a back pew. But, wouldn't you know it? I have to go and be a minister and not only, that but the state youth director!"

He let out a bitter laugh, and drew his fingers through his hair, then rubbed his temples.

Darcy watched him silently. Her arguments were ready, but she held her fire. This wasn't her decision to make.

Neil turned toward her, then drew her just a little closer. "Can I tell you something?"

She nodded slowly, unable to resist warming herself in what she saw in his eyes.

"It was you, Darcy, who showed me that I don't still love her, that maybe what I felt for her was never really love, at all. What I feel for you is so different. It's so deep and peaceful and so full of..." He broke off awkwardly. "I shouldn't be saying these things to you. I mean, nothing's changed, has it?"

"Neil..." She lifted one of his hands to her cheek. "Can't we try to find her? I mean, why can't we work together to find out what happened to her? Don't you want to be free from this? Don't you want..." Her voice cracked and tears splashed down onto his hand.

He immediately gathered her close, and laid his lips on her hair. "Yes! I *want* you, Darcy. I do, with all my heart. But I've followed every imaginable trail. Wherever she is, she doesn't want to be found. I'm sorry, sweetheart." He pulled back and let her see his raw emotion. "But this just isn't going to happen for us."

He released her and stood up, making a move to leave, and she rose to block his path, intent on some sort of resolution.

"Then what *does* happen?" She studied him, longingly. "Do we just pretend that we don't love each other? Do we exchange meaningless pleasantries when we meet, and act as if we barely know each other? I can't do that, Neil. Can you?"

He didn't try to answer. What good would it do?

Darcy couldn't let it go. She loved this man, and she wasn't about to simply let him slip away, without a fight. "Give me one good reason why we can't try to find her and put an end to all this."

"Darcy..." He turned and paced around restlessly, his hands in his pockets, his eyes staring vacantly ahead. He tried to push back the same old feelings that always came, when he entertained the notion of looking for his wife, but to no avail. A tomb-like coldness clutched his heart, and bitterness surged to the forefront of his emotions. He spun around and planted a look of bleak resignation on her.

"Just leave it alone!"

She stared at him in complete disbelief. "That's your answer? 'Just leave it alone'? I'm not even worth *trying* for?"

He gave her a long look, then pulled her into his arms, hugging her with a desperation that she could feel. "You're worth... oh, Darcy, you're worth everything to me, but you just don't understand."

"What is it I don't understand?"

Neil looked down into her eyes for a long moment before losing his resolve, and kissing her firmly and hungrily.

Tears were coursing down both their cheeks now, as he released her and opened the door. "We just have to let it go," he said hopelessly, closing the door firmly behind him, as he left.

Chapter Eleven

Hailey glanced back over her shoulder at her quiet sister-in-law, as she started her car. "All set, Darce?"

"Yeah, I think I have everything."

"How 'bout you, Missy?" She cast a fond eye over at Meredith, who was resting comfortably in the front seat.

"So far, so good," she quipped, reclining her seat slightly and hugging a thin bed pillow close. "Am I cutting off your leg-room, sweetie?" She tossed her question to Darcy, who was stretched out across the back, with one foot up on the door's armrest.

"No, I'm good. My legs are up on the seat." Darcy raised herself up and leaned forward. "Are you sure you're up to this, Merry? I mean, after your fall and everything."

"If I wasn't, don't you think Mr. Etheridge would be yanking me out of this car, by now?" She grinned and winked. "I'm much better now, no worries. Just turned out to be a little blood pressure thing."

"Listen to her!" Hailey maneuvered her car around the drive and out onto the main road. "*Little.* She probably thinks Mt. Everest is a speed bump."

Darcy widened her eyes. "Why aren't you in the hospital, girl?"

"Because Joel ordered them to fix me right there, on the spot, that's why." She smiled at Hailey's light giggle.

"Actually, I'm under a whole bunch of orders, and on medication, at least for right now. My O.B. wasn't too thrilled about putting me on anything, but he finally decided it was the lesser risk. Joel said I could go today, as long as I brought my stupid cell phone, and didn't do anything more strenuous than lift the cheeseburger he finally said I could have. The one Hailey's buying me," she added with a grin and a light punch to her friend's arm.

Darcy shook her head. "How high did it go?"

Meredith shrugged characteristically. "I really don't remember, but it sounded scary at the time. All I know is it put me on the floor. Doc Lynch says it's not unheard of, for us preggies to peg out the meter. Other than an occasional headache, I'm pretty much okay, now."

"Well, you need to be careful, Merry, especially when you're by yourself." Darcy sat up straighter, and leaned over her shoulder, to inspect her. "Hailey said you got all cut up."

"Like a Thanksgiving turkey." She held up her still bandaged hand for Darcy to see. "You should check out my knees. Probably have a scar on the right one. Ooo, a scar!" she added, widening her eyes and grinning over at Hailey. "Joel won't let me get a tattoo, but I may start doing my concerts wearing cut-offs, so the kids will see my scars, and think I'm cool."

Hailey rolled her eyes and laughed. "Cut-offs, huh? I don't remember cut-offs being a part of Joel Etheridge's wardrobe policy. You must secretly love it, when your husband shows up on stage, and carries you off. I think you rankle him on purpose."

Darcy was still looking at Meredith's bandaged hand, then noticed a gash on her upper arm that was healed enough to not need a bandage, but still ugly looking. She winced, and drew her breath in audibly. Meredith reassured her with a little laugh, "I'm okay, honey. It's just Joel's baby boy. That's what kids are good for, ramping up your blood pressure. He's not wasting any time." She didn't look too upset about it.

There was a quiet lull before Hailey peered at Darcy through the rear view mirror. "Listen, pet, are you sure you want to go through with this? I don't mean to get too personal, but I can tell there's a problem, and I can only assume it has to do with you and Neil McCallen."

"Why do you assume that?" She asked tonelessly, lying back against the seat, with a tired expression.

"Your failure to light up like a Christmas tree, when his name is mentioned, for one thing. You seem to have given up on that Yuletide thing you had going."

"You don't miss much, do you?"

"You sound like Ross." Hailey smiled back at her. "Was I mistaken, or was there something brewing there, at one time?"

"Maybe. At one time. I don't know." Darcy let her eyes wander aimlessly around. She wasn't sure why, but she really didn't want to talk about Neil with Hailey and Meredith. Normally, she'd be spilling her guts. If it were anything else besides a wife, lurking in the shadows! She let a soft sigh escape, and closed her eyes.

Hailey pulled onto the freeway and headed west toward the little town of Dickson, where the campground was located. It was a privately owned setting, that was commonly rented to different church groups, for their summer outings.

"I don't mean to bug you," she ventured slowly, as she carefully started around a lumbering eighteen-wheeler, "but I'm just a little concerned about you having to spend an entire week at youth camp with this guy, if things aren't good between you. Talk about awkward!"

"It doesn't matter," Darcy informed her, in a flat manner. She caught Hailey's worried expression in the mirror. "It just didn't work out. I'm not mad at him, or anything."

Meredith threw Hailey a knowing glance, before shifting around in the seat so that she could see Darcy better. "What chance do you think you have, locked up in a car with the two women most unlikely to stay out of your business?"

She smiled faintly at Meredith's teasing grin, but gave her nothing else in return.

Hailey shook her head in curious surrender, and Meredith settled back and focused her eyes on the passing landscape.

The two slipped into a casual conversation, while Darcy pretended to nap. She apparently did such a good job, that she jumped up, startled, when Hailey stopped the car and announced their arrival, all too soon. She rubbed her eyes and stared blankly out the window.

"You don't have to do this," Hailey assured her, noting the dread that washed over her pale face.

"Yes, I do." Darcy drew in a deep breath. "I'm already registered and it's too late to get a replacement. Besides, I'm full-time, now. The state office expects all full-time youth leaders to take an active roll in camp. Registration is actually mandatory."

"How are you going to manage, honey, if things are gonna be weird between you and Neil?" Meredith inquired in a gentle voice.

She lowered her head and blinked quickly, two spots of hot color burning fiercely on her cheeks.

"Never mind, baby." Meredith had once known, only too well, the pain of not being able to be with the man she loved... an ache made even worse, whenever she had to see him. Her heart went out to Darcy. "It'll be tough, but you'll manage."

They got out of the car, stretched, and looked around, then began gathering Darcy's belongings.

"Would you guys mind just loading me up out here?" Darcy asked hesitantly. "You don't have to go in."

Hailey shot Meredith a keen look. "Well... okay, Darce, if you're really sure that's what you want." She shielded her eyes against the sun, and looked around the campground at the various counselors, who were unloading their gear. They were all arriving some four hours early, for orientation and in order to be ready to give their undivided attention, when the campers got there.

She turned to help her sister-in-law, and stopped short at the look of absolute sorrow in her eyes. She traced Darcy's gaze directly to Neil McCallen, who was standing next to his car, caught staring helplessly back at her. His tortured expression was identical to hers.

"Jeepers!" Meredith hissed under her breath. She laid a commanding, but compassionate hand on Darcy's shoulder, and placed herself on their visual path. "Listen to me, Darce," she advised, in all seriousness. "I've been exactly where you are, right now." She tightened her grip a little. "Look at me."

Darcy reluctantly dragged her eyes away from his, and encountered Meredith's sharp, no-nonsense expression. "I hate to sound callous, baby, but unless this is some small tiff that can be fixed by a simple apology, you're just gonna have to suck it up, and get on with it."

"Merry, don't use that awful expression!" Hailey complained, irritably.

"Sorry," she muttered. She locked her gray eyes onto Darcy's, and changed her grip to a caress. "Sweetheart, what I'm trying to say is that you're here to do a job. That comes before anything else. You've got a huge wad of kids to look after, and we don't want anybody drowning in a pool, or getting bit by a snake, because you're phoning it in."

"Missy..." Hailey began.

Darcy left off her study of the pine straw around her feet, and held up a silencing hand. "No, Merry's right," she decided, with a lift of her chin. "I might as well get a grip now, before it overwhelms me."

Hailey studied her for a long moment. "You said your car won't be fixed before the weekend, even if we could get it to you," she said slowly. "What about letting us come to get you, when this is over?"

She managed a shaky smile. "Thanks. I'll call and let you know. It's only a cracked distributor cap and a bad thermostat, but Stan doesn't think he can get to it, with the hours he's putting in. He said if he could, he and Bett would either get it to me, or Bett may be able to pick me up. It all depends." She gave her a big hug, and reached for Meredith next.

"You girls headed straight home?" she asked them, a little too brightly .

"Not if Meredith's still feeling okay, when we hit Nashville. We're going baby bed shopping."

"Plus, *cheeseburger*," Meredith reminded her.

"Merry, you be sure and tell Hailey, if you start feeling funny," Darcy warned.

"Won't have to. She asks me every five minutes."

Hailey loaded Darcy down with luggage, constantly snatching suitcases away from Meredith, as she tried to help. She stopped and surveyed things with a critical eye.

"Sure you can manage, Darce?"

"I'm fine."

"We're praying for you."

"Thanks, Hailey."

Hailey lingered, reaching up and smoothing Darcy's hair, with a maternal touch. "Okay, pet. We love you."

Quick tears hurried to her lashes, but she smiled in spite of them. "I love you too. Do me a favor and leave, huh?"

They traded more hugs, and unwillingly left Darcy to fight her own battles.

Joel looked up from a stack of letters, and a contract Delores had left for him to read through and sign. "Heading home, Marshall?"

"Guess so." He strolled in and rested casually on the arm of a chair. "Looks like everybody else has. You gonna pack it up?"

"Not just yet. Delores left me with plenty to do, and since Meredith's off with Hailey, I thought I'd try to get caught up. I've taken off several days, the past couple of weeks, but I guess I don't have to tell you that."

"Merry doing better?"

Joel swiveled his chair around a little and began massaging a stiff neck. "Much better. Getting rowdy again." He leaned back into a long stretch. "I was really starting to miss our little sparring matches, to be honest. But this morning, I made the mistake of saying I didn't have time for breakfast, after she had finished making it, and I ended up wearing it. That's when I knew my gal was up to snuff."

Marshall joined his hearty laughter. "Are you serious? You really ended up..."

"With egg on my face." Joel informed him. "And in my hair and all down my shirt. We won't even talk about the orange juice."

Marshall threw his head back, and roared. "That's our girl!" he declared, wiping his eyes.

Joel grinned and crossed his arms. "I couldn't get mad. This is so much better than the pale, little moppet that's been haunting the house lately, that I'll gladly take it. In fact, I think I'll find some other way to rile her tonight, so she can read me the riot act."

Marshall shook his head and lifted himself from the chair. "Well, good luck! You're probably the only person I know, who can take her on, and make a decent showing. Just tell me one thing. Have you ever won a round?"

"I got her to marry me." he reminded him, with a smile. "I'd call that winning."

"Can't argue with that." His associate moved toward the door, turning back inside the frame. "You're sure you don't need me around, old man? I can definitely stay, if you need me to."

"Nah, get out of here." He waved him off. "Give my love to Bobbie."

"I'll do it!" Marshall returned his wave, and slipped out.

Joel sat still a moment, reliving the events of the morning he had just described to Marshall. He began to shake with silent laughter, his expression melting, as he remembered the way his little wife's stormy countenance immediately changed into one of consternation, as she realized where her hair-trigger temper had taken her.

She had stared up at him with those beautiful eyes and backed away, as if she half expected a paddling. She might have gotten one too, if she weren't pregnant! Instead, Joel was powerless against her appealing gaze, and wrapped her up in his arms, and gave her an eggy kiss. They both began to laugh, and Meredith apologized by getting him all cleaned up, and sending him on his way with more than a little affection.

He rested his eyes on her picture, and quietly thanked God for blessing him with his "little one" before forcing himself to concentrate on the job at hand. He barely lifted his head, as he heard a muted tap on his door. "Just can't stay away, Marshall? I don't pay you by the hour, you know."

"That's why I haven't applied for a job here!"

He jerked his head up quickly, obviously startled to find Janis Sheridan smiling at him from the doorway, and realizing that Marshall had forgotten to lock the front door, on his way out.

"Sorry, Miss Sheridan, I thought you were my associate. He just left, so recently in fact, that I thought he had come back in." Joel stood up, and regarded her curiously. "We didn't have an appointment, did we? I don't usually let Delores schedule anything this late."

Janis moved smoothly toward him and stopped in front of the desk.

"Well, no, Joel, we don't, and I know I'm being a little presumptive, to just show up like this. The thing is, I'm on my way to a meeting with some of my affiliates, and I'm worried that I don't have all my facts straight. I was just hoping against hope, that you might still be around, and that Delores might let me talk to you."

"Dee's cleared out for the day," he replied, ignoring the fact that she had used his first name. "I'm afraid I'm the secretary, as well as the entire staff. What is it exactly, that you need?"

"May I?" She indicated a chair with a flourish of her manicured hand.

"Of course, pardon me."

"That's perfectly alright!" Janis seated herself slowly, deciding, at the last moment, not to cross her long legs seductively. Not just yet. She reached inside her briefcase and pulled out a sheaf of papers. "First, I wanted to touch on something you'd said, the last time we talked. You told me that much in your industry depends heavily on airplay?" She received a nod, and continued on with her rehearsed script.

"I've been trying to figure out what determines radio play in this town. I did try to talk to the station managers but..." She broke off and swept her lashes coquettishly. "I guess this is going to sound a little vain, but I can't seem to get past declining to give out my phone number, and removing a few of the men's hands from my knees."

She raised her startling green eyes, in a seemingly shy manner. "I must say, I'm more than a little surprised to encounter that sort of behavior in the Christian market."

"Are you?" He was apathetic. "Why is that, Miss Sheridan?"

"Please call me Janis," she invited graciously. "I just thought that members of the religious community were sticklers for fidelity, and that sort of thing. Some of the hands I removed had wedding rings on them," she added, deceitfully.

"Well, I'm sorry to hear that, but not necessarily surprised. A lot of men claim a relationship with Christ, and do it with all sincerity, but if He's not ruling over their flesh, then they are, themselves, and doing a poor job of it. And, of course, you can't discount the enemy's influence."

He leaned back into his chair, and unconsciously resumed manipulating the knotted muscles at the base of his neck, then repeated his earlier question. "What is it you need to know?"

She leaned forward with a smile she knew to be quite effective. "Well, just what I said. What does determine whether or not a song gets airplay?"

Joel shrugged. "Beats me."

She faltered a little. "What do you mean?"

"I mean, who really knows? Some say it depends on how commercial a song is. Define *commercial*. Some say it depends on the song's repetitive value. You know, clever, hooky lines and redundant grooves, that echo in your head... whether you want them to, or not," he added dryly.

Janis narrowed her eyes, and regarded him thoroughly. "But by those definitions, your wife's music is hardly commercial, yet she's one of the most well-known artists this town has ever produced."

"Ah, but 'there's the rub'," Joel quoted, leaning forward onto his elbows. "This town had nothing to do with producing Meredith. She's God's own production, and she sets her own instinctive course by swimming against all the eager salmon. Against the flow, if you follow me."

"Then how do you explain her success?"

"Anointing, for one thing, though that doesn't necessarily have anything to do with whether or not a person makes it as a Christian artist, in this town. Not that other artists aren't anointed, just that it isn't the number one criteria for getting a record deal, unfortunately, for a lot of effective and anointed people. The big concern is one, can you move a lot of units? Two, can you get radio play? Three, do you look good, while doing it? Not like the Jesus Movement of the seventies. It was more real then, somehow. Less about money, and more about ministry."

Joel wished, and not for the first time, that he'd been a part of those years, before collecting himself, and continuing. "Meredith's deal is that the people love her. She pays absolutely no attention to what the guys in the suits tell her she has to say. She essentially thumbs her nose at the radio industry. She gets out there with the people. She hangs with the homeless, and the addicts, and the poor, and just the basic sector of society, as well as random churchgoers.

They let her know what they desperately need to hear. and she makes sure they hear it. People constantly call the radio stations, demanding her music because she fills a need. The broadcasters and advertisers seem to have finally gotten it through their skulls to give the people what they ask for... at least where Meredith is concerned."

"I see." Janis was quickly tiring of the apparent pride with which Joel Etheridge talked about his wife. "Sort of a grassroots approach."

"Not consciously, but perhaps. I'm hoping it's a sign of the people refusing to get caught up in the politics of the music and radio industry, and making themselves heard. By people, I'm not talking about Bobby Briefcase and Larry Let's-do-lunch. I'm talking John and Mary Doe who have to work at a thankless job, to pay for one CD or concert ticket, and who deserve to have been ministered to, when it's over.

"These people shouldn't have to be told by the industry what they need to hear. They know what they want. And it's usually a lot deeper than clever clichés, and redundant guitar riffs, that sound like the same guy played on everybody's project, which is generally the case, around here."

He stifled a tired yawn, then lifted up a corner of the stack of paperwork he'd been working on. "You'll have to forgive my opinionated viewpoint, Miss Sheridan. I'm obviously not the best choice to give you a purely statistical perspective, especially in the area of radio airplay."

She smiled coyly and shuffled her own papers. "That's quite understandable, Joel. I can certainly understand the satisfaction you take in seeing your wife defy such an obstinate system." She crossed her legs, slowly and deliberately, hiding a disappointed frown, as he naturally averted his eyes to his papers, that seemed to need his undivided attention.

"Well..." Janis lifted her heavily mascaraed lashes, and gave him a look of appeal. "If you don't mind my robbing one more moment of your evening, I wonder if you would take a quick glance at these figures I've compiled, and tell me if I've come anywhere close to the target."

Joel continued to peruse the letters and contracts Delores had left for him. "What kind of figures have you been working on?"

"Demographics, mainly. I've been breaking down the responsive age groups for each of the prominent artists I've been researching. I have Meredith's completed, and I thought you'd better see if I'm accurate, before I turn everything in at tonight's meeting."

"Sure. Let's take a look." Joel extended his hand to take her list, but she pretended she hadn't seen and, instead, came around to his chair.

"The way I've done this," she began, laying the sheets in front of him, and leaning over to point, "is to break everything down according to categories. You see, this is the column representing annual record sales." She leaned even closer, her low-cut blouse falling slightly open. "And this," she lowered her voice to a hum and smiled to herself, as she realized her expensive perfume was still quite aromatic, "is the section for concert attendance. And of course, this last column reflects the statistics of letters and requests for merchandise. I got that from your girls downstairs."

Joel was silent for a moment, looking over the information she had given him. She waited for his response, remaining hovered in close proximity.

"You didn't include video in any of this?" He asked finally, still not looking up.

"Why, no, I didn't!" Janis caught at her throat in feigned despair. "Is that an important factor, Joel?"

"Only if you consider the fact that her videos have been the most requested ones for the past two years, and immediately go viral. I understand that the requests came primarily from the teen through college sector."

"I see. Is that something I can simply include in my notes, do you think?" She turned to fasten her eyes on him, her face only inches away from his.

"That depends. You don't think your affiliates will require data, to back up the claim?"

Janis made no reply and, after a moment, Joel glanced up to find her surveying him, with unveiled desire in her strange eyes. A rush of thoughts pelted him all at once, holding him mute with their force, so that he seemed to be returning her gaze.

Mistaking his silent realization with mutual attraction, she displayed her loose fitting garments to full advantage, and moved to plant her lips on his. Immediately, she cried out in pain, as Joel's fingers dug sharply into the flesh of her upper arm.

"Joel! Stop! What are you doing?"

He leaped up from his chair and pulled her around the desk, snatching up her briefcase with his free hand. His face was white with emotion, and the muscles around his mouth throbbed with quiet rage.

"I'm sorry! No, wait!" she whimpered, real terror finding its way into her voice, as she realized what Oliver's response would be, when she had to face him. "Please! I don't know what came over me!"

He said nothing, but continued to drag her through his door and out to the one leading to the elevator.

"Joel, please! You're hurting me!"

Joel threw open the main office door, and flung her briefcase through it with such force, that it hit the opposite wall and bounced off, splitting open as it landed on the floor. Without consideration for the pain she was claiming, he firmly pushed her out after it.

"Please!" Real tears sprang from her eyes, not of repentance, but at the horror that faced her, when Oliver Sullivan was ready to deal with her.

"That's enough!" Joel's voice was like a thunderclap. "My wife was right about you, all along! I don't know what your game really is, Miss Sheridan, but it's over. If I ever catch you anywhere near this office, or my wife, you'll regret the day you ever stepped foot in Nashville!"

"No, let me..."

"GET OUT!" He slammed the door with a shuddering blast and locked it securely. His head was swimming with anger, and his pulse hammered dangerously. He stood there looking around blindly, not able to focus for several minutes. Finally, he made his way back into his office, and stopped short when he saw Janis Sheridan's papers on his desk, and scattered around the floor. He muttered something darkly under his breath, and shoved them into the trash, then slumped heavily into his chair, hardly able to believe what had just happened. He had to make a conscious effort to breathe normally, and it took him a good while.

"Dear God," he sighed out loud. "What has happened to my discernment? I'm supposed to be protecting my wife, and all I've done is tell her she was being silly about Janis Sheridan! Please forgive me for not listening to the Holy Spirit."

He straightened up in his chair after another moment, then realized how very desperately he so needed to hear Meredith's voice. He silently thanked God that he'd insisted she take her phone today, and his stern features relaxed at the sound of her husky voice.

"Baby farm! You sow 'em, we grow 'em!"

"Sweetheart!"

"Well, if it isn't Old McDonald, himself."

He smiled and cradled the receiver, as if it were his wife's hand. "I've missed you."

"Trust me, you didn't!" Meredith let out a giggle and he chuckled quietly.

"Will you knock it off with the reproductive jokes, and say something mushy to me?" he demanded, in faint exasperation.

"Boiled okra."

"Stop it," he murmured, his recent turmoil already fading into oblivion. "Where are you, baby?"

"We're headed down Hillsboro. Or we would be, if we weren't having to stop at every red light and, of course, there's one at every block. If you miss one, don't worry, you're gettin' the next one! Whoever timed these stupid things, apparently had no where to go, himself."

"Going home, then?"

"Yep. Long day. But I feel okay; my feet are just tired," she hurried to add, anticipating his next question.

"A foot massage might be in your future. I'm about to head home, myself."

"Why don't you do that, Mister Man?" She coated her words with love and he trembled at the way she stirred his heart.

"I'm on my way." He looked down at some of Janis Sheridan's papers that had fallen from the edge of the trash can to the floor and frowned.

"Meredith..." He said her name with a quiet urgency that put her on high alert.

"What is it, sweetie?"

There was the slightest hesitation. "I love you."

She wrinkled her brow, not missing an indefinable "something" in her husband's voice. "I love you, too, Joel. Come home, and see for yourself."

"I'll be there soon." He laid the phone down and gathered up his belongings, hoping that Janis Sheridan wasn't waiting out front. He needn't have worried, it seemed. The briefcase was gone and she was nowhere in sight. He sped along to the parking structure and hopped into his Cadillac, concerned only with getting home to his wife.

Janis Sheridan watched his departure from her own car, her eyes smoldering with hatred. "Fine, Joel Etheridge," she hissed through clenched teeth. "I'll stay away from your office. As for your wife, however..." She paused, and an ugly gleam came into her eyes. "I'm not making any promises."

Chapter Twelve

Darcy looked down at her folded hands, and moistened her dry lips, nervously.

"I'm sorry this was so uncomfortable."

She glanced up at the sound of Neil's voice. It was the first thing he had said, since they passed Nashville.

"It's no one's fault," she offered, in a small voice.

"Well..." He looked out the window of his car at Wally and Foster, digging out in the garden. "I know you would rather have ridden with your friends, or had your own car. For your sake, I wish it could have worked out for you. But still, I..." He looked over at her, and forced a smile. "Never mind. Let's get you unloaded, then."

She came around and waited, while he unlocked the trunk. Wally and Foster, as of yet, hadn't noticed their arrival. Darcy watched her little blonde buddy, in order to distract herself, as he held up something, probably a worm, and inspected it closely.

"Is this everything?"

She looked down at the pile of bags Neil had lifted out and now indicated, and hesitated a moment, remembering the jacket she had left in his car, and the evening he brought it back. The flush of scarlet that crept into her cheeks did not go unnoticed. "Yes, that's it. Thank you."

He began hanging luggage on his shoulders, and grabbing the handles of larger cases.

"Neil, you don't have to..."

"I want to."

Darcy blinked quickly, and led the way to her apartment door. She knew Bett was watching from the kitchen window, and just wanted to get it over with and get inside, before she discerned too much. She fumbled clumsily with her keys, suppressing a strong urge to try to kick the door down. At last, she came up with the right one, and the door yielded.

Neil stepped in behind her and slowly released his burdens onto her living room floor. He straightened up and gave her a long searching look.

"Are you alright?"

"No." She made herself return his gaze. "I'm sorry, I'm not."

"Neither am I."

They both stood there uncertain of what to do next. Neil made no effort to hide the longing in his eyes, and Darcy unwisely let herself be caught up in their depths. With a quick movement, he closed the space between them, and gathered her up against himself.

"I'm so sorry, Darcy," he whispered, burying his face in her hair.

She made no reply, but pulled him closer and tried to lose herself in this feeling. They stood that way for several long, silent moments, before Neil slowly pulled away.

"I just keep messing things up, don't I?" He gave her a sad smile, and stepped toward the door. He allowed himself to drink her in, with one last look, that did nothing to cloak what he was feeling. "Goodbye, Darcy."

She stood in silence, until the door clicked behind him with a bitter finality.

"Goodbye, Neil." Her whisper turned into a quiet sob.

It was some time before she was able to shake herself out of this frozen moment, and secure her emotions, in order to face Bett and the kids. She sought refuge in the shower first, letting the warm water beat down on her, soothing her into a more composed state. She took the time to dry her hair and dress, then crossed the yard toward the Greer's house.

"Deck!" She turned around, as Wally hailed her. He came toward her with a dutiful stride, Foster hot on his heels.

"Deck, don't God got wings?" he demanded.

"Hi, yourself!" She found herself managing a smile. It was good to see him.

"Hi," he inserted, impatiently, as if she hadn't been away all week. "God does too got wings, don't He?"

He waited for her to weigh in, his arms crossed importantly over his little chest.

"Wings?" Darcy gave him a puzzled stare. "Well... I guess so. Why?"

"See!" He flashed Foster a triumphant look.

"He's got *hands*," Foster declared, tossing his red bangs out of his eyes. Both junior philosophers stood their ground, apparently waiting for a final decision.

"David did say in Psalms, 'Hide me in the shadow of Your wings' and 'In the shadow of Your wings I will take refuge.'" she volunteered, wondering where all this was coming from.

"Well, it says He's got the whole world in His hands!" Foster persisted.

"That ain't no bible verse!" Wally jeered. "That's just a dumb song!"

"Well, Foster, if it makes you feel any better, when Jesus died on the cross, He told His Father, 'Into Your

141

hands I commit My spirit.'" Darcy smiled at the effect her words had on him.

"Told you so!" He turned the tables on Wally, with a smug expression.

"Well, that ain't right!" Wally was downright indignant. "He can't have both! That'd be weird; have big ol' wings with hands stickin' out the ends!" "

If you think *that* sounds weird, try reading Revelation, sometime," she advised, turning on her heels toward the house, and leaving the two theologians to arrive at their own conclusions.

"Bett..." Her tired voice preceded her actual entrance, and she came into the kitchen with both hands in the air, as if she were trying to hold up a wall. "Please don't ask me a bunch of questions. I had a good time at camp and I'm doing okay, really, and no, I'm not planning on doing anything drastic. Can we just leave it at that?"

Bett grinned good-naturedly, from in front of the stove.

"Fine by me!" she declared, wiping her hands on her apron and coming over to give her a hug. "Anyway, I don't need to ask a lot of questions. I told you before, I'm not blind."

"Yes, you did," Darcy conceded wearily. "Not much gets by you, I'll grant you that."

"It doesn't get by me, the fact that things aren't working out between you two, like I'd hoped."

"Were you hoping?" She slumped down on a stool and tucked her hair back behind her ears.

"Yes, I was. If I ever saw two people meant to be together, it's you and the Incredible Hunk!"

Darcy shot out a gush of weak laughter, in spite of herself. "I knew you'd come up with some kind of tag for him, Bett, but I didn't expect that."

"Why not?" She settled on a nearby stool, and rested her elbows on the counter. "He's a fine specimen of manhood, if you ask me."

"Yeah, well you'd better hope no one asks you in front of Stan."

Bett chuckled pleasantly, and swiped something invisible off the laminate with one hand. "Like I said, I'm not blind."

"I've heard that," Darcy's comment was dry, and she rested her chin in her hands, and looked up at Bett with eyes that gave away too much.

"Listen, sweetheart." Bett sobered and laid a gentle hand on her arm. "I think of you like one of my own family, you know that."

"Stop it, you're gonna make me cry."

"Well, maybe that's what you need, a real honest-to-goodness cry," she replied, not without wisdom. "The point is, I know you're hurting right now, and I know it's serious. You two are in love, any idiot can see that. I know it would take something big to keep you apart, and because it *is* something big, I'm not going to tease you about him, or pry into it. I'm just telling you that when it gets too big, I'm right here. Fair enough?"

Darcy hopped up and came around to embrace her dear friend. "More than fair," she choked, giving Bett a tight squeeze. "And I will want to talk about it, just not right now. Okay?"

"Okay." Bett patted her on the back and released her, as she straightened up.

"Is my car fixed?" Darcy mopped at the corners of her eyes, and looked up hopefully.

"All ready."

"Great! Tell Stan thank you for me, and tell him to hit me with the bill tonight. And I *do* want a bill and not just for parts, either," she added with a stubborn expression, that put a stop to any argument that might be forthcoming.

"He not going to do all that work for nothing. Tell him I'm ready to go to the mat on this one." She put an extra measure of sternness into her voice, since both Stan and Bett often tried to give her a pass on everything, including rent, just because she was their church's youth pastor.

"I'm going to run over to Ross and Hailey's right now. I just need to check with them about something." She stopped at the door and looked back at her landlady, who was so much more like a big sister. "I love you, Bett."

"Go on, get outta here!" Bett flung a carefree wave toward her, as she took her leave.

Traffic was light, and Darcy covered the distance between her home and her brother's quickly. She noticed Joel and Meredith's black car parked in the drive, and hesitated, then prodded herself. It didn't matter. A little embarrassment seemed a small thing, if this trip turned out not to be a waste of time. Besides, she trusted Joel and Meredith as much as her own family.

She stepped up to the door and knocked timidly. It fairly flew open, and Hailey dragged her inside.

"Darcy's home!" she sang out, for the benefit of the others. She wrapped her up tightly, then passed her over to her brother, for similar treatment.

"Hey, squirt!" Ross planted a kiss on her cheek. "How goes the war?"

"I may need to enlist extra troops," she replied half seriously, reaching for Meredith and Joel in turn.

"I'm surprised you didn't just crash, as soon as you got in," Hailey speculated. "Not that we're not wildly excited to see you. Why didn't you let us come get you?"

"Well..." Darcy left the question unanswered and eyed them all soberly. "I have to talk to you guys about some things."

"Should we leave?" Joel lifted his brows at her, to invite agreement.

"No, don't." She held up one hand to detain them. "I need some help and I think I'd like to include all of you, if you don't mind."

"Sounds like a sit-downer," Ross observed, plopping back down onto the sofa, and patting a place next to himself, for his bride.

Darcy found a chair, and hurried through her thoughts, before beginning.

"I don't know if I'll get into every little thing," she started, slowly. "But I know everybody's been keeping tabs on Neil McCallen and me. I might as well go ahead and admit that we've recently discovered that we do have strong feelings for each other. But anyway," she rushed on, in order to stop anyone's attempt to tease her, "all that doesn't matter anymore, unless..."

She halted, uncertain of how to proceed. "I mean, it doesn't matter how we feel, because we can't do anything about it."

"Why not, Darce?" Ross asked with a tender note. He leaned forward and studied her closely.

"Because, he's already... he's married." She let her words sink in, not missing the angry crimson that tinged both her brother's and Joel's faces. Meredith closed her eyes, while Hailey stared at her in astonishment.

"That sorry pup!" Ross spat out furiously.

"No, wait, let me finish!"

"Finish *what?*" He glared at no one in particular. "He's either married or he's not!"

"It's not that simple."

"Let her finish, honey," Hailey breathed quietly. She laid her hand on his knee, and gave Darcy an encouraging nod.

"He married a girl about six years ago. I'm not gonna rehash every detail because, to be honest, I just don't think I'm up to it."

Her brother noted the dark circles under her eyes and inwardly seethed.

"I'll just say that it turned out to be a marriage of convenience, even though he didn't realize it would be, when he took her to the altar. He'd asked her to marry him before, and she always turned him down, but then, out of the blue, she suddenly wanted to get married right away. It turns out she was pregnant with somebody else's baby, and accepted his proposal to avoid a scandal. The father was a married producer here in town."

Mixed expressions traveled quickly around the room, but none more alarmed than Meredith's.

She stared intently at the floor, trying to snag some suggestion of a memory that was eluding her, but only for the moment. The conversation around her faded into the background, as she trained her eyes on the carpet pattern and worked through something she'd known about, but had obviously forgotten... some girl backup singer and... what was that producer's name? She'd not heard anything about a pregnancy, but she did remember that the girl had left town abruptly, and that the producer apparently headed for parts unknown, not too long afterward. She furrowed her brow to summon fragments of past events, until Darcy's voice drew her back to the moment.

"She hit him with all this on their wedding night," she was saying. "He never... they never consummated their marriage. She had a miscarriage a few months later. They were together almost two years, even though she didn't seem to be able to stand him. He left for three months to go on a mission trip and when he got back, she was gone."

Darcy drew in a deep breath and steadied herself. There. It was out.

"What do you mean, baby?" Meredith tilted her head to one side and waited. "Gone for good?"

She nodded. "There was no note, or anything. All her clothes and things were gone, so the police wouldn't get involved. Neil tried to contact her family, but there wasn't much of one that he knew anything about. No one knew anything, or if they did, they weren't talking."

She looked at her brother carefully. "It's been four years, Ross."

He caught her gaze and held it, as his dark brooding face gradually softened.

"I'm sorry, Darce. Listening to the rest helps, but it doesn't completely erase my instincts to punch out any guy who would drag my sister into something like this."

She offered a tentative smile. "I didn't come here just to tell you this story."

He raised questioning brows, and she ventured into her real mission. "I came to ask your help. I want to find her."

"What do you mean, *you* want to find her?" Ross's frown immediately found its place, again. "Why isn't McCallen here, asking for help to find her?"

She dropped her eyes and hung her head.

"Do you mean to sit there, and tell me that the man doesn't even have the decency to do his own detective work? If he had no intention of continuing his search for her, then he never had any business telling you that he has feelings for you!"

She lifted her eyes to meet his, with a defiant air that her brother had often seen, and knew meant trouble.

"Maybe not, but he did! It's a little too late to hate him for it, don't you think?"

"I never said anything about hate," he shot back. "But I *am* saying that I have absolutely no respect for a man who would lay something like this on my sister, and then not even have the backbone to settle things, himself! Why should it fall on *you* to do this? Why can't he get off his can, and conduct his own search?"

"Ross..." Hailey laid a restraining hand on his arm.

She sat forward on the edge of the sofa, and gave her sister-in-law a smile. "Ross is just reacting like any brother would, who loves his sister, Darcy, but of course, you already know that. Tell us what you know about the wife."

Darcy chewed on her bottom lip and began hesitantly. "Her name is Madeline Holt. I'm pretty sure she doesn't go by McCallen. She was a singer. Neil said she did a lot of studio work for different projects, and she was trying to get a deal, around the time he left."

She lifted her hands in a helpless gesture. "That's about it. Sorry, I know it's not much. I guess I was just thinking that since Ross is a cop, he might be able to point me in the right direction, to begin a search. One other thing," she added. "Neil *did* say that her car was found at the Nashville airport, so it looks like she was planning on putting some real miles behind her, when she..."

She stopped short and stared at Meredith's strange expression. "What is it?"

Everyone followed her eyes and noticed Meredith's cheeks flushed with excitement.

"Kirby Yeager!" she whispered out loud, to herself. "Yeah, and then he just dropped off the radar!"

A flash of instant recognition and complete disgust whipped across Joel's face, and he whispered something, himself. It was probably just as well that only his wife heard what he said.

She gripped his fingers and looked around the room wildly. "Honey, is Perry still at the studio, do you think?"

"He was still there when I called him just after lunch," he answered, recognizing her intent to pursue something that had occurred to her.

She pulled herself up and headed toward the kitchen. "Gotta use your phone, Sissy."

She disappeared and seemed to be gone forever. After a while, the telephone rang sharply, and was immediately snatched up in the kitchen. An eternity crawled past before she returned, her breathing shallow and her eyes glistening.

"It's the same one!" she announced triumphantly, realizing at once that no one there knew what she was going on about.

"Listen!" She crawled back up next to her husband, and tucked her bare feet against his leg. "First, I just wanna go on record that I agree with Ross. Neil's a jackass!"

Her husband sent her a swift look. "I don't believe anyone heard Ross use the word *jackass,* Missy."

"Well, he *is,*" she scowled, and then relented, offering Darcy an apologetic smile. "I'm sorry, baby, it's just that I do agree with Ross that Neil should be the one pursuing this. You can understand why people would feel that way, can't you?"

Darcy pursed her lips and nodded mutely.

Meredith's expression took on sympathetic warmth, before she continued. "But since *you* are, it's time to help and not hinder, so, let me see if I can do that. Back... oh, I don't know, at least four years ago, maybe longer... not long before we met, Joel..."

Meredith innocently raised her eyes to his, and thrilled him. She grinned, taking in his reaction. "I was doing one of those spec projects. That's how I met Perry Mitchell. He and Marshall had me in there, laying a few tracks."

Joel prodded her lightly with his fingertip, and she picked up the pace.

"Okay, so anyway, there was this girl there, doing BGVs. Background vocals," she explained, unnecessarily. "And that's who it was, Madeline Holt! She was actually pretty good, too. The thing is, Perry Mitchell was producing the whole thing, and I couldn't help but notice that he seemed to be interested in her. But then, there's this other guy hanging around with her, so Perry never makes a move. And it wasn't Neil, either, Darcy, because I've *seen* Neil. And it wasn't that producer, either. We *all* knew that sleazebag, but I'd never seen this guy, before.

"So, the thing is, Perry gets kinda bummed, because he wanted to ask her out. I mean, she wasn't wearing a ring or anything. But then, there's this guy, right? Anyway, the last day of recording, can you believe it, he hears the guy..."

Meredith stopped and gave her husband a mute warning, after he'd felt it necessary to jab her toward the finish line, again. He laughed quietly, and she did, too.

"Okay. Perry told me a few minutes ago that his name was Craig. So!" Her hands became as expressive as her eyes. "Perry hears this Craig calling her Sis, and he's all happy, 'cause they're obviously brother and sister." She grimaced adorably. "But it never worked out for Perry, because she split the next day. I mean, she probably assumed she was done, but they called to get her back in for some pitch work, because, even though she started out solid, her vocals starting sounding washed out and... well, pitchy. But they were never able to locate her after that, to dub her in."

Well... I guess it's the Madeline that Darcy is looking for," Hailey admitted, slowly. "But that trail's gone cold, now."

"Oh, yeah, I left something out!" Meredith slapped herself, a habit she had, whenever she messed up.

Joel pulled her hand safely away. "Why don't you just put it *in*, then, instead of giving yourself a concussion?" he chided.

"Remember, the phone rang a little while ago?" She skimmed on, without waiting. "That was Perry, calling me back. See, Perry remembered Brady Fowler knowing Craig. He was our drum tech. Brady, not Craig," she added, just to be sure she hadn't thoroughly confused everyone. "Brady's from out West and he recognized Craig when we were in session, because they went to UCLA together! Ran track, both of 'em. How 'bout that?" She was growing more excited by the minute.

"So, Perry gave Brady a ring and then called me back. Brady said the last he heard, Craig Holt was living in either Riverside or Redlands, California. They're both pretty close together, so it shouldn't be hard to figure out which. He told Perry he had a phone number somewhere, but he'd have to dig it up. I told Perry to expect a call from you, Darce, to get it. And of course, *I'll* know that guy if I see him again, so all we've gotta do is hop on a plane and go dig him up!" she ended happily, completely oblivious to the startled expression on her husband's face.

"Excuse us, please." He stood, hauling Meredith up with him, and piloted her through the room. "We'll just be a minute," he tossed over his shoulder.

Hailey giggled in anticipation. "Uh oh!"

Joel tugged his wife into the kitchen, leaned her against the counter, and fenced her in with his arms. "I hope you don't think I'm actually going to let you do this." His words were quiet but calculated.

"Ever since I got pregnant, every little thing with you turns into a long argument," she observed sullenly.

"Not necessarily.   Watch this. You're not going. Argument's over. I just won."

Meredith fired a glare at him.

"Stop that." He caught her chin, and tilted her head back slightly, as she tried to avoid his eyes. "Look at me."

Reluctantly, she complied, knowing that the battle was now lost.

"Do I have to remind you that we spent our wedding anniversary in an emergency room?" Joel corrected her attempt to look away again. "The last I heard, this is *my* baby you're carrying. My wife and my unborn child are *not* going to hop on a plane and go flying around the country, looking for God knows *who*, God knows where! Darcy's on her own. She can come and go, as she pleases. You, however, are *not* going and let me suggest that you do not try to defy me."

"I bet I'm not too pregnant to fly. We haven't even checked, yet."

Joel's demeanor indicated that he was clearly in no mood for any more. He fixed her with a look that advised putting an end to it.

"This is no longer open for discussion. You can pitch a fit, you can mumble little cuss words under your breath, you can throw any tantrum you have in mind, but the facts do not change. That is it, and that is all."

"Why, because you say so?"

"Yes. Because I say so."

He slipped his hand around to the back of her neck and came even closer, causing her to again realize that she was unarmed.

"Kiss me."

She grazed his lips lightly and began to wear on his patience.

"I said *kiss* me."

Without waiting, he secured her mouth in a way that settled this, and all other issues. Many moments later, they emerged from the kitchen, Meredith's eyes glowing like stars.

"Oh, goody, they made up!" Hailey crowed.

Ross winked over at his sister. "So how'd you manage to do that? We didn't hear any yelling."

"He gave me one of those kisses that got me pregnant, in the *first* place!" Meredith blurted out, as only she could.

Hailey howled, as Darcy gasped and flooded with color, and Ross shook with laughter.

"And on that irreverent note," Joel informed them, putting his arm around his wife, and steering her to the front door, "I am taking her out of here before your house fills up with frogs and locusts, and all your beverages turn to blood!"

Chapter Thirteen

Oliver Sullivan squinted at Janis Sheridan through the cloud of blue smoke that rose from his cigarette.

"Let me understand you, my dear," he crooned, when she had awkwardly finished her narrative. "What you're saying, however vaguely, is that you have essentially failed."

"Only as far as breaking up the marriage," she pointed out hurriedly. "I'm still working on something else!"

"Do you hear that, Warren? Miss Sheridan is working on something else." He smiled, as his large companion belted out a raucous laugh.

"Come, Janis, darling! Don't keep us in suspense. Tell us all about your latest project."

Janis swallowed hard and twisted her cocktail napkin around her finger.

"I've been concentrating my efforts strictly on Meredith Etheridge, now. If I can't get at them by interfering in the marriage, then I'll simply focus on her, especially in her precarious condition."

"We can do that ourselves!" Warren Patrick declared with an irritable scowl. He turned to face Oliver, with an impatient gesture. "This has dragged on long enough! I say we wrap it up!"

"Ah, but I am not overly concerned with what you say, my esteemed colleague." A slow smile spread over his evil face. "Poor little Janis has worked long and hard, and even though her results have been less than pleasing, I have found it in my heart to allow her one more chance.

"You do understand, my love," he added, appraising her with icy precision, "that my tolerance is wearing thin. Should this next endeavor go the way of your last, I'm afraid I'll have no choice, but to make an example of you. And that *would* be a pity."

Janis began using her napkin to wipe the sweat from her palms. "I won't disappoint you, Oliver," she promised, unsteadily.

"Of course not," he soothed, rising from his chair, and signaling for her to do likewise.

He placed a commanding arm around her shoulder, and handed her purse to her, before escorting her to the door. "We await your progress with mounting interest."

He gestured meaningfully toward the hallway, and Janis departed in haste and relief.

Oliver closed the door behind her, and turned to study Warren Patrick with a thoughtful expression.

"Warren, chap, you might ask room service to do something about that last bottle of wine they brought up." He strolled across the suite, toward his room.

"Oh, and one other thing," he added, stopping to turn halfway around, with a bored, careless wave of his hand. "When Miss Sheridan is done with her little task, remind me to dispose of her."

Warren watched him leave before indulging in a smirk of satisfaction.

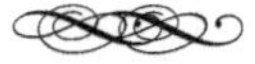

Meredith looked away from the stove with an annoyed scowl, as the bulb over the kitchen table popped and burned out. It was one of several bulbs that had blown out in the kitchen that week, and three, so far, today. She hadn't replaced the other two, thinking she still had enough light to function, but that third one burning out made it look like moonlight in the kitchen now, and not even a full moon.

Joel told her he'd called an electrician to come see if the voltage was too high, or if there was a loose connection, but he wouldn't be able to come until tomorrow, at the earliest. That did her little good at the moment.

"Well, this is just great! The cherry on the cake of my day." She rolled her eyes, and grabbed a dishtowel to wipe her hands.

"Move, Hook!" She stepped gingerly around her big gray cat, who was stretched out in the middle of the floor, and then into the utility room, to find another bulb. She came back and stopped to consider the job before her.

"Joel won't be too thrilled, if he finds out I did this," she admitted, under her breath. She twisted her mouth impatiently. Joel wasn't too thrilled if she did anything, besides sit still, and grow their baby.

Besides, Laura would be here in a little while for lunch and, since it was so dark and rainy out, she needed this light to see how to finish cooking their meal.

She judged the height of the light against the height of the chair next to her, and decided that she could reach it.

"Alrighty, I can do this." She gave herself a little pep talk. "It's no different than using a stepstool for the top of my closet."

She climbed slowly onto the chair and balanced herself, wishing the seat was solid, instead of padded. She felt okay, until she lifted her arm. She would have to maybe plant one foot on the table. She brightened. It was a huge, solid piece of furniture. All she had to do was stand on it, and she could reach the light easily. Getting down might be clumsy, but she could do it.

"Well, however I manage it, I'd better get on with it," she advised herself. She grasped the bulb in one hand, and raised her foot to the tabletop. At once, the room began to spin crazily, and it seemed as if the ceiling was falling on her. Her leg, that supported her on the padded chair, began to shake and, as she pulled her other leg back down, she missed the chair entirely.

No one but Hook heard her cry out, as she lunged forward, her head striking the sharp corner of the oak table. He came over and rubbed against her, then drew back in confusion, as something warm and wet covered his coat. He paced around, as if unsure of how to handle himself, before finally coming back and settling down beside his mistress. He was still lying beside her, waiting for her to stir, when the doorbell rang.

Laura began to tremble with a sense of apprehension, as her fourth ring went unanswered. Meredith's Jeep was in the drive, and Laura had called earlier to confirm their lunch, so she had to be around.

"Merry!" She tried the doorknob and found it locked. Silent alarms were going off in her head. This was all wrong!

"Oh, help me, God!" She pushed through a side gate and tore around the big house. When she pounded on the back door, then tried it, she found it unlocked, to her great relief. She pushed it open, and gasped as she saw her daughter-in-law in a crumpled heap.

"Lord Jesus!" Laura threw herself down over her.

"Get *back*, Hook!" She pushed the heavy cat out of the way, and pulled Meredith's long dark hair away from her white face.

"Meredith!" She drew back in alarm, as she realized that blood was streaming from beneath her head, then leaped up to grab the kitchen telephone and call 911.

An ambulance was dispatched immediately, and she hurried to call Joel's cell phone. It went straight to voicemail. She panicked and hung up, before she could think to leave a message, then closed her eyes tightly to try to remember the office number, and pounded it out.

"Etheridge and Associates."

"Get Joel!"

"May I say..."

"His mother! Get him now! Do it!"

Seconds passed, then Delores's voice sounded in her ear. "Laura?"

"Where is Joel?"

Delores's heart surged. "What's wrong?"

"Get him!" She began to sob. "He won't answer his phone! Get him now, please!"

Delores froze in place. "Laura... he's not here!"

"Oh, my God!"

"He forgot his cell phone and took off, late for a meeting. It's on his desk. I can find him, though," she said hurriedly. "Tell me what to say to him!"

"It's Meredith!" Laura stared at the seemingly lifeless form before her, and choked in despair. "She's hurt! It's bad, Dee! There's an ambulance on the way!"

Delores's mind raced. "Okay, I'll get hold of him. Where are you taking her, do you know?"

"Baptist, maybe! Oh, I don't know! I can hear the ambulance coming, Dee, I have to let them in!" She gulped and shook with fear. "Tell Joel to call the emergency dispatch and meet us. No, wait, call my cell..." Laura heard the sirens getting louder. "I don't know! I have to go!"

She slammed the phone down and, as she stood up, noticed a skillet of something catching fire on the stove. Instinctively, she turned off the burner, grabbed the handle and threw it in the sink, all in a blur of motion, before racing to the front door.

The paramedics wasted no time getting Meredith out to the ambulance, as soon as they saw the situation. Laura shook off someone's hand, and hopped in with the gurney, but managed to stay back, as they worked with her. She silently cried out for God's help, when she heard one of the EMTs inform the hospital, while en route, that there was possible brain swelling.

A team of medical personnel stood waiting in the emergency room entrance, and Meredith was instantly whisked away from Laura. She stood weeping, alone in the hallway, hugging herself, and feeling helpless and lost.

Joel bounded through the doors, ramming into a cart and sending it crashing. He grabbed Laura by the shoulders. "Where is she?" He shook her harder than he meant to. "Where is Meredith, Mother?"

"They took her," she whimpered, tears splashing all down her face. "I don't know, Son, they just took her!"

He looked around crazily and spotted a nurse. He released Laura and secured her by her arm. "Where is my wife?"

"Who..."

"I want my wife!" he gritted angrily. "You take me to her, now!"

Understanding came into her eyes. "Is your wife the pregnant woman they just brought in, sir?" She tried to keep a gentle tone in order to calm him.

"I want to see her!" There was going to be no calm. Joel's voice thundered to a roar. "Do you hear me?"

"Alright! It's okay." She removed his tight grasp from her arm and took his hand. "Come with me, and I'll find out where they've taken her."

Laura followed them through the corridors. The nurse stopped another one in the hall and spoke to her in subdued tones. She turned back to Joel.

"Sir, the doctors are with her, right now. One of them will be right out, just as soon as it's safe to leave her."

Joel made an impulsive move forward, and she blocked him, by pressing her hands against his chest and using a louder, more forceful approach. "If you don't stop it, sir, you're going to endanger your wife's life! The doctors have to concentrate, and your bursting in there and yelling could cause her serious harm!"

He looked past her with wet eyes, gripping his chest, as his breathing became more and more difficult. Laura put a hand on his shoulder.

"Be still, Son," she whispered. She looked up at the nurse. "Would someone let the doctors know that Meredith's husband is out here, waiting?"

The nurse was sympathetic. "Absolutely, right away. Just sit down here, and someone will be right out." She signaled an orderly, and gave him instructions that were promptly carried out.

"I'm Corey and I'm the charge nurse for this shift," she informed Laura, since Joel wasn't even listening. "I'll be at the desk. You call me if you need anything, at all."

"Thank you, Corey," Laura said, with a damp smile. She turned anxiously to check on her son, as the nurse took her leave, and managed to convince him to sit down with her. He looked at her with a glazed, stunned expression.

"What happened, Mother? Can you just tell me what happened?"

"She didn't answer the door, and it was locked, so I went around back. I was worried, because we were supposed to have lunch, and her car was there. So I got in, and found her on the kitchen floor."

She dabbed at her own fresh tears. "She was just lying there, not moving at all. I saw that her head was bleeding, so I called for an ambulance, then I called for you."

He stared ahead for a long moment, then began to shake. Laura pulled him close and held him, as his crying became audible gasps.

"Shhh... it's okay, honey." She stroked him lovingly, and immediately, and naturally, slipped into her role as his parent. "It'll be alright. God's watching over her."

Joel clung to her, and struggled to gain control over his churning emotions. "I just love her so much," he moaned brokenly.

"I know you do, Son." She looked up, as someone approached them from the double doors. "Joel, I think that's the doctor."

He sprang up and met the man halfway.

"I'm Dr. Chambers. You're Mr. Etheridge?"

Joel nodded, suddenly unable to speak.

"Why don't we move over here?" He led the way back over to their seats, and motioned for them to sit down with him.

Joel sank heavily into a chair and faced him, all the color drained from his face. "Has... has my wife...?"

"No, no!" Dr. Chamber's face instantly clouded, as he realized that his patient's husband thought the worst. "No, she's still hanging in there, Mr. Etheridge." He reached out and caught his hand, and squeezed it.

"I'm the attending neurosurgeon, in charge of your wife's care. We have to run some tests, but I need to tell you that there appears to be a good deal of inflammation. That's why your wife hasn't regained consciousness. This can be caused by a number of things, including something called subdural hematoma, which is blood that has collected, creating pressure.

"The skull, unfortunately, doesn't give way to allow for added expansion. There are ways to relieve the pressure, but we need to determine whether or not there is also internal bleeding, and we have to be on the alert for any clotting that may occur. Who found her?" His dark eyes darted back and forth intently.

"I did," Laura quavered. "I'm her mother-in-law."

"Mrs. Etheridge?"

She nodded.

"Mrs. Etheridge, I need to know something about the amount of blood you saw, when you found her. The paramedics left on another call, before anyone was able to ask them about it."

"It was..." she wavered in uncertainty. "Her head was... the blood was under the side of her head, so I don't know, for sure. I could see a pool, maybe the size of... of a saucer, I guess. I couldn't tell, without moving her. The uh... her cat had it all over him..." Her voice failed her and she wept quietly. "I'm sorry."

"No. You're doing fine. That's what I needed to know." He raised his compassionate eyes to study the haggard man who slumped before him, and recognized him.

"You're *Joel* Etheridge, am I correct?" he asked gently.

He barely nodded.

"Joel," Dr. Chambers said, laying a hand on his. "We're doing everything humanly possible for your wife."

"Her name is Meredith," he sighed, looking up at him wistfully.

"Yes. Meredith."

"Can I see her?"

"Very soon, now. We're going to have to do some testing, as I said, to determine what is going on, first. Joel, who is Meredith's obstetrician?"

"Ron Lynch."

"Good. I need to get him in here, to check on the baby. Can you hold up here for me, while I do all I can for her?"

Joel nodded, and wiped his wet cheeks.

"Good man. I just need a little more time to assess things, before we let you back there. I promise you, Joel, I'll come for you myself, when it's safe for you to see her."

He rose to leave, giving Joel a pat on the shoulder.

"Thank you." Laura stood with him.

"Yes." Joel forced himself out of his distraught state, however briefly. "Thank you, Doctor."

He smiled and hurried back toward the doors.

"Wait!"

Dr. Chambers whirled around at Laura's summons.

"I don't know if this is important." She moved forward, after a slight hesitation. "Meredith had a fall, almost a month ago. The ER physician said her blood pressure was really high. I don't know if that's important," she repeated, in a faint voice.

He eyed her gravely. "Yes, it's very important, Mrs. Etheridge. Which ER?"

"This one. I think a Dr. Fuller examined her. And Dr. Lynch was here as well, so he could tell you more about it. But I'm not sure that's what it was, this time."

"Why do you say that?"

"Well, she seemed to be trying to climb up on a chair. There was a light bulb lying near her on the floor. I think she may have lost her balance, trying to change it."

"What was close enough for her to hit her head on?"

She thought about it. "The dining room table has sharp corners. I didn't think to look at them, but it's a heavy oak table."

"Thank you, Mrs. Etheridge."

He sped on through the doors and she looked down at Joel, rigid against the back of his chair. He was staring up at her, pale and spent.

"She was climbing up on a chair, Mother?"

"I think so, Joel. It looked like it."

He shook his head slowly and tried to digest her words. "She knew better!" he sputtered furiously. "That little idiot!"

Anger, however, quickly surrendered to grief. He was overcome by the force of it, and moved away when Laura tried to soothe him.

She looked up with relief, as Gary rounded the corner, with Hailey and Ross behind him.

"Joel!" Ross immediately knelt in front of his friend and caught his hands. Hailey crouched down beside him and laid her hand on his knee.

"Joel?" Her face was red from crying. "Have you seen her? Is she okay?"

He shook his head, and raised his swollen eyes to hers.

"She's not?" Her watery voice shook with panic. "She's not okay?"

"I haven't seen her," he rasped.

Laura turned from Gary's embrace and came over to place a comforting hand on Hailey's shoulder. "The doctors are running tests to determine the extent of the damage, sweetheart. There seems to be swelling and she has a gash on her head. As soon as they're done, Dr. Chambers will talk to us and take Joel in."

"How did she get hurt?" Hailey gulped, unmindful of the tears running down into her collar.

"I can't be sure, but it looked like she was up on a chair, trying to change a light bulb. I think the hard corner of the tabletop may be what her head struck."

Hailey lowered her forehead down on Joel's knee and shivered. He looked down, in sudden realization of what this was doing to her. She and Meredith had been like sisters, for over ten years. 'Sissy' and 'Missy', he had tagged them. He laid a hand on her head and gripped Ross's hand tightly.

"She's gonna make it, Sissy," he heard himself say, in a strange, weak voice. "She's not gonna leave us. She's not, is she, Ross?"

He faltered, and Ross quickly wrapped his arm around him. "No, buddy. She's not gonna leave us."

"Joel!" He raised his head at his mother's voice, and saw Dr. Chambers coming toward him. Ross reached for his wife and lifted her up, so that Joel could stand.

The doctor flashed the others a warm smile, before taking Joel's hand in a secure grip. "Dr. Lynch is on his way and I've sent Meredith up for a CT scan. I wish I could have waited, since it's not something I recommend for pregnant women, but time is against us and a head trauma is nothing to fool around with. Dr. Lynch agrees. The CT will be able to tell us whether or not there is internal bleeding or a subdural hematoma. Remember, I explained that?"

Joel nodded mechanically.

Dr. Chambers glanced around at the concerned faces on either side of him.

"Joel, I need to inform you that Meredith hasn't regained consciousness, yet." He looked steadily into her husband's eyes, with a somber expression. "That causes me quite a bit of concern. I need to prepare you for the fact that immediately following her CT, we may be looking at emergency surgery."

Laura wilted and laid her head against Gary's chest, while her son gazed vacantly at the floor.

"What about the baby?" Ross hurried to ask. "Can she go through something like that, while she's pregnant?"

"If it becomes a matter of life and death, it's a risk we have to take." He leveled his gaze at Joel. "They'll be bringing her back down in a few minutes. As soon as they do, I'll come for you."

He nodded again, so desperately clinging to his every word. Dr. Chambers gently removed the hand that Joel was tightly squeezing and gave him a reassuring smile, before he headed back inside.

"I'll come for you," he reminded him with a firm note of promise. "In the meantime, try to stay calm, and know that we'll do everything we possibly can for your wife."

There was a long, drawn out silence in which nothing could be heard but an occasional sniff, and a devastated man's bitter anguish.

Gary brought Laura around and caught Joel by one hand. "Ross, you and Hailey join us. Let's talk to Father about Meredith."

Chapter Fourteen

Bett Greer studied the pattern of the laminate on her snack bar, as if she had never seen it before, while Neil McCallen waited anxiously for an answer to his question.

"Please, Mrs. Greer!"

"Mrs. Greer is Stan's mother," she informed him, dryly. "I'm not exactly decades older than you."

"I'm sorry. Bett, then." He searched her usually friendly face with an urgency. "Please, why can't you tell me where she's gone?"

"Listen, Neil." Bett left off memorizing her countertop, and fixed him with a meaningful look. "You might as well know that Darcy told me why you two can't get together. I have to admit, I'm real sorry about it. I was kinda pulling for you, but it looks like it's pretty much over. And since it is, why do you want to keep coming around, to constantly remind her of what the two of you can't have? If you ask me, it's downright cruel."

"I'm not trying to be cruel, Bett." He raised honest brown eyes to hers and allowed her to read the truth in them. "I know you're right. I should stay away, but I just can't seem to do it. I can't fall asleep without thinking about her. I can't wake up, without missing her. I wish I could stay away, I really do."

"Sometimes, you have to do what you *should* do and not what you want to do. Look." She gave his hand a maternal pat. "With things the way they are, all you're doing is creating extra pain for the both of you. You need to just get on with what you came to this area to do, and let God work things out between you and Darcy."

"Yes, but... couldn't you at least tell me *when* she's coming back?"

"I don't know, and that's the honest truth. Besides, why? What good would it do you to know? You need to let it go, Neil. What's done is done. Please don't keep coming around to stir things up. That girl is so in love with you, she can't see straight. I don't tell you that to flatter you, but to make you understand. Can't you see the harm in showing up, just when she begins to function again, and knocking the wind out of her?"

He lowered his head and nodded. He knew she was speaking the truth.

"I swear I don't want to hurt her, Bett," he said softly.

She gave him a smile of sympathy. "I know you don't."

"I just wish there was some way... I just... I love Darcy."

"And anyone with half a brain can see it! But unless you intend to find out how things stand with you and your wife, you have no right or business loving her. I hate to be mean, Neil, but there it is!"

"I know." He absorbed her words, not even trying to pretend that she was wrong. "But I can't help feeling like... what if she doesn't come back, at all? What if I've hurt her so badly, that she just decided to leave like... like Madeline did?"

Bett drew in a sharp breath at the agony in his face, and silently berated Darcy for making her promise not to tell him what she was up to.

"Neil, she just had to work through some things. You can't start thinking like that."

He breathed out heavily and closed his tired eyes. "Why not? I wasn't smart enough to think like that once before, and look what it got me."

Darcy closed her hotel room door wearily behind her and let her luggage fall wherever it landed. She kicked off her shoes and threw herself limply across the bed.

She still couldn't believe she had actually dared to come to California! What was she thinking? Who knew how long it would take for her to accomplish her mission, if she even *did* accomplish it?

Hailey was able to help her get a break on ticket costs, but this trip was sure to tap out her savings account. It was probably ill advised, as most impulsive things turn out to be, but here she was.

She rolled over and stared at the smooth white ceiling that was comforting to her burning eyes, starved for sleep. She let her mind travel back to the incident that made her angry enough to hop a plane, in the first place.

Perry Mitchell had given her the phone number that Brady Fowler had passed on to him. She wasted no time in calling, and when a man answered and heard her ask if he was Craig Holt, he admitted it freely and pleasantly enough. But as soon as Darcy asked if he had a sister named Madeline, his whole manner changed. He instantly froze over and insisted that she had the wrong number. When she persisted, he denied hotly that he was Craig Holt, and slammed the phone down in her ear.

She rose up on one elbow and stared at the telephone pensively. She wouldn't try to call him again. There was no sense in it. He would only deny everything and she'd get the same runaround, or he'd just hang up on her.

Well, she'd decide all that later. Right now, she'd go ahead and let Bett know that she had arrived safely, as she had promised to do.

She'd already realized at the airport that she'd left both her cell phone and her laptop. She'd have to buy a burner phone, but for now, she got an outside line and punched in the many tedious numbers required for a long-distance call, then lay back and waited to be connected. She frowned at the agitated way Bett answered the phone.

"Yes, hello!"

"Bett?"

"Darcy! Thank God! I've tried to call you a million times, but it keeps going straight to voicemail! Hailey's been trying to reach you, too!"

She sat upright, in reaction to the apparent distress in her friend's voice. "I plugged my cell phone in to charge before I left, and ended up forgetting it. What's wrong, Bett?"

"Something bad!" she gushed. "Honey, there's been an accident, and they rushed Meredith to the hospital!"

"Meredith!" She gripped the phone with white fingers. "Is it the baby? She's not losing the baby, is she?"

"I don't know. I mean, that's not why they took her in."

"Then what is it?"

"She had a fall, and busted her head open. Her mother-in-law found her unconscious, and called an ambulance."

Darcy forced herself to breath more slowly. "When did it happen?"

"Yesterday, around noon, I think." Bett hesitated a minute. "Listen, baby, they had to do surgery."

"Surgery! What kind of surgery?"

"Well, the blow to her head caused a lot of swelling and then, on top of that, when they ran one of those 'cat' scan things, they found something else they hadn't bargained for."

"A blood clot?" She held her breath and waited.

"Sort of, but not exactly. You remember when she had that big rise in blood pressure a while back, and fell?"

"Yes. But she didn't hit her head then, did she?"

Bett took a deep breath, and let it out in a sigh. "The thing is, she apparently wasn't as all right as she seemed to be, after that first time. When they did the scan, yesterday, they found an aneurysm."

"No! Oh, Bett... are you sure?" Even as Darcy said this, she knew it was a dumb thing to ask, but she didn't know what else to say. She felt faint.

"Yes. Hailey called me herself early this morning, but you had already gone. She said she was sorry she didn't call last night, but everyone was upset and Joel was all over the floor, so to speak, and no one was thinking.

"Anyway, hon, they figured that's what made her fall again, even though, according to Joel's mom, it looked like she was trying to climb up on a chair to change a light bulb, at the time. Hailey said it was a 'leaking' aneurysm, whatever that means. They had to rush her right into surgery as soon as they found it, baby or no baby."

"Oh, Lord Jesus!" Darcy breathed an unformed prayer. "Oh, dear God..."

She swiped at her wet face and pushed her hair back out of her eyes. "Why didn't they find out about this when she had her first fall?"

"I guess they had no reason to suspect it then. As soon as they took her blood pressure I think, if I remember right, they were more focused on whether or not she had preeclampsia and as you say, she didn't hit her head, last time."

"But what about the surgery, Bett? Did she... what happened?"

Bett began to wipe her eyes. "It's not good, Darce. Meredith's in a coma."

"Coma!"

"Actually, she never roused from the time they brought her in, and Hailey said they were all hoping that the surgery would cause her to come to, but yes, honey. She's in a coma."

There was nothing on the other end of the line but blank, empty silence, for the longest time.

Bett waited to let Darcy absorb things, before she said anything else.

"I... okay, then, I'm... coming back home. I'll just try to get a flight." Darcy couldn't get her thoughts to do what she wanted.

"Wait, honey. Listen to me. Even if you came home in the next five minutes, the surgeon says it's just a waiting game, now. There's nothing you can do here, but sit and stare, along with everybody else. Why don't you just stay put, and let us call you, if there's any change?"

"Well, I don't know..." Darcy collected herself. "Bett, do they know *why* she went into a coma? I mean, weren't they able to fix the aneurysm in surgery?"

"Yes, and they were even able to relieve some of the pressure and the collected blood, from what Hailey said. I think the coma has something to do with the swelling, but I'm not sure. She hit her head pretty hard, and I don't know how long she'd been laying there before Joel's mother found her. I just know that she was considered to be in imminent threat of death, when they took her to surgery.

"Right after that, they were saying that she was in guarded condition. Hailey says that, this morning, they're calling her condition stable, which sounds like an upgrade to me, even though she hasn't woken up. Dr. Lynch seems satisfied that the baby's not in any stress, right now. Why don't you just sit tight, Darce, until you hear something?"

She blew out a deep lung full of air, and mopped at her wet face.

"I'm going to get a burner phone when I go out to get a rental car, so I'll get that number to you when I do, but I'll also keep checking the front desk anytime I go out. Call me, Bett, if there's any change."

"You know I will," Bett assured her, comfortingly. "Don't you worry, Darcy. People are praying 'round the clock. God's gonna take care of Meredith. You just be careful, yourself, and let me know what's going on."

"I'll check in every day," she answered. "Okay, well... get a pen and I'll give you this number." She waited a moment, then gave Bett the hotel and room number, and she took it down and read it back.

"Okay, sweetie," Bett said, when she was done. "I'll call you if I hear anything. You take care."

Darcy rang off and sat staring at the phone for a long moment, before dragging herself up to wash her face with cold water from the bathroom tap. She wandered back in after a bit, and knelt down beside the bed, laying her head against the side and offering up prayer after prayer for Meredith, and for Joel and the baby.

She sat there for a long while, giving place to tears that, once flowing, could find no stopping place. She knew that behind the new tears that ran for sweet Meredith and her devoted Joel, came old ones that had been denied for too long, and would now have their way with her. She emptied herself out and then, with a shaky heave, rose to her feet and fretted to get herself into some kind of functioning state of mind. She still waffled back and forth with staying, or heading back to the airport.

Finally, she determined that the quicker she accomplished what she came here to do, the quicker she could get back home. She pulled out a huge telephone directory and, disciplining herself to face the business at hand, began to investigate for any listing that might turn out to be Craig Holt's.

She was hoping against hope that she might find a street address next to his name. If she did, she had every intention of driving to his house.

She decided that Bett was right. It would do no good to go rushing back to Nashville and since she was here, she would pursue Craig Holt as far as she could. She found nothing in his name, so she fished around in her purse for the number Perry had given her, hoping to match it against the list. Looking down at the huge number of Holts in Riverside and its surrounding area, she realized, with dismay, that this was going to be quite an undertaking.

She bit her lip and continued on with determination coming into her blue eyes. Somewhere, there was a Madeline who stood between her and any happiness she could even hope to have with the man she loved. She would find her, if it took forever.

She held out the scrap of paper and, one by one, began comparing the number to every listing in the book. It was almost an hour later before she closed the directory with intense disappointment, and lay back on the bed to think.

Nothing! None of the numbers even began with the same prefix as the one she had. She rubbed her eyes and let out a heavy sigh. His was probably unlisted or unpublished.

Okay, what next? She laid one arm over her forehead and stared blankly at the ceiling. Redlands! Meredith had said either Riverside or Redlands.

She jumped up and yanked open the bedside drawer, closing it again with an impatient bang. No directory, but a

Gideon bible. That, at least, was good news. She had packed in such a hurry that she had forgotten hers, and she was definitely going to need to hear from God, while she was here.

Darcy picked up the telephone, rang the front desk and was rewarded for her efforts, by learning that there was a directory for Redlands in the office, that they would be happy to loan her. She slipped into her shoes, grabbed her key and scurried out the door, returning with a new light of possibility on her face.

When her methodical scanning yielded no better results than before, she slammed the book closed and fought back more hot tears. She was just too tired, she decided, and it was late. At least it was, according to Tennessee's time zone. She gave up her fruitless detecting and dragged herself first into a hot shower, and then into bed, where she spent the night in fitful, reckless sleep.

Neil turned off the light and lay back against his pillows, blinking at the surrounding blackness, while his eyes slowly adjusted and the moon finally brought in less forbidding shades of gray.

"Lord Jesus," he heard himself murmur. "I just want do what's right. I just want to honor You. Why is this so hard? Is it really as cut and dried, as I've always heard it is? Am I still a married man, Lord?"

He rolled over onto his side and felt a tear roll across his face and onto the pillow, as Darcy's pretty face invaded his mind.

"Dear God," he sighed, reaching for the extra pillow and hugging it close. "Please show me if I'm sinning by loving Darcy. If I am, please help me to stop. But if I'm not... oh, Father, I need Your help. I want to be a Godly man. I don't want to be a stumbling block to these young people, that You've given to me to pastor. How can I just pretend that Madeline isn't out there, somewhere? And, without knowing what was really behind her leaving, without being certain that she was having another affair after we married, how can I just put her away with an annulment, without creating a controversy here in the church? Not everyone would agree with it, and some may not even believe me.

"I've lived here in Tennessee long enough, that there'll always be somebody showing up who knew Madeline, who knows we were married. I can't spend my life keeping secrets from those who should be able to trust me as their pastor, and I wouldn't ask Darcy to join me in deceit. Please show me what to do."

He clenched the pillow and buried his face into its soft comfort, while his groans and prayers lulled him into a long night of unconscious intercession.

Chapter Fifteen

Muted footsteps padded up and down the long corridor, as busy hospital personnel carried on with the day's routine. Delores and Bobbie stood outside the door of Meredith's room and waited, as Dr. Beatty, her personal physician, and her obstetrician, Dr. Lynch, checked on her condition.

Delores glanced at her watch repeatedly. Every now and then, one of them would raise eyes full of confusion and sadness to the other, and a silent question would pass between them, but neither one spoke.

Finally, Laura came out of the room and caught each one by the arm, steering them away from the door and down the hall.

"Joel's gotten to where the least little thing sets him off," she explained, noticing by their expressions that they must have thought she was coming out to give them some news of the doctors' findings. "He's especially irritable and teetering on the edge right now, and I could tell that he just wants to be alone with Meredith, so I told him we were going for coffee, if you girls don't mind."

"How is he, physically?" Delores asked quietly.

"Not real good. Won't eat. Won't sleep. Hasn't shaved. Bites your head off, if you voice any concern for him."

His mother sighed, as they turned the corner and moved toward the elevators. "He's like a caged animal, daring you to come close to either him or Meredith.

"I've stopped trying to reason with him, at least for now. I remember how I was when Paul was in the hospital after the wreck, just before the kids and I lost him. It wouldn't be right for me to deny Joel his own expression of grief. He loves Meredith so deeply. She's everything to him."

"Laura, what are the doctors saying?" Bobbie cast her a sideways glance and pressed to call for the elevator.

"Dr. Lynch still seems satisfied that the baby is doing okay," she replied, with a weary slump to her shoulders. "Dr. Beatty... well, he just stands there and looks down at Meredith, and doesn't say anything."

"Dr. Beatty has always been so fond of Meredith, even when he's fussing at her, and he's done his share of that," Delores commented. "I guess this must be hard on him, just waiting like everybody else, and not being able to help her, despite all his years of medical training."

"He's a good man," Laura agreed, stepping inside behind her friends, after the elevator had chimed its arrival and its doors slowly parted.

Delores eyed her covertly, not missing the pallor in her face, and the bags that were beginning to form under her eyes. "Did you go home last night?" she ventured, as the car descended to the first floor.

Laura looked up quickly, called back from some place her mind had wandered. "Hmm? Oh, yes, Dee. Joel didn't seem to want anyone around, so I left about eleven. Gary drove me back to Joel and Meredith's house to get my car, and followed me home, in case I fell asleep, even though the two houses are so close. I couldn't seem to convince him that sleep wasn't even going to be an option for me last night."

She followed Delores and Bobbie out of the elevator with a strange look in her eyes, as if something were trying to occur to her.

Dr. Beatty and Dr. Lynch both paused at the door and gave Joel one last evaluating look, before they took their leave.

"Get some rest, Joel," Dr. Beatty admonished, knowing that his advice would go unheeded. He followed his colleague out, without Joel even knowing they had gone.

Joel climbed onto the bed and laid his head on his wife's shoulder, closing his red eyes, and swallowing hard at the knot that lodged deep in his throat.

"Missy," he whispered, in a tired, thin voice. "I love you." He caught her seemingly lifeless hand, and lifted it up to his chest.

He touched her wedding rings lovingly, gently turning them slightly from side to side, noting their loose fit, in spite of Meredith's recent complaints of her hands and feet swelling. Laura had cautioned him to remove Meredith's very expensive rings for safekeeping, while she was in the hospital, and maybe he should, but he just couldn't bring himself to slip them off her finger.

He rubbed her hand gently. "Why did you do it, little one? You knew better. You knew, good and well, I wouldn't want you climbing up on a chair like that."

A bitter smile broke through the path fresh tears were making.

"So, of course, you just *had* to. Maybe I should have given you orders to climb at least one chair a day, then I couldn't have gotten you to do it, on a bet. Then none of this would have..." He broke off and buried his face in her gown, overwhelmed by too much emotion.

He raised his head after a while, and let his eyes wander to their baby, nestled inside his mother. He reached down and stroked it tenderly. "Mommy's gonna be okay," he murmured, in a soothing whisper. "You don't worry, little boy."

A faint light from somewhere far away crept into Joel's eyes, as he remembered the moment and the way Meredith had chosen to tell him they were having a baby.

He was cleaning the windows on the large French doors between the dining and living rooms, because Hook had a habit of licking them and smudging his face against them, and because Meredith absolutely balked at having anything to do with window washing, even though she griped incessantly, whenever they were dirty. She had grabbed the window cleaner and had gone around to sit on the floor on the other side, spraying each pane with great care.

Joel hid his surprise at what seemed to be her efforts to help, and tossed a rag around, grinning as it landed on her head.

"There!" he had told her. "You'll need that, if you're gonna do it right."

"Stop it!" she snapped, jerking off the rag and throwing it down. "I'm not cleaning any windows!"

"Silly me, what was I thinking? Well, I'd like to know what you call what you're doing, then," he declared, sliding around to her side, and dabbing at the dripping window cleaner with his own cloth.

Meredith popped his hand in exasperation. "Don't *do* that!"

"Knock it off, hothead! We can't just leave it on there."

She grabbed his wrist tightly, and fixed him with an impatient glare. "Now I have to do it all over again! Get back on your side!"

Joel had been tempted, at that point, to make her eat the rag, but he returned to his side of the door to finish cleaning the windows in silence, a stormy scowl hinting at a similar mood to follow.

Meredith ignored him and, once again, slowly and meticulously, began applying the foaming window cleanser to each small pane. Joel leaned back on one hand with a irritated set to his jaw, then began to pay attention to her process.

She was writing something, even though her letters were backward. A moment later, his dark brooding faded away and a tiny, suspicious grin began playing around his mouth. She had spelled out b-a-b-y!

He looked at her with every question he could think of spilling into his eyes and when he suddenly made a move to reach for her, she jumped up, sprayed the rest of the cleaner all over him, and tore off laughing up the stairs.

He had dashed up after her and held her down, while he rubbed his white foamy head all over her, until she cried "Uncle". They laughed together for a moment, until the cleaner began to burn their eyes and they both had to forget about b-a-b-y, and run to wash up.

Joel let out a ragged breath, and raised himself up to gaze down into his love's beautiful, still face.

"Oh, God! Meredith! Where *are* you?" His plea was directed at both God and his wife. He searched intently, his eyes begging for any sign of awareness, and was once again disappointed.

"Please come back to me, Missy. *Please* don't leave me!"

There was a hesitant tap on the door. When Joel failed to respond, Ross and Hailey pushed it open slightly and, at once, wished they hadn't intruded.

Joel gave them a glazed, almost hostile look that mellowed, as he slowly realized who he was looking at.

"Oh, hi," he offered in a muffled voice, giving his face a hasty swipe. "Come in."

"Are you sure, buddy?" Ross gripped Hailey's fingers securely, and waited by the door.

"Uh... yeah." He pulled himself upright into a sitting position that would still allow him to shield Meredith from any danger, real or imagined.

Hailey stopped short in her tracks, and just barely managed to suppress a shocked gasp, as she took in Joel's ghastly appearance. He was a wasted man! He had only been at the hospital just over forty-eight hours and already, his beard heavily shadowed his face, his graying hair was beginning to seem white in places, and his eyes looked like they weren't even real.

She successfully choked off any plea she was about to make for him to eat, and get some sleep. So far, the slightest hint of concern from anyone only netted them a curt, and sometimes angry retort from Joel. Instead, she crossed the room to the other side of Meredith's bed, and leaned over to kiss her white cheek.

Joel watched her sharply, as he did anyone who even got close to his wife.

Hailey was mindful of his guard, but stroked Meredith's face with a loving finger, anyway.

"Hi, Missy," she breathed.

Joel relaxed. He knew he needed to get a grip. He allowed himself to look away to his friend, who had come over and taken a chair next to the bed.

"How are you, Ross?"

Ross seemed surprised by the question but recovered smoothly, "I'm fine, Joel. And how 'bout you?" He laid a brotherly hand on his knee. "You holding up okay?"

Joel looked back down at Meredith's frozen features and grappled for a response.

"No," he said finally, simple and direct. "I'm not doing good with this, Ross."

"I know." Ross patted him lightly. "That's okay. That's what you have us for, to help you with it.

Joel almost smiled, as close as he could manage. "Thanks. You off, today?"

"Took off. I had some unused time coming, so Hailey and I thought we'd just kinda hang out, in case you needed anything."

"You guys don't have to do that," he answered softly, watching Hailey whisper loving words and prayers into her best friend's ear, stroking her brow with her fingertips.

"We wanted to," she told him, never taking her eyes off Meredith's face. "I wanted to be with Merry, just a little, if we're not in the way."

Joel made no effort to assure her otherwise, but he made no objection to their presence either, so Hailey settled in to keep a quiet vigil over Meredith.

Ross made the same critical analysis of Joel that his wife had earlier. "Buddy, you're not getting any sleep, are you?"

Joel shrugged carelessly.

The door swung open as an aide came cheerfully in, carrying a tray. She placed it on the overbed table, flashed everyone a smile, and turned to continue on with her other duties.

"What is *that?*" Joel's cold, abrupt tone caused her to spin back around in surprise.

"That's lunch."

Joel slid off the side of the bed, and eyed the young girl narrowly. "And do you think that's funny, bringing a lunch tray to a woman who's in a coma?"

"Joel..." Hailey tried to break in.

"*Answer* me!"

The aide bit her lip, and stared nervously down at the floor before saying, "The tray is for you, Mr. Etheridge."

Joel's face fell, as the realization of how rude and irrational his behavior was, fully hit him.

He hung his head and began to press at his temples as if to try to coax logic and reason to return to him.

"I'm terribly sorry." His apology to the aide came from a weak and feeble place. "Please forgive me, I'm so sorry," he added, not able to raise his eyes to hers.

She took a swift look at his absent, beautiful wife and her heart went out to him.

"Don't worry about it, Mr. Etheridge," she comforted. "You didn't know." She favored him with an understanding smile that Joel realized he didn't deserve, and closed the door behind her, as she left.

He stared down hard at the floor with glassy eyes. "I'm really sorry, Ross and Hailey, to have behaved that way, and in front of you. I don't know what's gotten into me. I just... I can't seem to... function."

He lowered himself back down across Meredith's chest, cradling her stomach, and began to moan softly.

Ross leaped up from his chair and laid his arm across Joel's back, as Hailey reached across the covers to caress his hand.

They both began to pray for their dear friend to somehow cope with feeling so lost without his wife, and so helpless, unable to rescue her. After a bit, Joel raised his head, and shoved his fingers through his tousled hair.

"Thank you both." He stopped to clear his throat. "I guess I've just been spiraling out of control, and not being much good to Meredith, or anybody else."

"Listen, you don't owe anybody any apologies," Ross corrected. "I don't even want to think about how I'd be, if I were in your place." He hesitated, and cast a wondering look at Hailey, then ventured into something he had been avoiding bringing up.

"Joel, I think you should know that the media is aware of Meredith's condition."

"The media," he repeated dully, a frown creasing his brow. "Yes. I forgot about them."

"Marshall is handling them, at least he was, when we came up the hall. Dr. Chambers has ordered this room restricted to immediate family, and the names that Laura put on a list at the nurse's station and, since this room's right next to the station, they manage to stop anyone going in and check them against the list. They even stopped us, and they know us."

An expression of gratitude and relief washed over Joel's face. "That's good to know. The last thing I want is for a bunch of reporters to cram in here, trying to get a scoop."

"Well, Marshall took them all into a lounge, and is giving them enough to keep them busy for a while."

"If you see him before I do, thank him for me, will you, Ross?" Joel gazed back down tenderly at his wife then watched as Hailey continued to dote on her. "She's so beautiful, isn't she?"

Hailey nodded her agreement. "She's breathtaking."

"And she picked me." His eyes lit up in wonder.

"That's because her Father picked you," she replied. "Not to mention the fact that she's been head-over-heels in love with you, since day one."

"Since day one, really?" He looked up quickly, with undisguised pleasure surging into his sad, handsome face.

"Joel, trust me. I knew her way before you did."

Flashes of all the confidences and secrets, pain, and joy that best friends share rushed into remembrance, and she beamed up at him. "Since day one."

He let his gaze drop onto Meredith's motionless form, and lifted her hand to his mouth. He pulled back suddenly and looked down at her stomach, then at Hailey, with a grin. He took her hand and laid it on Meredith's tummy and watched, as her eyes filled up with wonder.

"Our son," he announced, with quiet pride. "I keep hoping he'll wake his mommy up."

"He just might, if he keeps thrashing around like that!" Hailey caught the anxious, yearning look on his face.

"She'll wake up, Joel. I know she will. And when she does, believe me, we'll *all* know it!" She made him smile.

Ross winked at her approvingly. "What we have to remember and be thankful for is that they were able to get to the aneurysm in time, Joel, and that the swelling is going down. God's blessed Meredith with some first-rate doctors, and she couldn't be in better hands."

"I know," he acknowledged faintly. "I know you're right. I've got to start thanking Him, instead of letting fear do a number on me. It's just that I feel so isolated from the world and everybody in it, without Meredith. People say she's still with me, but it doesn't feel like it. There's no laugh, no pretty eyes; there's no pouting and challenging me over every little thing.

"I always felt her presence before, even if I was in the middle of a meeting and she was miles away, in concert. She was still as much with me, as if she were in my arms. But now she's... something inside me is missing."

He broke off and looked at Ross imploringly. "Do you understand?"

"I think I do. And it's the most natural thing in the world, for you to feel that way. You two are one flesh."

"Even like this?" He looked down at her stillness, his shoulders drooping with the weight of sheer loneliness.

"One flesh. Maybe that explains what I'm feeling. If Meredith's not here, then neither am I."

Chapter Sixteen

Joel slowly opened his eyes, and blinked in groggy confusion, as he tried to focus on where he was. Realization came slowly, and he lifted his head to look down at Meredith's still figure. He let out a deep sigh, as he saw at once that there had been no change. He bent down and kissed her unresponsive mouth, and caressed her stomach with a gentle hand. Their baby seemed to be resting peacefully.

There was such a strange serenity on Meredith's face. It was a little unsettling. For a second, he became alarmed, then relaxed, as the warmth and softness of her skin reassured him that she was okay. He settled back, and breathed a simple word of thanksgiving.

The door swished open quietly, and Joel glanced up at the nurse he expected to see. Hot anger immediately blinded him, along with the flash of a camera. There was a quick scuffle of feet, as the photographer made a hasty retreat, and Joel leaped up and flew after him, in a heated rage.

Hospital employees viewed him with confusion and alarm, as he yelled, "Where did he go? Where is he?"

Only one nurse had seen the man bolt from Meredith's room, and realized what was going on. She pointed and exclaimed, "He ran out the exit door, Mr. Etheridge! He's taking the stairs!"

Joel shot down the hallway. "Watch my wife!" he thundered back over his shoulder, and the nurse hurried toward her room.

People stopped and gaped, as he dashed out the exit. He descended the stairwell without even knowing it and, once he spied the man he was after, his speed seemed to increase supernaturally.

The man gasped, as a strong hand caught him tightly by the collar and twisted him around. He closed his eyes, as Joel's big fist lifted to smash him in the face.

Joel stopped himself, just in time.

"Who are you?" he demanded savagely.

He took too long to answer, and Joel slammed him roughly up against the wall. He snatched the camera away from him, snapping the strap in two.

"Please don't break it!" the frantic trespasser begged. "It's really expensive and it isn't mine! I'll get fired, if anything happens to it!"

Joel looked down at him in disgust. "Who do you work for? What's your name?"

"Mike," he answered, quickly this time. "Mike Daniels."

"*Who* will fire you?"

Again, he hesitated too long and Joel jerked on the man's collar. "If I have to beat it out of you, I will," he gritted, through clenched teeth.

"Alright, alright!" He gasped for air. "I can't breathe!"

Joel smoldered, as hot wrath urged him to make good on his threat to thrash what he wanted out of the man. He finally managed to restrain himself, and relaxed his hold, although more violent options were still on the table.

"Start talking!"

"I'm a free-lancer," the man gushed, in distress. "I was lying, I admit it. It's my camera, but please don't break it!"

He closed his eyes again, as if he thought a punch was coming.

"Is this how you make your living, Daniels? Sneaking into hospital rooms, where you have no right or clearance to be, and taking pictures of helpless patients in comas?" He tightened his grip on him.

But, it's... it's not just *any* patient," he protested, hurriedly. "It's Meredith Clark! That's news in this town!"

Joel continued to eye him menacingly. He slowly released him and flipped the back of the camera open, ripping out the film, to the unscrupulous reporter's dismay.

"Here's your expensive camera," he said shortly. "If you come anywhere near my wife again, I'll make you eat it! Do you understand me, Daniels?"

"I... yes," he finished lamely. "I was only doing my job, Mr. Etheridge. That's all."

"You call what you do a job?" he scoffed. He pushed him away with contempt. "Leave, while the leaving's good, Daniels."

He didn't need to be told twice. He cradled his camera close and hurried out of the building.

Joel made his way back up the stairs, a stormy look of turbulence still flashing in his wild eyes. He charged down the hallway and into Meredith's room, the spoiled film gripped tightly in one white fist. Several of the hospital staff applauded, in a silent, suppressed fashion, as he closed the door behind him.

Gary and Laura glanced up at his entrance, but he was too worked up to even acknowledge them.

"One of the nurses told us what happened," Laura explained, moving toward him with her arms crossed. She looked down at his hand. "You got him!"

Joel followed her eyes down to his clenched fist.

"Yes," he answered simply. He let the film fall into the trash then crossed the room to check on Meredith.

Laura picked up the strip of film and shoved it into her purse.

"Just in case someone is tempted to retrieve it," she said, as Gary questioned her with his eyes. "I'm sure it's probably ruined, but let's not take any chances."

"How does she look to you, Mother?" Joel asked, in a hushed voice from the bed.

She came over and put an arm around his shoulder. "Like a painting. Peaceful. Beautiful. You know, honey," she added, gazing down at her daughter-in-law fondly, "I believe, with all my heart, that Meredith is just spending some time with her Father, during all of this."

"Do you?" He looked up quickly, unsure of what she meant.

"I really do. I think Father is filling her with something deep and wonderful. And I think when He's done, she'll come back to us." She halted at the look of hope in her son's face.

"I have no scripture for anything I've just said. I can't prove it, I can't even make sense of it. It's just something I feel. Call it whimsical, but I believe it."

Joel stared down thoughtfully. "I think I'll believe it, too," he said, with faint conviction.

Laura looked up at Gary, who smiled with love. She moved back over to him, and he laid a supportive arm across her shoulders.

"Mom... Gary? Would you mind watching Merry for a few minutes?" Joel turned to look up at them, expectantly.

"Of course, Joel!" Gary seemed relieved. "Are you going try to get some food down, and maybe a little fresh air?"

"Maybe," he hedged. "I won't be gone long, just a few minutes."

"Take all the time you need."

"Thanks." He bent down and kissed Meredith, giving her a long look, before hurrying out of the room.

"Well, bless him!" his mother said fervently. "It's about time he took care of himself. Meredith would have a fit, if she knew how he's just let himself go, since she's been here."

After a moment, the door opened again and Dr. Lynch strolled in with a nurse behind him, carrying Meredith's chart.

"Good morning!" he greeted them briskly.

"Hello!" Laura smiled back.

He glanced around the room searchingly. "I don't know that I've ever seen Joel not here."

"He's actually stepped out, we hope to get something to eat," Laura offered.

Dr. Lynch nodded with approval. He approached the bed and studied Meredith's dormant form quietly. After a few minutes, he fitted his stethoscope and, lifting the sheet up, listened to her baby, with an intent expression. He smoothed the covers back over her and raised one eyelid and then the other.

"Let's hook up a monitor," he said to his nurse, in a subdued tone. "Keep a watch on Baby's heart and let me know if anything significant is noted. Otherwise, I'll come back by this evening."

She nodded, and wrote his instructions down swiftly.

"Is there a problem?" Laura interrupted hesitantly.

"No, not necessarily," he remarked in his crisp manner. "I just want to check on Baby, and make sure everything is progressing nicely."

He shot her a quick smile and caught Meredith's wrist with inquiring fingers, glancing at his watch to time her pulse.

"Okay," he decided. "We'll be back by sometime this evening, around six or so."

His nurse opened the door and followed him out into the corridor.

"Do you think everything's alright, Gary?" Laura asked, with uncertainty.

"God's in control, honey so yes, I do."

Joel came in a moment later, looking back behind him, out the door. "Was Lynch just in here?"

"He just left," Gary volunteered.

"What did he say?" He watched their faces carefully.

"He didn't indicate that anything was wrong, but they're going to hook up a fetal monitor. He said it was just to be sure everything is continuing, as it should."

He nodded in relief. "Okay."

"Joel, you weren't gone very long," Laura observed. "Did you even get any breakfast?"

"I didn't go for breakfast," he admitted. "I made a phone call. I've arranged to hire security to make sure no reporter gets in this room again!"

Laura looked up at him soberly. "Honey, do you really think that's necessary?"

"Yes, Mother, when some guy can just waltz in here and start taking pictures of my wife, I think it's necessary!"

Gary shook his head at Laura's forthcoming argument. She relented and let the matter drop.

"I saw Beatty and Dr. Chambers both down the hall," Joel said to no one in particular, lifting one of Meredith's hands and caressing her fingers. "One of them will probably be in here, soon."

He looked up. "Mom, do you have a manicure set with you? Meredith's nails probably need some attention."

"Sure, honey! Here, I'll do that for you."

"No, *I* want to do it!"

She halted, stung by his tone, then fished the case out of her purse. "Sure, Joel."

He relented. "I'm sorry, Mother, I really am. I didn't mean to growl at you. I guess that reporter just got me rattled." He offered her a faint smile of apology. "I just want to be able to do anything at all that I can for Meredith. That's all it is, Mom. I'm sorry."

She handed him the manicure set and kissed his cheek. "Not a problem. We're good."

Joel began grooming Meredith's nails with careful, loving hands. Dr. Chambers and Dr. Beatty came in without his being aware of it, until he heard Laura and Gary greet them. He stopped and looked at them with an expectant air, then moved back, to give them access to his wife.

"Well, let's check on Meredith," Dr. Chambers proposed, in his best morning voice.

He studied the chart the nurse offered him and murmured some instructions, scribbling down his orders, before handing it back.

Dr. Beatty stood by the foot of the bed, as his colleague continued to assess his patient, silently analyzing Joel, his experienced eyes taking in much more than those of a casual observer.

"Well, Etheridge." Dr. Beatty placed his hands on his hips and looked Joel squarely in the eye. "You look like hell!"

"That right? Have you ever *seen* hell?" Joel challenged him, sarcastically.

"I have now. Eat something, take a nap and for the love of God, shave that mess off your face! If Meredith wakes up and sees you looking like that, she might just go right back under, and who could blame her?"

Dr. Chambers had to laugh at that. "Beatty's right, Joel. You're not helping Meredith at all, going to pieces. It's like I've said before. Right now, this is about waiting. Not eating or sleeping, and allowing yourself to sink into despair, aren't going to help anyone, especially your wife. And I'd have to agree, if I were Meredith and *you* were the first thing I saw, I might just check out again, myself. And take my word for it, I've *seen* some stuff!"

Joel smiled grudgingly at the two physicians. "Okay, point made."

"Good!" Dr. Chambers declared. "Lynch been in?"

"He came by earlier. He's ordered a fetal monitor."

"Well, that's not unusual, Joel." Dr. Beatty sensed his concern. "Done all the time."

Joel nodded. "That's what I thought, but it's good to hear someone say it."

Dr. Beatty clapped him good-naturedly on the back, before moving to the door. "See ya later, Grizzly!"

Dr. Chambers fired Joel a wink, and followed him out.

Laura and Gary lingered, while Joel settled back down and continued to clean and smooth Meredith's nails. When he was done, he reached over to touch her IV and to satisfy himself that it was working properly, then fussed with her sheets. He couldn't seem to find anything else to do in that moment to help his wife, and his head dropped with fatigue.

They approached and stood behind him, gazing down, as if in silent prayer.

At last, he raised his eyes. "All her beautiful hair," he remarked sorrowfully. "I thought they'd leave some of it."

"They had hoped to be able to. But it'll grow back, sweetheart." his mother comforted. "You'll see."

"Yes." He touched her bandages gingerly.

"We're just gonna be downstairs," Laura explained, after Gary had come up to the bedside to offer a simple prayer for Meredith. They slipped out, and Joel climbed up wearily beside his wife, resting his head next to hers, and allowed himself to drift into a light slumber.

He sank into a pleasant dream about the two of them hiking up to Grotto Falls in Gatlinburg. He dreamed of the night he gave her an engagement ring. He dreamed of their wedding, and of the week they spent just driving up the East Coast, stopping wherever and whenever the mood hit them. His dreams were kind to him, as if his Heavenly Father were sending them, to comfort him.

He was awakened by a slight noise, and roused himself immediately, remembering the reporter who had intruded, earlier. He blinked, disoriented, and then forced himself to stand.

"Iris!"

Joel's sister hurried across the room and caught her brother into her arms. Her husband followed, gripping his neck in a tight embrace.

Joel pulled back and looked at them, as if unable to believe his own eyes. "Did Mom know you were coming?"

"Well, she knew that we might, if we could. We got in last night, but it was too late to wake anybody up." She grasped his hand lovingly, then moved over to gaze down at Meredith.

"Oh, Joel, she's just as beautiful as she was, at the wedding!"

"Yes, she is." Something about having his beloved Iris there was like medicine to Joel. He put his arm around her and reached for Jack, with his other hand.

"I can't even tell you how good it is to see you guys." Joel gave his brother-in-law a tired smile. "How've you been?"

"Same old thing, so that's good, I guess. We're more concerned with how *you've* been."

"Everyone is," he replied, placing a hand on one hip and rubbing a stiff neck with the other. "I'm just... you know..."

Jack nodded and let his eyes wander back to Joel's wife.

Iris laid a gentle hand on the baby. "Bless him, Lord Jesus," she breathed.

Pain crowded into Joel's eyes. "Iris..."

Marshall and Bobbie Edwards had come quietly into the room with Meredith's producer, Perry Mitchell. Perry's eyes immediately filled with tears, at the sight of his dear friend Meredith, but he made no move to approach her.

"Is it alright to come in?" Marshall raised his brows, as if in question, then widened his eyes. "Iris! Jack!"

"Good to see you, Marshall," Jack said in a muted tone, gripping his hand warmly. "Bobbie!"

"This is Meredith's producer, Perry Mitchell. I don't know if you've met." Bobbie indicated him with a small gesture.

"I met him at the wedding. Hello again, Perry." Jack greeted him in a low voice, but cordially. He motioned for them all to follow him to the far end of the room, then looked back at Joel and his sister, with worry in his eyes.

Iris was staring wide-eyed at her brother, with tears spilling down her face.

"Iris," they all heard him say brokenly, clinging to her hand. "Do you think God's punishing me, because of Kayla?"

"Joel!" Iris looked blanched and stricken, and Bobbie gave a little gasp. "Oh, no," she moaned softly.

Jack's face washed over with grief and he gestured toward the door. "Maybe we should give them a minute."

Perry studied Joel and his sister in sober bewilderment, before leaning in, and asking, in the faintest whisper, "Marshall, what's going on? Who is Kayla?" He looked back at Joel, with grave concern, and his heart went out to him.

Marshall lowered his eyes to the floor without speaking.

Bobbie moved over and laid a hand on Perry's arm.

"I always thought you knew," she said quietly. "Let's go find some coffee," she suggested, as Iris wrapped her arms around Joel, desperately trying to comfort him.

"I'll explain what I can. We can talk outside."

Chapter Seventeen

Darcy gave the classified section of the local newspaper a shake to straighten it, then took a second look, to make sure she'd really seen what she thought she had. She had come down for the hotel's continental breakfast, and was seated in a far corner of the lobby, with the paper spread around her in a manner that discouraged anyone from seeking her company.

She opened her mouth and stared at the page, her heart leaping in her chest. There was the name Craig Holt and a picture! He was listed with several other agents for a realty company in Redlands. She took a breath and made a valiant attempt to gather her whirling thoughts together.

What if it wasn't the same Craig Holt? There were a lot of C. Holts in both the Riverside and Redlands directories, but none of the numbers matched the one Perry had given her. Her spirits sank for a moment. Almost all agents gave their home numbers and none of these matched, either, if any of them was his home number.

Something occurred to her now that hadn't before and she became even more disheartened. What if her call had upset him so much, that he changed his number? If that were the case, she'd never narrow him down because she wouldn't have a way to connect him to the number from Perry.

What she needed was a plan. Darcy gathered up the classifieds and swallowed her coffee in a gulp before hurrying to the elevator. She dashed into her room, grabbing the "Do Not Disturb" sign and hanging it on the knob to hold the household staff at bay.

"Okay," she breathed, making a conscious effort to corral her rampant emotions. "Okay, let's think how to do this."

After a moment, she decided to call the number under Craig Holt's picture. Even without a number to match what she had, she felt she'd know his voice again. What she was going to say, she didn't know. Darcy had an impulsive streak that frequently got her into trouble.

She needn't have worried. It was apparent, right away, that she had reached an answering machine. She drew in a sharp breath. It was the same voice! This was the man!

The recorded message apologized for the fact that no one was there to take the call, assured the caller that this call was important, and suggested that the caller leave a message at the tone or call the following additional numbers. Darcy grabbed a pen and listened intently. She scribbled down one set of numbers, then a second, and hung up the receiver with shining eyes.

That was it! The last number was the one Perry had given her!

She wrinkled her forehead, as if she were trying to figure something out. If Craig Holt routinely gave his home number out, then why was it unlisted? That didn't make any sense. Maybe it was to combat telemarketers. She gave a little shrug and silently chided herself for getting hung up on non-essentials.

"Take it easy. Slow down," she coached herself out loud, as she was accustomed to doing during stressful situations. "Now's when you need to take your time with this, and not slip up."

She lay down across the bed and gave her situation considerable thought and planning. After a while, she was convinced that she had hit on the right solution and hopped up to carry on with her quest. She grabbed her purse, ripped the sign off the doorknob and pursued her trail.

It was after one o' clock when she pulled into the lot of the realty company in her rental car. She scanned the paper again to choose a listing that Craig Holt seemed to be representing exclusively.

She toyed a moment with the idea of using her mother's maiden name, since she didn't remember if she had told him her name when she called him before. No, she decided. She wouldn't do that. That was the same as lying, and God wouldn't honor it.

"God, help me to do this without being deceitful," she prayed, as she climbed out of her car. She entered the busy offices of the real estate firm and looked around to see if she could spot the match for the newspaper photo.

"May I help you?" A pleasant voice cut into her concentration. Darcy turned to find a pretty young woman smiling in question.

"Yes, please," she said hurriedly. "I'd like to see the agent who is showing this house." She held out the folded page of the classified section.

The receptionist studied the picture then handed it back. "That would be Craig Holt's listing."

She looked down at the switchboard. "It looks like he's on the phone but if you'd care to wait, I'll let him know you're here. May I have your name?"

"Darcy Decker," she supplied in a rush, before she chickened out.

"Miss Decker?"

"Yes."

"Well, it shouldn't be too long, Miss Decker."

Darcy thanked her and took a seat near a large coffee table, picking up a magazine and pretending to look at it.

The receptionist was right. A man's cheerful voice interrupted Darcy's feigned reading attempt, after only a moment.

"Miss Decker?"

She heaved a sigh of relief. Her name failed to register with him. She must not have given it to him, before.

"Yes." She stood and shook his offered hand.

"Craig Holt. Sorry to have kept you waiting."

Darcy studied his brown hair and blue eyes and wondered if Madeline looked anything like him. He was a handsome man. She found her voice. "I've only been here a short while."

"Well, come have a seat and let's see what we can do for you."

He led the way in, indicating a chair with a sweeping motion and settling in at his desk.

"So, you've spotted a house you might be interested in?"

"Well..." Darcy struggled to remain honest. "I was just looking through the paper this morning and I decided that I wanted to be shown this one." She laid the paper on his desk and tapped the photo with her finger.

Craig glanced down. "Oh, yes. That's a little beauty." He reached inside his drawer and pulled out the original photo of the newspaper picture. "Here. You can tell a lot more about it, not having to filter through all that printer's ink."

"I see what you mean." Darcy studied it long enough to seem interested before giving it back to him.

"It's only two bedrooms," he warned. "Do you have a family, Miss Decker?"

"No, it's just me."

He sat back in his seat and compressed the tips of his fingers together. "Well, it's a small house, but one person could do a bit of rattling around in it, especially if you're used to apartment living. Most singles in Southern California are. But I couldn't help noticing from your accent that whatever part of the South you're from, it's not Southern California."

She smiled. "Is that an observation or a question?"

"Well, I guess one leads to the other," he pointed out, with a grin.

She was sure she had told him before that she was calling from Tennessee. Besides, his sister had lived in Tennessee. No, that would be a dead give-away.

"North Carolina," she supplied, and then redeemed herself by mentally adding, *originally.*

"Tar Heel state. I've met several people from your neck of the woods." Craig smiled and tapped the newspaper. "You'd like to see this place, then?"

"Yes, I would, actually."

"Well..." He looked down at his calendar for a moment. "I'm sorry to say that the earliest I could get to it would be Monday."

He looked up and caught the obvious disappointment on her face. "Think you can make it through the weekend without buying a house from someone else?"

Darcy gave him a wry smile. "I'm sure I could manage to restrain myself."

"Great! I'm showing places this evening and all day tomorrow, and on Sunday, my wife has this thing she's making me go to. Something at the Redlands Bowl. Probably some kind of doggie fashion show, if I know her."

Darcy laughed with him.

"Well," he added, touching a photo she couldn't see, "Donna's job folded suddenly when her company was bought out by another, so she spends a lot of time at home, lately. The least I can do is make myself available when she needs to get out of the house."

Darcy leaned over and retrieved the folded newspaper. "Well, Monday will do fine."

"How's one?"

"One's good. I have the whole day open." She picked up her purse and stood up. "Thank you for your time, Mr. Holt."

"Well, you're very welcome. Oh, wait!" Craig flipped over a business card, and scrawled down the street address of the house. "You'll probably be needing that," he predicted with a grin, handing it across the desk to her. He rose and offered his hand.

Darcy thanked him again and wandered back out to the parking lot in deep thought.

That was a very nice man. He certainly didn't seem the type who would deliberately allow Neil to wonder for years where his wife was. None of this was clicking into place.

She drove back to the hotel, musing over her brief meeting with Madeline's brother. And he *was* her brother; that much she was sure of. His strange behavior on the telephone settled that issue, as far as Darcy was concerned.

She unlocked her door and hurried over to the phone to give Bett her daily call and to find out how Meredith was doing.

Bett answered after several rings, just as Darcy had about decided that she was out.

"I almost hung up, Bett."

"Oh, hi, honey!" She was a little out of breath. "Wally and Foster found a snake in the back yard, and just marched in here with it, like it was a vase of roses! I just finished chasing 'em out of here. I made 'em take it out back to the field. Wally acted like he thought he was actually gonna be allowed to keep it!"

Darcy laughed, as she imagined his reaction to Bett's raining on his parade. "Tell him I miss him," she said. "I miss all you guys."

"Well, we miss you, too, you can be sure of that."

"Bett..." Darcy sobered. "How's Meredith?"

"Well, hon, about the same. Doesn't seem to be much change. Dr. Lynch was a little concerned about the baby, though, and now they're running one of those fetal monitors."

"Why? Is something wrong?"

"Well, I haven't heard anything, if it is. He said it was just a precaution. To be honest, it was just after lunch yesterday when Hailey called me, so I probably need to check in and see how things are."

"Okay, well if something's going on, I want to know about it."

"I know, sweetie. I'd call you right away, believe me."

Darcy propped her feet up on the foot of the bed and pulled a scrunchie out of her hair.

"Listen, Bett, I guess I've stumbled onto something here."

"Yeah? What kind of something?"

"I've found him."

"You're kidding!"

"No, I'm not."

Bett sank down on a stool and waved Wally back out the door. He was covered in mud. "Did you actually see him, Darce?"

"Yeah, but only briefly. It turns out that he's a real estate agent, so I came to the office and got him to agree to show me a house on Monday ."

"Then he doesn't know who you are, yet."

"No, and that's really not fair. When I see him again, I'll have to tell him. I just didn't want to do it there in the office with everyone around, in case it got ugly."

Bett hesitated before speaking. "Darcy, when do you think you'll be back?"

"Oh... I'm not sure. Soon, I hope. Why, aren't the kids doing okay?"

"Oh, sure. Faron Waldrop's holding his own, even though he said he'll be only too happy to see you."

Darcy laughed. "Tell Faron I really appreciate his covering for me."

"Darce..."

Darcy knew that tone. "What is it?"

"I probably shouldn't be hitting you with this, while you're right in the middle of everything." There was a note of reluctance in Bett's voice. "It's just that... well, Neil was here the other day."

"Neil." Darcy's eyes immediately filled up. "When?"

"Actually, the day you arrived in California. There was just so much going on with Meredith and everything then, that I wasn't sure it was such a good idea to tell you."

"Well, what did he want?"

"He just seemed really desperate to know where you were, and when I wouldn't tell him, he begged me to at least tell him when you'd be back."

Darcy stood up and began twisting the phone cord. "Well... what did you tell him, Bett?"

"I told him I didn't know when you'd be back and that maybe he shouldn't make things worse by pursuing you if he has no intention of finding out how things are, where his wife's concerned!"

"Oh, Bett!" She fell back down heavily into her chair. "You told him you knew?"

"Well, I'm sorry, but yes, I did! And he said he knew I was right but that he didn't seem to be able to help himself." Bett paused then rushed on. "Darcy, to be brutally honest, I think it's mean not to tell him what you're doing."

"Bett, no! Please, you promised!"

"I know I did and I don't intend to break that promise, but if you could have seen him. Darcy, he was a hurting man. He said..." She stopped, wondering if it was a good idea to go on.

"What did he say?"

Bett plunged ahead.

"He was afraid you'd just taken off and weren't gonna come back, like Madeline did."

Darcy's shoulders slumped and she dabbed at her eyes. "We've already agreed that our relationship can't go anywhere, so he shouldn't be expecting me to just stay put for him, but still... I didn't figure he'd be thinking like that."

"Well, he is. I guess it's one thing if you both formally said your last goodbyes, but he's imagining you just up and disappearing on him and, I have to say, if you'd seen his face, you'd know how painful that would be for him. Darcy, please let me tell him. I believe it would help him, if..."

"No, Bett, you can't do that! I tried to talk to him about finding Madeline and he wanted nothing to do with it. He just flat out told me to leave it alone, and he was serious. I'm doing this for *me*, now. *I'm* the one who has to know. Please don't tell him, Bett.

"I don't know what his reaction's gonna be, when he does find out that I came out here, but I'll just have to deal with that, when the time comes. But not now. I can't deal with that, now."

Bett sighed and shook her head. "Okay, but I don't like it. If you won't let me say anything to him, then the least you can do is get on back here, and tend to him."

"I will. As soon as I know what I came to find out, I'll be on the first plane home."

Bett relaxed a little. "Okay. You keep calling in, honey. We don't like you way off out there by yourself. Wally's afraid you'll be in an earthquake."

Darcy smiled. "Well, just tell Wally... tell him if an earthquake comes, I'll hide under Father's wings. He'll know what that means and he'll be okay with it."

She rang off and, after working through the emotions created by what Bett had said about Neil, she lay down for a much needed nap.

"I think I'll do just that, God," she murmured, closing her eyes and hoping sleep would come quickly. "I'll just hide under those wings Wally was talking about."

Chapter Eighteen

Pastor Barry Todd's secretary hopped up and hurried out to the hallway.

"Lee!" The church's maintenance man wheeled around, before tapping on the pastor's door.

"Hey, Claudia! I didn't see you in there, when I walked by."

She motioned him away from the study and indicated that he should follow her back to her office.

"Everyone's been complaining about that, ever since I moved the desk around this way. I wanted to be able to see out the windows but now I can't see who's in the hallway and they can't see me." She grinned ruefully. "I guess I should have thought about all that before I started moving everything around."

Lee Mullins nodded and smiled knowingly. "You and my wife! I make sure I go to bed before the lights are out. You never know what you're about to fall and break your leg over." He gestured down the hall with a nod. "Pastor in?"

"Well, he is, but he's with someone, right now. He asked not to be disturbed, so it must be pretty important."

He nodded again. "Well, I was just gonna shoot the breeze, anyway. I might come by and pop my head in this afternoon, if he's still around."

He eyed her predicament critically. "What d'ya say we move this stuff around into something you can live with?"

Claudia laughed and held out a welcoming arm. "I say let's hop to it, and thank you! I don't expect Pastor Barry will need me for at least another hour, the way things look."

Pastor Todd got up from his desk, and came over to join Neil McCallen on the sofa. He eyed him closely, and mulled over everything he had just heard.

"Neil," he finally said. "Are you telling me that you have absolutely no clue at all where your wife is? You don't know anything? I mean, wasn't her family able to tell you anything, at all?"

Neil rested his elbows on his knees, and stared down at the carpet. "To be honest with you, Barry, during the entire time that I was with Madeline, I hardly found out anything at all about her family. She never seemed to want to talk about them and I guess I figured there'd be time enough for that, later on."

He lifted his head and gave him a tired look. "Her parents were both dead, she did tell me that. There was an aunt on her mother's side and a cousin, but Madeline never had anything to do with them. When I finally located them and went to see them after she left, they seemed glad to know she was gone and, if they knew her whereabouts, which I doubt, they certainly weren't gonna let me in on it."

"And you say you tried where she had been singing?"

"I tried everywhere, I told you that." An edge crept into Neil's voice. "They had already learned that she was gone, because she didn't show up for a session, but that was all they knew, or at least the ones I talked to. A receptionist at the studio said Madeline had been in the company of a man, but she didn't know who he was. She said she had never seen him before that week or since then."

He rubbed his temples slowly. "So, I figured she had met someone while I was gone, or maybe taken up again with the man who fathered her child. Who knows? She might have been seeing someone all along, and I guess I would have been too stupid to know it."

He settled back with a sigh. "Anyway, she didn't want to be with me, that much was clear enough."

Barry studied him thoughtfully. "How long did you look for her, Neil?"

"Why?"

"Just tell me."

"I don't know. Two or three months. I quit, after that, and then, a couple of years later, I tried again. I even went to a town in Ohio, where she claimed to be from." He laughed cynically. "No one had ever heard of her!"

Barry was quiet. This was one of the most startling things that Neil could have laid on him. All this time, a married man, and never even mentioning it! Not that it interfered with his duties as youth director. Neil was above reproach in his conduct, and was one of the best counselors he had ever had the pleasure of working with. But to be left hanging like that, for all these years! His heart went out to him.

"Barry..." Neil's hesitant voice interrupted his chain of thought and he looked up.

"There's something else. It gets even more complicated than this."

"How *could* it get more complicated than this?" Barry widened his eyes expressively.

Neil shrugged, and gave him a faint smile. "It just does." He pressed his fingers together, and studied them for a moment. "I'm in love with someone."

"Brother!" Barry declared fervently. "You sure know how to thicken the plot." He shifted around, in order to read his friend's face. "May I ask who this someone is?"

"You know her," Neil said softly. "Darcy Decker."

Barry straightened up, and let his jaw drop slightly. "Well... not that I don't think Darcy's a great choice, Neil. She's as fine a girl as a man could ever choose. But the question is, are you in a position to be choosing, in the first place?"

"Oh, believe me," Neil returned caustically, "I *know* what the question is!"

He lay back against the sofa, despondently. "The worst thing is that, like a fool, I let her know how I feel about her. I know, I had no right to do that. It's just that I enjoyed her company so much, and more and more, I found myself missing her to distraction, when I couldn't be around her.

"I'm completely in love with her, and she has the same feelings for me. That should make me the happiest man in the world, but, of course, I'm not allowed to be happy. You can only imagine what it did to her, when I told her why we couldn't be together."

"Neil..." Barry touched his arm briefly, to encourage him to listen. "You can't just let this matter hang suspended, like this. You've got to find Madeline, and settle the status of your marriage, once and for all."

"No. I don't." Neil bit his words off sharply with a grim cast to his face that Barry had never seen before.

"But you say you love Darcy, and that she loves you. Surely, you don't intend to spend the rest of your life running away from love, because of what Madeline did to you."

Neil's countenance had frosted over.

Barry narrowed his eyes, clearly mystified. "Why won't you look for her, again? I don't understand. What are you afraid of? Are you worried that you still have feelings for her? Is that what you don't want to face?"

He watched his friend's appearance harden, becoming even more unyielding. "Oh, I have feelings for her, alright." His words were filled with loathing. "I hate her!"

As soon as the words were out, Neil's eyes met Barry's, with a look of horror. What had just come out of him shocked him into disbelief. "Listen to what I just said," he whispered. "Where did that come from?"

He bent over and buried his face in his hands. "I didn't know I had that in me, Barry."

"Neil," the pastor ventured, in a quiet tone, "you've been packing this unforgiveness and resentment around long enough, haven't you? Don't you think it's about time you asked God to help you forgive Madeline? Not for her, but for you. Listen, this is eating you alive. This kind of buried animosity and rage can manifest into a cancerous mass of disease, that Satan will use to destroy you."

He watched to see if his words were sinking in. "Don't you know that you'll never get beyond this point in your life, until you sever all those things that keep you tied to your past? Harboring all this anger against her only hurts you, not Madeline. You're the one you're punishing. Let it go."

Neil began to shake, as dammed up pain finally broke through the walls of a fortress he'd spent years building.

"Just let all that old junk go, buddy," Barry encouraged quietly. "It's time to move on."

He reached over to lay a compassionate hand on Neil's shoulder, then lowered his head. "Father God, please give Neil the grace and strength he needs to work through this. Help him to lay down his anger toward Madeline, and even see her through Your eyes. Help him to forgive her and to be released, Lord Jesus."

Neil started to weep in earnest, tears that had frozen long ago, now thawing and running hotly down his cheeks.

"Lord," he moaned brokenly. "I'm so sorry. I really am. I don't want to hate Madeline, and I'm sorry I said it. Please help me. I want to forgive her. Help me."

His words trailed off into silence. He mopped at his face with his fingers, and sat still and quiet for a long, healing moment.

"Thank you, Jesus," he finally whispered, rubbing his eyes. A strange peace, unlike anything he had ever known, began to settle on him. For a moment, it was as though he couldn't even understand what it was, that had kept him so bound up, all these years. He raised his emotional eyes up to look at his pastor.

"And thank *you*, Barry," he said, hoarse with feeling.

"You did it," Barry returned, with a smile. He gave Neil a brotherly pat.

"Neil," he said, as he watched years of stress leaving him, "It might be too soon for you to make any decisions, but I want to state my position, for what it's worth. Actually, it's worth a lot, because it's right out the Bible. The Word says in one place, 'how long will you waver between two opinions' and, in another, 'a double-minded man is unstable in all his ways.' Perhaps a bit out of context, but I think you understand what I'm saying. Been feeling a little unstable, lately?" he asked, with a kind twinkle in his eyes.

"You could say that," Neil confessed, breaking into a smile.

"Listen, my friend," Barry urged. "No more of this, okay? Make a decision and then stand firm in it. If you love Darcy, go and find out if it is a love that God will bless. Find out what your situation is. Maybe you'll be free to love her completely, to take her as your wife. That's what you want, isn't it?"

"Yes," Neil breathed, almost too softly to be heard. He grinned, self-consciously. "That's what I want."

He stood up, along with Barry, and gave him a grateful hug. "Thank you again, Barry."

"You can thank me by following through on this and by keeping me informed," his pastor replied, weaving bluntness with affection. "It's like Darcy's friend, Meredith Etheridge always says, 'Fish or cut bait'. Good advice!"

Laura Etheridge let herself in the back door with Joel's key, and bent down to pick up Hook, who was beside himself with joy to see somebody. *Anybody!*

"Hey, Mister Hook!" she cooed, as he purred loudly next to her ear. "Are you hungry? Dumb question, huh, bud?"

She set him down and laughed, as he led the way into the utility room, to show her where the food was kept.

"Meredith would probably smack me," she confided to him, as she took down a can of food. "I think that you're supposed to have dry food today but, doggone it, Hook, I also think you deserve a little pampering. You've been a lonely fellow, here, all by yourself, haven't you?"

She bent down, as Hook watched her with adoring eyes, and dumped the salmon into his dish. He proceeded to do what he did best, while Laura checked his water supply, then scooped out his box and added some fresh litter.

She continued on through a list of chores she thought needed taking care of: bringing in the mail and the papers, putting some potpourri out to freshen things up, pouring out bad milk, throwing moldy bread out, and washing out the skillet she had thrown into the sink the day she found Meredith on the floor.

She wiped her hands on a towel when she was done, and looked around thoughtfully, to see if she had forgotten anything. She cringed, as she saw some blood still on the floor where Meredith had been, and the light bulb next to it. She certainly didn't want anyone else seeing that!

Fishing around under the sink, she came up with a sponge, a bottle of pine cleaner, and some rubber gloves. She washed up the blood and threw the bloody sponge in the garbage, then picked up the bulb, miraculously unbroken. She shook it next to her ear and decided it was still good, then looked up at the overhead light. Better take care of this, too.

Carefully, she stood up on the chair and stepped onto the table, making the change in bulbs with no difficulty, then hopped down and threw away the old one.

"Okay, Hook," Laura sighed, giving the kitchen an appraising look. "Let's see what else. Extra clothes for Joel. And a razor," she added, smiling to herself.

She slipped upstairs and filled a small suitcase with whatever seemed useful, tossing in Joel's bible and, without knowing why, a tiny layette she spied that had been placed in the new baby bed. She brought everything down and, as she made her way back out to the kitchen, stopped in her tracks when the blinking light on the answering machine caught her eye.

She pondered whether or not to bother with it. Probably just well-wishers calling to check on Meredith, but maybe there was something important. Even if Joel couldn't care less about business right now, maybe Marshall would want to know.

She snatched up a pad and pen and settled down to listen. There were scant messages, here and there, but what

Laura really noticed was the number of hang-ups. Not just someone deciding not to leave a message, but more like a deliberate waiting, before clicking the receiver down tauntingly. It was almost as if the caller were intentionally trying to be annoying.

She kept her pen ready and finished listening to the messages. Suddenly, she looked up with a frown and hit the button to repeat a message.

There, she really had heard it! Someone was laughing, a muffled, mocking sound. It was clearly feminine, and it was followed by the predictable hang-up.

Joel and Meredith's answering machine was the sort that kept track of the date and time each call came in. Laura bit her lip and puckered her brow, as she realized that the last four calls, including the one with the laughter, came on the day Meredith had her fall, all before noon, in fact. She wasn't sure why that was significant, but it bothered her, for some reason. What also bothered her was the realization that there were no more such calls, after Meredith's accident. Now, why was that?

Had this been going on, back when she called Gary, and then her children, about that strange feeling she was having? Joel had insisted that everything was fine when she had called him, but then he would have, even if there had been a problem. Joel could be very closed, when he wanted to be, and other times, he was just so caught up in the grind of the music industry, it seemed he was completely oblivious to what else was happening, outside of that world.

She reset the machine and leaned back on the couch to think. Something kept trying to jog her memory, but she couldn't quite pin it down.

She knelt down beside the couch, and decided to ask the Holy Spirit to make her sensitive to anything He was trying to show her. After a while, she stood up with a determined look in her eyes. Something was going on, and somehow, she felt certain that Joel held the answers. She didn't know what it was, but she was going to get to the bottom of it!

She grabbed up Joel's suitcase and marched to the back door with a purposeful stride.

"Hold down the fort," she instructed, glancing over her shoulder at the fat and contented Hook. "I think it's about time to go annoy my son!"

Chapter Nineteen

She was really dreading this, and she knew she wouldn't be able to go on much longer with this charade.

Darcy watched Craig Holt pull up next to the curb of the house he had agreed to show her, and gripped the steering wheel tightly. He waved and smiled, and she knew she had no choice now, but to go through with it.

She climbed out of the car with nothing even close to enthusiasm and slowly approached him.

"What's this?" he questioned, continuing to grin pleasantly. "You're supposed to act excited to be here. This is no time to play hard to sell a house to!"

"Sorry," Darcy offered, smiling back faintly. "Just trying to shift gears."

"Beast of a day?"

"Something like that."

Craig unlocked the front door, and swung it open, gesturing her in grandly.

"Here you have the main ballroom," he quipped, flashing even white teeth at her and looking around, as if he hadn't seen the place before, either.

"Impressive," she commented, realizing, as she did, that she sounded like Neil. "How fortunate that it can also double as a living room, if I get in a bind."

"Ah, humor raises its sleepy head!"

He whipped open his note pad and scanned his own scribbling briefly. "There are a few imperfections, according to the seller, that we should just get out of the way at once. Water spots on the kitchen ceiling. They replaced the roof six months ago but they never touched up the ceiling. If you're dead set that they take care of it, I'm sure I can persuade them."

Darcy let her eyes wander around as she would be expected to, successfully concealing her churning stomach. She really couldn't see the wisdom in letting this drag on any longer. She wandered over to the large front window and stared out, praying for help to say what she had come to say.

"Nice neighborhood, isn't it?"

When she failed to respond, he came over and cleared his throat, laughing as she jumped.

"I said nice neighborhood. Yes?"

"Oh... yes," she stammered awkwardly.

Craig tilted his head to one side and gave her a frankly curious look. "Are you sure you're up for this today, Miss Decker?"

"No. I'm not."

"Want to reschedule? I won't even try that line on you about having lots of other people who are chomping at the bit, to buy this house."

She smiled nervously. "I appreciate that but... well, the thing is... I'm afraid I haven't been completely honest with you, Mr. Holt."

"Craig," he suggested. "The realtor is the servant of the buyer and should be addressed by his or her first name."

"Craig," she said faintly. She looked all around the living room, anywhere but directly at him.

"Miss Decker..."

"Darcy."

"Darcy, what's wrong? I'm not the world's smartest man, but it doesn't take an analytical genius to figure out that you're just not into this. You said you've not been honest. What are you, wanted by the law, or something?" His eyes crinkled with gentle humor.

She took a deep breath and decided that now was as good a time as any. "You may wish that it was that simple."

She glanced over at the big hearth and sank down onto it, her legs suddenly choosing not to support her.

Craig questioned her silently, then came over to join her, appraising her with kind curiosity.

"Why don't you just come clean?" he suggested.

Darcy leveled honest blue eyes at him. "I'm not who you think I am."

"You're not Darcy Decker?"

"Yes. But I'm not here to buy a house."

"You're not," he echoed quietly.

"No." She flushed with embarrassment. "I'm sorry."

He knitted his brows. "Well... if you're not in the market, then..." He cut her a sideways look, with a grin. "Are you some kind of mad stalker, or an ax murderer? Should I be afraid?"

She smiled, in spite of herself. "I'm no ax murderer but you may end up considering me a stalker."

He continued to wait, but made no attempt to mask his polite confusion.

"You and I have spoken before, Craig. Several weeks ago."

"We have?" He looked down idly at the floor, but nothing seemed to click with him.

"I called you." She waited and, after no response, braved ahead with barely a whisper. "From Tennessee."

Craig lifted his head and stared straight at her, as if he were haunted, and she was the ghost.

"Don't do this," he implored her.

"I didn't want to," Darcy said softly. "But I knew, when you got so upset with me on the phone, that you really are her brother and I had to come."

He jumped up and made his way across the room to the window, burying his hands in his pockets, and staring blankly out at nothing. Finally, he spun around and flashed hurt eyes at her.

"Why did you come here? I told you, I'm not the one you want. Why couldn't you just take my word for it, and let it go at that?"

Darcy came over to face him, with nothing left to lose. "Because you *are* the one. You're Madeline's brother."

"Well, what if I am?" His face became twisted with emotion. "What business is it of yours? Why can't you just leave me alone?"

"I can't!" She gave him a helpless, vulnerable look.

Understanding dawned in his eyes, immediately followed by anger.

"*He* sent you here, didn't he? Don't even try it," he warned, mistaking her look of surprise for one of denial. "He's the reason you're here!"

"Neil doesn't know that I'm here."

Craig gaped at her in bewilderment. "Neil? I'm talking about Kirby Yeager! Who the blazes is Neil?"

It was Darcy's turn to look shocked. "You don't know who Neil is?"

They locked eyes and just stood there, each unsure of what was going on. Suddenly, Craig grabbed her wrist and pulled her toward the door.

"This is over," he stated flatly, dragging her out onto the front porch and locking the door firmly. He hurried to his car, ignoring all her pleas for him to stop, and wasted no time disappearing into traffic.

Darcy watched him go, with hot tears of frustration coursing down her cheeks. She knew he'd be angry, but she didn't think he'd refuse to talk to her, once she finally had him alone.

She wiped her face, and trudged out to her own car, sitting there in disbelief for a long moment, before finally heading back to the hotel.

"So much for your big plan," she muttered to herself, darkly. "Now what?"

She returned to her room in defeat, and drew the heavily lined drapes together. There had been no call from Bett to return, so she turned off the light and laid down in the darkness, trying desperately to come up with something that would redeem the mess she had made of things today.

The evening found her still discouraged, but as she opened her eyes the next morning, something just seemed to lock into place. She sat up straight, her heart pounding, and hurried to get ready to go out. "On to plan B," she announced, under her breath.

She dashed downstairs for a quick breakfast, realizing, as she choked down her food, that there was no need to hurry. What she was planning didn't need to happen before late afternoon, anyway. Well, she'd take care of the preliminary steps now, and have that much out of the way.

She drove to the car rental agency, and made arrangements to change cars.

"Is there something wrong with the one you're driving, Miss Decker?" The man at the counter questioned her pleasantly, but with concern.

"Not at all. I'd just like something smaller, if that's possible."

He nodded, as if understanding completely. "A lot of people prefer driving smaller cars, here in California, especially when you're having to maneuver in and out of heavy traffic."

"Yes." She smiled and signed the papers he laid in front of her. She then handed him her key, and took the new one he offered her.

She strolled through the lot, looking for the space number he had given her. Her eyes lit up, as she saw that this car was black. She had completely forgotten to ask for another color, and that was important. The other car had been red. She hopped in and went back to her room, to wait until time to leave again.

Four o' clock found Darcy sitting in the parking lot of the real estate company, dark sunglasses hiding much of her face and her bright hair secured under a cap. She glanced at her watch and wondered what the company's normal office hours were.

An hour later, she found out, as several employees left the building, all at once. She spied Craig Holt almost immediately, and started her car, in order to move in directly behind him as he left the lot.

She accomplished this smoothly, and followed him out into the street and east onto the 10 Freeway, making sure to keep just enough distance to not be considered a tailgater, but staying close enough to keep any other cars from cutting in front of her. She knew very little about where she was, and she was certainly not about to lose him!

Traffic crawled along, everyone bent on leaving the city behind for the day. Darcy had been told that this is what created most of the evening congestion, and marveled at how far people were willing to commute in Southern California.

She endured the snail's pace impatiently, relieved as she noticed it gradually picking up, the closer she got to Redlands.

At last, Craig exited off the freeway and took a road that led them south beyond the reaches of the clustered community. The countryside almost began to take on a rural aspect, something Darcy didn't expect to find.

They passed several orange groves and the road began to wind back and forth, steadily climbing. Craig took a side street unexpectedly and Darcy had to hit her brakes. He didn't look back and she heaved a big sigh of relief, telling herself to keep her eyes on his car, and not the scenery.

He turned on his blinker and she slowed down, as he turned left into the drive of a pretty, white, stucco house with a nicely kept lawn. She continued on past, looking back in her rear-view mirror to see him hop out with his briefcase, keys in hand. That must be his home, she decided, and the second car, a silver Thunderbird, must be his wife's.

Darcy drove down to the next street and turned around, waiting at the curb, until she thought she had given him enough time to go inside. She headed back down the street until she came to the white house, and slowed just enough to note the house number. Pulling back out to the main road, she looked up at the sign on the corner, and stopped to scribble down the street address.

She had to smile, as she suddenly remembered Craig asking her if she was a stalker. She certainly was exhibiting those tendencies! Well, her stalking was done. She had gotten what it was she'd come for, at least for now.

"Okay," she breathed with a light of accomplishment shining in her eyes. "If I can just find my way back out of here."

The rental car had no GPS system, and her burner phone was no help. She stopped at a gas station by the freeway, and purchased a map of Redlands, just in case she couldn't remember her way back to Craig Holt's house. She settled in for the drive back to Riverside, her mind a hive of activity, racing even faster than the uninhibited westbound traffic.

She remembered what Craig had told her about his wife now spending so much time at home. "Maybe she wouldn't mind a little company, then," she muttered.

Janis Sheridan leaned back into the pillows on her bed and closed her eyes, wishing that she hadn't answered the telephone.

"My dear Janis!" Oliver's lazy purr set her nerves on edge. "Please tell me all about your latest escapades and, by all means, don't spare the drama."

She licked her dry lips. "Don't you read the papers, Oliver?" she asked, trying for a nonchalant tone.

"Let's just say, for the sake of an argument, that I haven't yet indulged myself," he returned, smoothly. "Why don't you fill me in on your most recent exploits?"

"Well," she answered nervously, "if you *had* read the papers, you would know that Meredith Etheridge has been hospitalized and is in a coma. She's in guarded condition."

"Let us hope not too well guarded, for your sake." Oliver abandoned all attempts at cloaking his malice and adopted a blatant, threatening manner.

"I specified a complete end to Meredith Etheridge, and her so-called ministry, and if anything less transpires, you will answer for it."

Janis grasped the phone tightly, and drew in a deep breath. "I'm concentrating all my efforts on taking her out."

"You've concentrated all your efforts on taking her husband!" he fired back. "I had no objection, as long as it was a method by which to accomplish my purposes. But you failed dismally, my dear. Do not fail again. Is that understood?"

"Perfectly."

Oliver laughed quietly, and returned to his languid, dulcet tones, with apparent ease. "My darling Janis, do you not realize that I am your only ally? Warren has made no secret of the fact that he desires to erase you completely out of the equation, something he's rather good at doing. If it weren't for my insistence that you be allowed to continue with your little project, you would be among the ranks of the missing, by now. And you *will* be, Janis, if you fail me again. Nothing personal, sweetheart. Just business."

He ended the conversation abruptly, much to Janis Sheridan's relief. She sat up and stared at the phone for a long moment, waves of fear, hatred, and resentment washing over her.

You know, Oliver," she simmered, in her own silky tones, "I'm getting just a little tired of your threats. You're not the only one with power."

Janis opened the drawer, and pulled out the box she kept inside. "I said I'd take her out, and I will. And then, just for amusement, I might also take you and Warren out. Just business, you understand. Nothing personal."

She laughed at her own cleverness, as she opened the box and removed the icons of her perverted worship.

Chapter Twenty

Laura sat up in bed, her heart knocking against her ribs. She noted, with tremendous relief, that it was daylight. It had been an incredibly long night, spent intermittently drifting in and out of bizarre dreams, and calling on the Lord to calm her.

She pulled her knees up to her chest, and hugged them tightly, as she remembered the one recurring dream that had awakened her several times. Her telephone kept ringing, over and over, louder and louder, until the volume got so loud, she was forced to answer it. Each time she did, a woman's hysterical laughter pierced her ears, and then the caller slammed the phone down, only to call right back.

In her nightmare, Laura tried to turn the phone off, she tried leaving it off the hook, she even unplugged it from the wall, but it continued ringing with shrill persistence. She was plagued by the dream all through the night and now, as she dragged herself wearily out of bed, she was hit with fatigue, as if she hadn't slept at all. She wished she hadn't even gone to bed.

She looked over at her telephone, warily at first, as if it had followed her out of her dreams, and then pulled it toward her, punching in Gary's number quickly, before she could change her mind. She knew it was very early, but she felt an overwhelming need to talk to him.

It rang several times and finally, after hearing some groping noises, the welcomed sound of Gary's sleepy voice gave her courage.

"Gary, it's me."

"Laura?" She could almost see him sitting up straight and looking surprised. "Honey... what is it? Is it Meredith?"

"No, nothing like that," she hurried to reassure him. She should have realized that he would interpret such an early call as trouble. "I'm sorry, I know you were still sleeping, Gary. I just... well, I feel stupid now, but I had such weird dreams all last night, and I felt as if talking to you might help."

"Don't apologize, Laura." He was wide-awake now. "You never have to have a reason for calling me, I don't care when it is. You know that."

"I know." His gentle concern warmed her heart. "Gary, I was wondering if you and I could meet for breakfast this morning, before I go to the hospital. These dreams harassed me, literally all night long, and I feel sure there's something behind them. I really think God is showing me something, and I need to talk to you about it."

"I couldn't think of a better way to start the day," he said softly. "I'd love to sit across a breakfast table from you. Who knows? If I play my cards right, maybe you'll let me come over and sit on *your* side of the table."

She laughed and leaned back against her pillows. "Could we maybe shoot for soon? Say in about an hour?"

"I'll come over and we'll ride together," he said. "And now that you've got me awake, let me tell you that I love you."

"I just happen to love you, too," she returned, with a smile. "What are the odds?"

Laura laid the receiver down, her smile still hovering around her lips.

A few hours later, she walked into the hospital's lobby, having had a wonderful talk with her fiancé, and feeling as if she had a pretty good idea of what was going on. She not only had a clearer perspective now, but every intention of grilling her son, until she knew exactly what it was that needed to be dealt with.

She had planned on talking to him the day she'd listened to the messages on his machine, but when she saw him at the hospital, he was in no state to be interrogated. A television network had actually managed to get a call through to Meredith's room, and Joel was livid. She'd completely forgotten everything, the minute she saw him.

She believed that when Joel told her things were fine, he really thought they were. But he knew something; he just didn't realize what. Laura was sure of that much.

She got off the elevator, greeted the nurses at their station, nodded pleasantly to the guard and strolled into Meredith's room, halting in her tracks as she saw Dr. Lynch with his hand on Joel's shoulder and Dr. Chambers holding his elbow.

"What is it?" she asked sharply. "What's going on?"

Joel lifted red eyes to hers and hung his head without answering. Iris came over and pulled her mother to one side.

"Dr. Lynch told Joel that the baby has been showing signs of being in distress this morning, Mother."

Laura put a hand to her throat and stared at her.

"It's starting to look as though they may have to do a C-section on Meredith."

"But..." She swallowed hard and searched for what she was trying to say. "How would Meredith be able to handle it? What about her blood pressure?"

She was visibly shaken and Iris indicated, with a touch, that they should step back toward the door.

"Dr. Lynch said a C-section wouldn't be his first choice, and if Meredith were able to be roused enough to be induced that would be best but, since that's not the case and because the baby's heart-rate is decreasing, he's concerned enough to prepare to proceed. But, Mom, Meredith's condition has been upgraded, remember that, and her blood pressure has been stable. She'll be okay."

"But would they sedate her? If she's in a coma, would she still need..." Laura couldn't finish her question. She couldn't process any of this.

"Probably general anesthesia. Dr. Chambers told us there've been studies using scans that suggest that coma victims do feel pain," Iris explained in a whisper, not wanting to further upset her brother. "They're going to make sure Meredith doesn't."

Laura nodded, as her words sank in. "No," she said faintly. "No, we don't want Meredith to hurt."

"The anesthesiologist has worked with both of Meredith's doctors plenty of times, Mother. They're both confident that he'll take good care of her."

Laura nodded, then patted Iris's arm absently and made her way over to her son.

"Joel."

He blinked at her as if he were dreaming. She held out her arms and he went into them.

"She's going to be alright, sweetie," Laura assured him, suddenly convinced of it. "I know she will, and the baby will be just fine. Too many people are praying and believing God."

Joel lifted his head and nodded, not trusting himself to speak. He pulled himself slowly out of her embrace and went to lean over his wife.

Dr. Lynch gave Laura a smile of recognition, while Dr. Chambers finished consulting with his nurse and left the room.

"Mrs. Etheridge, we're going to watch Baby just a bit longer, to decide if surgery is going to happen. But as things stand, I'm concerned with what the monitor is showing me, this morning. I'm going to have the nurses check things over the next hour but if things deteriorate, or haven't improved by then, we're going to have to deliver."

"She's been off the ventilator for a while, now. Do you think she'll have to have it, again?"

"Right now, I'd say no. She's been breathing on her own just fine." He touched her arm lightly. "I don't expect so, but we'll see. Everything's going to be monitored closely. Let's not worry too much in advance."

She nodded silently.

"The baby's far enough along and everything should be fine." He flashed her another encouraging smile. "So you might be a grandmother a little sooner than you expected."

She made an effort to respond to his optimism and he reached over and squeezed Joel's shoulder.

"Buck up, Daddy!"

Joel glanced up and managed a weak copy of Dr. Lynch's smile, as he gave them all a wave of camaraderie and hurried out.

Laura patted Joel's arm, and went over to give Iris a hug. "Sweetheart, I'm gonna step out and call Gary. He'll want to be around for Joel."

She let herself out quietly and Iris wandered over to keep a close eye on her brother.

"You okay, Joel?"

He kept his eyes firmly glued to Meredith's face, and acted as if he hadn't heard.

"Joel?" She touched him lightly on the back. When he finally straightened and turned to her, his face was wet with anguish.

"Oh, sweetie!" Iris caught him around the neck and held him tightly. Sharp heaves racked his frame as he began to weep out loud.

A sudden realization hit Iris like a rogue wave, as she remembered the only other time she had seen her brother cry like this. She knew, at once, what was triggering this grief.

"Look at me, Joel." She took his hands and held them tightly, tugging at them when he made an attempt to look away. "Stop it, now. You have to stop thinking like this." She kept her words tender but firm, and her eyes were full of mercy. "You have to stop."

"Iris..." He sounded as if he were breaking in two. "What if something happens to our baby? It'll be because of me, because of what happened to Kayla. And, my God, what about Meredith? She's already lost one baby!"

"Hush!" Iris hissed, shooting a worried look down at Meredith and giving him a little shake. "Be *quiet!* What if she can hear you, Joel? We've talked about all this. You have to let this go."

"I did it!" He ignored her, softly moaning like a hurt animal. "I killed her, just as surely as if I'd done it with my own hands. Oh, God, I'm so sorry!"

He pushed himself out of her grasp and crumpled down onto a chair next to the bed, shaking with the force of his torment. Iris bent over him, wrapping her arms around his shoulders, protectively.

"Joel, you listen to me. You have to listen to me, honey. I was just too hurt and angry that night. I didn't know the whole story. Sweetheart, I'm so sorry I called you a murderer!" Her own eyes began to rain.

"Joel, Kayla was going to get that abortion, whether you gave her the money or not. Mother told me that you'd already refused to give her money and then you found her on a street corner, trying to prostitute herself to get it. Jack and I both know now that you gave in to her because you felt that your hands were tied. I'm sorry, sweetie, that we allowed so many years to pass, before we were able to deal with things, but we really have forgiven you and we love you, Joel. It's not your fault that she died. Please understand that! It wasn't you, Joel, it was those butchers at the clinic and Kayla was going there, with or without you. There's nothing you could have done."

She came around to kneel in front of him, heartsick to realize that for so many years, she had allowed her brother to carry such an overwhelming burden of guilt and remorse.

"I should have come to you!" His voice was ragged and thin.

"I don't think it would have changed anything, if you had. You saw her yourself, Joel, out on the streets. We'd have pounced on her, and tried to control what she did, but you saw the extreme lengths that she was willing to go to. I admit that part of our anger was that you didn't come tell us right away, but on this side of things, we know, Joel, and so do you, that it wouldn't have changed anything.

"Listen to what I'm saying. Don't you realize how much Jack and I have struggled to cope with our own part in this? For whatever reason, our baby felt she couldn't come to us. She was so afraid of our reaction that she felt that her solution was less severe. Honey, Kayla was our only child. If Jack and I can understand and forgive you, you have to forgive yourself and let it go, just like we've had to forgive ourselves. We had to, and so do you."

She stroked his forehead and studied him carefully. "You're just really exhausted and emotional right now and you're not thinking clearly. If you were, you'd realize that God isn't anything like what you're making Him out to be. He loves you and Meredith so much and this baby is a gift from Him, to the both of you."

She continued to watch him, her soft eyes swimming with compassion. "Remember, Joel, that verse you quoted to me when I was sixteen, and I had just found out I was pregnant with Kayla?"

He looked at her hungrily, with swollen, watery eyes and she continued.

"It was Psalm 103. Remember? I do, because I memorized that whole passage. 'The Lord is compassionate and gracious, slow to anger and abounding in loving-kindness. He will not always strive with us; nor will He keep His anger forever. He has not dealt with us according to our sins, nor rewarded us according to our iniquities.' Look at me, Joel."

He had dropped his head but lifted it back up now to meet her eyes.

"Listen. 'Just as a father has compassion on his children, so the Lord has on those who fear Him. For He Himself knows what we are made of and He remembers that we are dust.' Joel, God is not punishing you. All your sins and mistakes are forgiven. You know that, don't you, sweetheart?"

"Yes," he whispered.

"Then you should also know that it makes no sense to blame the Father, for what the enemy is trying to do."

"No, I wasn't trying to blame Him, Sis," he answered, rubbing his eyes with a shaky hand. "I guess I just feel that He would be well within His rights, if He *was* punishing me."

"Well, He would be. If He wanted to exercise His rights, we'd all be in hell. Joel, God wouldn't have put you and Meredith together, and blessed you with this tiny baby, if He was just going to snatch everything away from you. Don't you know better than that? He's not mean."

A distant light began to flicker in his eyes. "Yes," he responded in a little stronger voice. "I do know that, Iris." He laced his fingers into hers and gave them a gentle squeeze. "But I needed you to remind me."

"Well, let me remind you of something else. Meredith needs you to not only pray for her, but to believe for her. Remember that verse that talks about the stronger receiving the weaker one into his faith? You are Meredith's covering, Joel. No more falling apart. It's up to you to remain strong in your faith, and to support your wife and child with that faith. Now..."

She boxed him harmlessly on the chin, the way she had done, since they were children. "No more crazy talk. If Meredith hears you running on like that, she'll sit up and pop you silly!"

"I wish she would." Joel gazed over at his wife wistfully, then back at Iris with a long, loving look. "I've missed you all these years, baby sister."

"Well, I'm here, now."

"Thank God!" He stood to his feet and lifted her up, giving her a sturdy hug. "Today is Merry's birthday." He looked down at Meredith with a tenderness that brought the ghost of a smile to his lips. "Maybe our son's birthday, too. That would mean a lot to her." He looked over at his sister.

"Would you do me a favor and sit with her just a bit, Iris? But call for me, if Dr. Lynch comes back in?"

"Of course." Iris watched curiously as he bent over and laid a hand on his baby and his lips tenderly on Meredith's. "Where are you going?"

He straightened up and gave her the closest thing to a grin she had seen on his face in ages, then flicked his fingers across his bearded face. "To get rid of this."

When Joel emerged from the room's private bath, not only was his face clean but his eyes were clear. Iris knew that he had been talking to God.

Laura had returned, while he was shaving and, as he came back into the room, she stood up and laughed.

"I knew I had a handsome son, somewhere under all that hair!"

He managed a smile and even a little wink for his mother, although he still looked tired and worn out. He looked down at Meredith's face with a sigh, but also with intentness, as if he were seeing something else, instead of his wife lying between life and death.

He bent down and put his lips close to her ear.

"I believe you can hear me, little one," he whispered. "So hear me when I tell you that I need you more than life, itself. You come on back to me, sweetheart, and help me raise our son. I love you so much, Merry."

He lifted himself up just a little, and examined her face with eyes full of all that he felt for her.

The door opened and a nurse gave them all a smile as she came to stand in front of the monitor. She opened a chart and made some notes, then left without speaking. Moments later, Dr. Lynch came back in with her to look at the monitor, himself.

He stopped and took in Joel's improved appearance with surprised delight.

"Don't I know you?" he teased, grinning at Joel's wry, self-conscious smile.

He focused his attention on the monitor briefly, a frown creasing his forehead.

"Joel," he said, turning to meet him with a steady gaze. "It's your baby boy's birthday."

"Today's his mother's birthday," Joel confided, quietly.

"Is it?" Dr. Lynch glanced back at her chart, noting it for himself. "That'll be special for both of them, won't it?"

"Yes," he answered simply.

"It will be," he insisted, with a pat on Joel's arm.

His nurse raised the sheet as he removed his stethoscope and fitted it into his ears. He listened for a moment, moving it around Meredith's body.

"Okay." He straightened back up. "We'll be prepping Mommy in a few moments, and then get her on into surgery." He hesitated, again studying Joel.

"Under normal circumstances, even with C-sections, fathers are usually present, but I know you do understand, Joel, that these aren't normal circumstances."

He waited for Joel's nod before continuing. "I'd appreciate your willingness to remain outside, until we're done. I know you feel strongly about being in there with us, but this situation's a bit more demanding than most and, whenever that's the case, it's best for all concerned if there are no distractions."

"I agree." Joel surprised him with his quiet reply.

"Thank you for that."

The nurse took his stethoscope and he came back over to Joel, taking one of his hands and one of Laura's.

"Dad, Grandma... try to stay calm, and hang in there for me."

"We'll be fine," Joel assured him.

"I know you will." Dr. Lynch smiled with confidence, as he left.

Gary made it to the hospital just before the aides were ready to roll Meredith out to surgery. Hailey and Ross had only just arrived, themselves. He gave Laura a kiss, then lifted Meredith's hand and one of Joel's, as if fusing them together, and led them in a prayer of protection and acknowledging the Blood covering over Meredith and her child.

Joel walked down the hall beside the gurney, grabbing it as they got to the operating room doors, and pulling it to a stop. He bent down and kissed Meredith lovingly.

"Sweetheart, I'll be right here waiting," he said, in a gentle voice. One of the aides looked at her co-worker with tears welling up in her eyes.

"You're gonna do just fine, and then you come back to me, okay? I'll be right here. I love you, little one."

He gave her one more lingering kiss and then raised up, clinging to her fingers until the gurney cleared the doors, forcing their hands to separate.

Joel stood staring after her, with an odd expression on his face. He shifted slightly as he felt Laura's hand on his back.

"Mother?"

"Yes, darling?"

He blinked rapidly, with his hand on his chest, and she knew something was rushing around in his head. He turned and gave her a strange look. "I just kissed Meredith before they rolled her in..."

She waited, as he gazed toward the doors and, after a few seconds, he looked back at her in wonder.

"She kissed me back!"

Chapter Twenty-One

"Darn it!" Bett Greer shoved a basket of laundry out of the way with her foot, and hurried to open the back door. Her face betrayed any attempt at poise.

"Neil, hello!"

"Hi, Bett." He peered through the screen hopefully. "May I come in?"

She looked around quickly, obviously flustered, and then pushed the door forward. "Well, sure. Excuse me, though."

Neil followed her in and took a seat at the counter, as she rushed back over to her huge pot of bubbling plums.

"I can't leave these, just yet," she explained, over her shoulder. "I have to keep 'em stirred, once they start boiling."

"What are you doing?" he asked politely, not really caring, but attempting to curb his impatience.

"Making preserves." Bett wiped her hot forehead with her sleeve, and continued plowing her big wooden spoon back and forth, through the rolling plums. "I guess you're probably wondering why we don't just buy stuff like this at the store."

He grinned, as she read his mind. "Well, that just seems so much easier than standing over a hot stove, like that."

"Yeah, but you haven't had *my* preserves." She fired him a teasing wink, and dumped a bowl of sugar into the pot. "I need to keep one eye on this," she informed him, "so please don't think I'm being rude, if I don't join you just yet."

Neil gave a scant laugh and then sobered quickly.

"Bett... I know I'm probably not going to have any better luck today, than I did the last time I was here, but I have to try. Is there any chance at all, of your letting me know how I can find Darcy?"

She had been prepared for the question, but not for the look of hopelessness that accompanied it. "If it were up to me, Neil, I'd take you there, myself. Unfortunately, it's *not* up to me."

He nodded and fingered a bread wrapper twist-tie that someone had left on the countertop. Bett paused long enough to give him a quizzing glance.

"You knew that already, so why even ask?"

"I just had to try."

"You know, Neil, you and I talked about this, already," she pointed out. "You know how I feel about it. I can't see any good in your coming around here, keeping things stirred up, if you're not going to do something to fix things for you and Darcy."

"Well, that's why I'm here... sort of." He looked up at her, as she lifted the pot from the stove and onto a folded dishtowel.

"For a while, I haven't been sure if I had a right to end the marriage. I've been feeling trapped between being an example for the church, and doing what I longed to do, just move on and put it all behind me. I know Madeline had a relationship with another man before we were married, but I don't know if she was unfaithful, afterward. I don't know for sure that she was with anyone, when she left. There was talk of another man being around just before, but I don't know who he was, or if they had anything going on.

"I mean, what if she left on some stupid impulse, but she had been faithful, and then she came back? Wouldn't I have to forgive her and take her back? This is what I've been struggling with."

He smiled at Bett's cynical expression.

"I know, I know. It's been four years. She's not coming back. Besides, how long is a man supposed to wait? Am I supposed to just remain in limbo, for the rest of my life?"

"You're the only one that can answer that, Neil," she declared, skimming the foam off the top of the plums and plopping it into the sink. She positioned a prepared Mason jar and began filling it with the hot preserves. "But I can tell you this. You can't just keep popping up in Darcy's life, without making some decisions, one way or the other."

"That's what I've come to say, Bett." Neil met her eyes directly. "I *have* made a decision."

Bett regarded him steadily for a quiet moment, before turning her attention back to filling the jars. "I'm listening."

"I've been talking to Barry Todd about it. We've met several times, in fact, for prayer and counsel. Of course, it would be easier if I knew where Madeline was, but... well, Bett, I've decided to file for an annulment."

She was silent, as she laid the lids on the mouths of the jars and fastened their rings firmly into place. Neil was beginning to wonder if she had heard him, when she glanced his way, before speaking.

"You've decided. But have you talked to an attorney, yet?" she asked, turning the jars upside down and studying them closely.

"Yes. I'd spoken to him about this off and on before, but I never could resolve to go through with it, until now."

"And why is this time any different?"

Neil looked uncertain. "What do you mean?"

Bett slowly began setting the jars back upright and placing them on a thickly folded towel in the corner.

"I mean, you say, yourself, that you've discussed this with your lawyer, on more than one occasion. You've obviously considered getting an annulment in the past. But you *didn't*, did you? Why should you be expected to, this time?"

"I was never in love before," he said simply.

"But now, you are," Bett finished for him, in her deadpan manner.

"For the first time in my life, if I've learned anything from the past." Neil's face had absolutely nothing to hide. "I love Darcy with all my heart, Bett."

She mopped her hot face, and pushed her blonde hair back out of her eyes, before filling the huge pot with soapy hot water and her spoons and leaving it all to soak. She came over and pulled out a stool, meeting Neil McCallen with a frank, blunt expression.

"You'd better be sure, Neil, that's all I've got to say. Darcy is like one of my own, and if anybody hurt her, I'd just as soon smack him, as look at him!"

He smiled at her fierce loyalty. "I promise you, Bett, the last thing I would ever want to do is to hurt her."

"You say that now. But who's to say you're not harboring some unfinished business with your wife, or maybe some unresolved bitterness and one day, you might wind up taking all that out on Darcy?"

Neil reached out his hand and touched hers gently. "You know, if you'd have said that to me the last time I was here, I couldn't have denied it was possible. Maybe even likely. I can tell you today though, honestly and before Heaven, that I'm not holding anything against Madeline. I've forgiven her, Bett. Completely."

Bett saw the truth in his eyes and slowly gave in to a broad grin. "Well, if that's the case, you have my blessing."

"That's a relief!" He laughed and picked up the twist-tie again, toying with it. "But I guess it's too much to hope for, that you'll tell me where she is?"

"I wish I could. I really do."

"Well... do you know, Bett, *if* she's coming back?"

"Of course she's coming back! You're the state youth director, for crying out loud! Do you think she'd just bail on those kids for good, and not even tell you?"

He shook his head and smiled.

"Okay," Bett sighed. "I'll tell you this much and that's it. Faron Waldrop's been looking after her kids while she's been away. I know you knew that. But he and his family are leaving on vacation soon, and she told them she'd get back before then, so they wouldn't have to change their plans."

"How soon?"

She grinned and chose to look away, instead of rolling her eyes. "At least by this time, next week."

Neil jumped up and grabbed her, almost squeezing the breath out of her.

"Thank you!" he gushed. "Thank you, Bett!"

"Save your thanks. I'd prefer your using the time between now and then to square away your legal entanglements," she advised dryly, having no trouble at all shifting from a smile to a scowl, a skill she'd honed by being a mother.

"I actually have an appointment this afternoon to start the paperwork," he assured her. "Unfortunately, because of Madeline's absence, things probably won't progress as quickly as I'd like, but they *will* progress. That's the main thing."

"I agree." Bett got up and followed Neil to the door. "The next time I see you, be prepared to convince me that you've got your ducks in a row, Neil, or you may end up wearing these preserves."

He gave her a jaunty little wave, and she laughed quietly at the way he almost danced to his car.

Darcy pulled her rental car up to the curb, and sat staring out the window at the Holt's residence.

"Here we are," she sighed. "Twenty-seven-fourteen, still here, just waiting on me." She glanced over at the silver Thunderbird in the driveway. That was good. Mrs. Craig Holt was home, then.

All morning, Darcy had been trying to come up with some plausible excuse to get inside this house. Finally, she decided to abandon her scheming, and just be honest. She was tired of having to skirt around the truth, to get to talk to anyone.

She stepped out of her car with a bracing lift to her chin, and a deep breath to steady her nerves. It was now or never, so she began her approach up the concrete drive.

She paused in front of the large gray door and breathed a quick prayer for help and strength, before committing to a sharp knock. In only a short minute, the door was swung open and Darcy found herself confronted by an attractive, brunette woman, with a pleasant, but inquiring smile lighting up her face.

"Hello," She offered a greeting, after Darcy seemed unable to come up with one of her own. "May I help you?"

"Mrs. Holt?" Her mouth seemed incredibly dry.

"Yes. Donna. And you are...?" She lifted her brows in question and waited.

"I'm... well, Donna..." She hated this, especially since she knew fully well that she was about to be asked to leave. "I'm Darcy Decker," she finished in a rush.

Donna Holt's expression remained friendly and unaffected by this revelation, much to Darcy's surprise. Was it possible? Had Craig deliberately not mentioned her to his wife?

"What can I do for you, Darcy?" Her soft voice cut into Darcy's jumbled thoughts.

She groped around for the next thing to say. "I was wondering... I know this is going to sound like an unusual request, Donna, and I realize I'm a complete stranger, but I was hoping I could talk to you for a few minutes. I came to see if you could answer some questions for me."

More curiosity wrinkled Donna Holt's forehead. "Well, sure, I guess. I have no idea how I could possibly be of any help to you, but I'll try. Come on in."

Darcy followed her into the spacious formal living room and took a seat opposite Craig's wife, an ornate coffee table separating them.

"Can I offer you anything?" her gracious hostess asked.

"Oh, no thank you," she stammered. "Thank you, I'm fine."

Donna smiled mildly, without bothering to hide her complete intrigue with who this woman was, and what she wanted with her.

"You thought I might be able to help you with something, Darcy," she reminded in a calm tone.

"I was hoping so, yes," she admitted. "Donna..." She broke off and gave her a questioning look. "My name didn't seem to ring a bell with you. Am I right?"

"Well, no it didn't. It's a pretty name and one I'm sure I would've remembered, if I'd ever heard it before. Should it have?" she asked curiously, tilting her head to one side. "Rung a bell, I mean?"

"I had expected it to."

"I'm sorry. Have we met, Darcy?"

Darcy leaned forward and riveted her clear blue eyes on the woman across from her.

"No, we haven't, but I was sure your husband would have mentioned me to you."

"Craig?" Donna looked surprised. "Are you a client of Craig's?"

"No, I'm... I'm the one who called him several weeks ago. From Tennessee."

"Tennessee?"

Darcy could see that none of this meant anything to Mrs. Holt, other than a means of confusion.

"I guess I don't understand," Donna faltered, seeming to pale a little. "Are you here to tell me... something about you and my husband?"

Darcy gasped and reached her hand quickly across the table to cover Donna's in a reassuring manner. "Oh, no! Oh no, no, *nothing* like that! Oh, I'm sorry, Donna, I didn't intend for it to sound like that!"

Relief spread hurriedly over Donna's pretty face. "I didn't mean to assume anything, Darcy, I just didn't understand why Craig wouldn't have mentioned your call, if you weren't a client. I guess my imagination just ran away with me."

Darcy sat back in her chair and let her eyes wander around the beautifully furnished room without seeing it, as she sorted out how she needed to proceed.

"I understand why he didn't mention it," she dared, at last. "It's because of Madeline."

She finally got the reaction she had been expecting. Donna drew in her breath sharply, and sat up straight in her chair. She lifted a hand to her mouth and gaped at Darcy with wide brown eyes.

"What do you know about Madeline?" she demanded.

"I know your husband is her brother," Darcy confessed, in a meek tone, intended to keep from further agitating her.

"Did he tell you that?"

"Does it matter?" she countered, quietly. "It's true."

Donna closed her eyes a moment and opened them again, slowly, as if she were hoping Darcy would be gone. She stood up and looked down at her, not unkindly, but steadfastly. "I think you need to go now, Darcy."

"Oh no, please, not you too!" Darcy jumped up with urgency. "Please just let me tell you why I came!"

"I'd better not." Donna moved suggestively toward the door.

"Donna... please..." Darcy's heart began beating in her ears. She was too close to let this happen again! "I don't mean any harm, I just have to find her! I *have* to! If you could just tell me where to look, that's all I ask. Please, you don't understand!"

"No, Darcy, *you* don't understand." Donna caught hold of the doorknob and pulled the heavy door open wide. "If Craig finds out about this, he'll have a fit! I can't talk to you about this. I'm sorry. I don't know why it's so important that you find Madeline, but I can't be the one to help you with it."

"It's Neil!" Darcy was unable to stop tears of despair and frustration from springing forth. "I love him, Donna! And he loves me, I know he does! But I can't... we can't ever be together unless Madeline... unless she decides whether or not she's ever returning to the marriage!"

Donna had been about to take Darcy's arm and lead her out to the front stoop. Now she stopped short and turned incredulous eyes on her.

"Neil?" she asked, in a faint voice. "To what marriage?" She searched Darcy's face thoroughly. "I don't understand."

"It's been four years, Donna!" Darcy was in an agitated state, overcome by disappointment, and hadn't seemed to hear her.

"Four years, and not a word! How long is a man expected to live like that? I know she's your husband's sister, and I don't mean to attack her, but it's a pretty sorry thing, to do what she's done to someone as wonderful as Neil. Especially since he's a minister, and feels bound by his vows.

"Meanwhile, she's off doing who knows what, who knows where, and Neil is forever frozen in time! She can do as she pleases, but he can't even... fall in love." Now she began weeping in earnest.

Donna stood there in stunned silence for a moment, then wrapped compassionate arms around Darcy. "I'm really so sorry," she whispered, starting to choke up herself, as the mystery of what Darcy was saying began to reveal itself to her. "I'm so sorry!"

"Please," Darcy lifted her wet face and begged her. "Please, won't you help us? Won't you just tell me where to find her?"

"I can't do that." Her heart stung her, but Donna remained staunch in her decision. "I made promises to my husband about Madeline long ago, and I won't go back on my word. I wish I could help you, but I just don't see a way to do that without betraying a confidence, not to mention my husband's trust."

Darcy felt sick. Her shoulders suddenly drooped with the weighty realization that all was lost. She dabbed at the corners of her eyes with her fingertips.

"Okay," she mumbled, in a dull voice. "I had to try. I guess it really is over, then."

She stepped out onto the stoop and down the steps.

"Wait!"

She stopped and turned back, unwilling to hope for much. Donna reached back inside the door and came out with a pen and a scrap of paper.

"I'm not promising anything," she insisted firmly. "But I'll take your number, in case things with Craig change."

Darcy stared down at the pen and paper, then clutched them in shaking hands, and scribbled down her hotel and room number. She laid it in Donna's hands and managed to offer her a weak smile.

"I'll only be here a few more days," she said, with a sniff. "I have to get back to Tennessee by Monday."

Donna smiled back and laid an understanding hand on her shoulder. "I wish I could do more, Darcy, but it's my husband's decision whether or not to help you. All you and I can do is hope and pray."

Darcy nodded. "I will do that," she promised. "I have to do that. It's all I have left."

She let out a cleansing breath and tried to manage another smile for this good and kind woman. "Thank you, Donna, for anything you can do."

"Remember," she cautioned, lifting her hand from Darcy's shoulder, after a gentle pat. "No promises."

"I understand. Thank you."

Donna watched her make her way slowly to her car and down the street, her head swimming with everything she had just heard.

She couldn't forget the devastation in Darcy's hurt eyes, or get the sound of her tearful pleading out of her ears. She considered her promise to Craig and wondered if it wasn't about time they revisited this subject.

Who was Neil? Had she really understood Darcy? Was it true? Had Madeline really been married?

Chapter Twenty-Two

Hailey turned around, as she heard Laura call her name. She smiled and waited for her to catch up.

"I'm just heading into the cafeteria for some coffee before I go up, Laura," she explained, after a quick hug. "Want to join me?"

"I could use a gallon of it!" Laura declared fervently.

She followed Meredith's designated "sister" in, and leaned wearily against the railing, next to the stacked cups. "I'm afraid I haven't been doing too well in the slumber department, lately."

"Got a lot of things on your mind, don't you?" Hailey glanced sympathetically at Joel's mother.

"You could say that." She didn't elaborate further until they'd paid for their coffee, and were making their way to sit down.

"I'm mainly tired. The thing is, I had been having some dreams that kept waking me up at night. Well, the same dream, over and over, actually. Gary and I talked about it and I've been meaning to talk to Joel, but then things changed here and I haven't, yet. I can't figure out what it means, but I can tell it's something significant. "

"Nightmare?"

"Well, yes, in the sense that it unnerved me and made me feel pursued, somehow."

They settled into a booth, in a far corner. Hailey leaned back comfortably against the padded back and eyed Laura with a little smile.

"So," she began lightly. "You might not be physically up to snuff, but I notice you have that same silly grin on your face that Joel has."

Laura laughed happily. "I just love being a grandma!"

"It shows! And that's a hefty boy, too, Laura, even if he is a little early. Meredith didn't look big enough to be packing around a kid that size!"

"Six pounds, seven ounces," she crowed, knowing this was old information, but supplying it anyway. "He's long, too. I'm sure he'll be tall, like Joel." Laura continued to smile proudly.

Hailey leaned forward on her elbows. "I had to leave before anyone said. Did Joel tell anyone the baby's name yet, or is he waiting for when Meredith wakes up?"

"Thanks for saying *when*, Hailey." She cradled her coffee cup in both hands and blinked, as a few sentimental tears crowded into her soft eyes. "Joel and Meredith already had the baby's name picked out, but they weren't telling anyone, not even me. Remember how no one could get a straight answer out of either one of them, so we all quit asking?"

Hailey rolled her eyes with a giggle. "They'd come up with something stupid, every time we'd try to find out. Remember that one time, when Meredith announced to us that they were naming the baby 'Haggai' and Joel acted all upset with her, and said he thought they'd agreed on 'Habakkuk' and that he didn't appreciate her just changing it, without even consulting him?"

They both shook with laughter, remembering how convincing Joel had been, with his fake outrage, and how Meredith played along, and informed him, very matter-of-factly, in front of everyone, that when he started carrying the baby is *his* belly, then he could name him.

"Oh, I know! I just wanted to bang both their heads together!" Laura declared. Her face softened. "When Joel finally told us the baby's real name last night, Iris almost hugged him in half."

"Why?"

"They named him Kaylan Paul Etheridge. Paul, after Joel's dad and..."

"Kaylan, after Kayla!" Hailey finished, her eyes shining. "Oh, Laura, that's so perfect!"

"Iris and Jack think so, too!" She sipped her hot coffee gingerly before setting down her cup and grinning up at Hailey. "Don't you just love all that dark, curly hair?"

"He's the most beautiful baby I've ever seen! How could he *not* be with those two, for parents? And I guess he couldn't help but have hair like that, with Joel and Meredith, both so dark and Joel's hair so curly."

"Well..." Joel's mother laughed heartily. "It's been a while since Joel's hair was dark. But I love all that gray. It makes me feel a little old, but he looks so much like his dad now, that I don't mind."

"Is it difficult, Laura, making room in your heart for Gary, when you loved Paul so much?"

Laura thought about it for a moment. "Gary is... he's my life continuing on. He's like a new chapter in my story, if that doesn't sound too trite. Paul and I had our own chapters and they were beautiful. I wouldn't take anything for them, and sometimes I still flip back through them in my mind and reread them, for old times sake. I probably always will. But my story's not over. God's sort of... let me see how to put this... He's sort of using Gary like a pen to finish the tale. Does that make sense?"

Hailey stared at her in amazement. "That makes wonderful sense, Laura."

She smiled at Hailey and lifted her cup. "Good. I was afraid I was rambling. I wish everything in my life made as much sense as Gary does." She suddenly looked tired again.

Hailey hesitated before asking, "Can you tell me your dream, if I'm not meddling?"

"It's the weirdest thing, Hailey. It's kind of involved, but there's this telephone that just keeps ringing, no matter what I do to stop it. I turn it off, I unplug it. Once, I even smashed it, but it just kept ringing."

"Do you ever answer it?"

"That's the part that gets me. I finally *do* answer it and when I do, someone just laughs, like a madwoman, and hangs up."

Hailey sat up straight and looked at her strangely. "So, it's a woman, then?"

"Yes..." Laura returned her penetrating stare. "Why are you looking at me like that? Does all this mean something to you?"

Hailey studied the handle of her spoon closely before speaking. "Laura, did Joel and Meredith ever tell you why they changed their phone number?" She glanced up when Laura didn't answer right away, and was startled to see her shocked expression.

"Of course!" Laura put her hands to her face and expelled a long breath. "Everything's been so crazy the past few days that I had completely forgotten about that!"

She met Hailey's eyes. "No, they didn't tell me, I didn't mean that. But when I went over one day last week to feed Hook, and to do some things around the house, I checked the machine for Joel. There must have been as least ten hang-ups, Hailey!" She clapped her hand to her head in frustration.

"How dense can I be? Listen to this... someone laughed on the answering machine and then hung up, just like in my dream... a woman! Why, in the world, didn't I remember that? I knew it was strange at the time, and I'd intended to ask Joel about it, but I absolutely forgot, even after I'd had that dream!" She shook her head.

"How in the world could I forget that? The dream should have instantly reminded me. And here's something else… there weren't anymore calls after Meredith fell. They just stopped. No more."

Hailey laid the spoon down and leaned forward.

"Listen, Laura," she began tentatively, remembering a promised she'd made to Meredith to not mention the calls. Meredith would just have to forgive her, she decided.

"The reason they changed their number, was because Meredith started getting a lot of phone calls like that. It was a woman. That's what she would do, just call and hang up. Sometimes, Meredith thought she'd hear a laugh. It never happened when Joel was home, only when she was alone, as if the caller knew she was alone. The thing about it is, even after they changed their phone number, she still kept getting calls. It was downright creepy!"

"Did Meredith know who it was?"

Hailey nodded, and pushed her cup over to one side. "There was this woman, Janis Sheridan. She called the house one morning, asking for Joel. The way she did it kinda ticked Meredith off. She never could prove anything, but she was sure it was Janis Sheridan calling and hanging up. Joel told her she was being silly."

Laura drew her brows together sternly. "Oh, he *did*, did he?"

"I'm afraid so. It made Merry really unhappy. I mean, he didn't make fun of her or anything. He just didn't believe that it was Janis Sheridan, and that bothered Meredith. She was sure about it, and when Joel didn't believe it, she got very depressed. Then, when Joel noticed the depression, but blamed it on her pregnancy, it just got worse. Anyway, she finally just quit saying anything about it, even to me."

Laura pondered all of this for a moment. "Hailey, what did this woman want with Joel?"

"She said she was here working on some kind of documentary. Joel bought it, so maybe that part was legit."

"Not if she was the one making all those calls, it wasn't." Laura pushed her chair back and stood up, her face grim. "Would you mind terribly, dear, if I head back to Meredith's room? I think it's time Joel and I had a little chat."

Hailey looked at her with an agreeable nod. "No problem! Ross said he was coming by, so if you run into him, just send him this way, okay? I'm going to lounge down here for a bit and make some calls."

"I'll do it!" Laura gave her a hug and Hailey watched her make her way to the elevators, with a thoughtful look on her face. She smiled slowly.

Joel Etheridge was in for a grilling, and Meredith's best friend decided that he deserved it.

Joel looked up briefly as his mother entered the room.

"Come here," he instructed quietly.

Laura moved to the side of the bed and stood beside him, the two of them gazing down at Meredith's lovely face.

"Do you think she's not as pale as she was?"

Laura bent down and looked at her cheeks. "Well, you might be right, honey. Merry does seem to have some color, this morning."

"The nurse said she saw something change in Meredith's face when she was checking her drain."

Laura drew in her breath. "What did she mean by that? Pain?"

"She said it was like a grimace, so maybe. I asked her if that meant they'd give her pain meds and she said she was noting it in the chart and that both Lynch and Dr. Chambers would have to be made aware of it. Chambers is supposed to come by this afternoon."

Laura took Meredith's slender fingers into her own, and quietly examined her face for any further indication of feeling. She stood there watching for a moment, then said, "Well, the last thing we want is for Merry to hurt at all but, at the same time, it might indicate that she's beginning to rouse, don't you think?"

Joel stroked his wife's face tenderly. "Mother, I was just so sure she'd wake up by now. She seemed to respond to me before her C-section, remember I told you?"

"Yes, I do. And she will again, Joel. People are talking to Father 'round the clock about Meredith. She'll be back with you and Kaylan soon, I just know it." She gave his shoulder a squeeze. "Come with me a minute, Son."

"Where?" He stepped even closer to his wife. "I don't like to leave, especially now."

"You won't be leaving. We're just gonna stand outside the door. I need to talk to you."

"Why can't we talk in here?"

Laura moved toward the door and motioned him to follow with a curt nod. "Get out here."

He looked at her curiously, but complied without further protest.

Laura reached behind him and pulled the door to. She smiled at a passing nurse, then caught Joel by the sleeve.

"You hear all sorts of things about people in comas," she began. "Some people believe they can hear what's being said, even though they're unable to respond. I just didn't want to take that chance."

"Why?" Her son continued to be puzzled. "What would you want to talk about, that Merry shouldn't hear?"

"Janis Sheridan." She saw the quick color pass over his face.

"What *about* Janis Sheridan?"

"Is she still around?"

"Mother, how do you know about Janis Sheridan? Did Meredith mention her to you?"

"No, but she *should* have. Answer me. Is she still around, Joel?"

"How should *I* know?" He was unable to keep from snapping at her irritably. Janis Sheridan's very name still managed to rile him. She was the last thing he wanted to talk about!

"Well, I think you'd better make it your business to find out!" Laura's tone took on an edge, not unlike her son's. "That woman is up to no good, or I miss my guess, Joel!"

"Then perhaps you miss your guess, Mother," he returned, his words tinged with sarcasm. "I'm sure Janis Sheridan is long gone from Nashville."

"Really! But you don't *know* that, do you?"

"Well, what if she *is* still around? What's that got to do with Meredith?"

Laura stared at him helplessly. He absolutely didn't get it! Had she really done such a poor job teaching her children about spiritual warfare? This man didn't have a clue!

"Joel," she said quietly. "All that stuff about Janis Sheridan being in Nashville to work on a documentary... did you buy all that?"

He let his eyes wander down the hall. "I did, at first," he admitted faintly.

"You did? But you don't anymore. Why? What made you change your mind?"

"Mother, do we really have to do this now?"

"YES!"

Several of the nurses at the station joined Joel in gaping with surprise at Laura's raised voice.

He pulled her around to one side, clearly annoyed. "What the heck is the *matter* with you?"

"I was just about to ask *you* the same question!" His mother was every bit as irritated as he was.

"Look," he said in a low tone. "You're obviously upset about something, so let's just get this row plowed, so I can get back to Meredith."

She shook his hand off impatiently. "Just answer my question! I said, what made you change your mind?"

He looked down at the floor uncomfortably. "She came on to me one night, at the office."

"And what was she *doing* at your office at night?" Laura demanded, when his answer turned out to be just what she had expected.

"I don't know. Marshall had just left and when I heard someone walk in, I thought he had come back, but it was Janis Sheridan. She said she was on her way to a meeting and needed some last minute information. Everything seemed to be on the level. She was all business, just like she had always been. Then, before I knew it, she was trying to kiss me."

The memory of that night caused an angry flush to creep onto his face but, at the same time, it felt good to finally be able to confide in someone. He had wanted to talk to Meredith about it, but she had been so emotional during that time, and before he could decide she could handle it, she had the accident. Now he breathed a sigh of relief and waited for Laura's response.

She looked at him evenly, for a long moment. "Joel, did you ever really understand why your wife wanted your number changed?"

"She got some weird calls. Some obsessed fan or something."

"Oh, *hardly* a fan! And obsessed is right, but not with Meredith."

Joel waited.

"Son, didn't it ever make you wonder? I mean, the fact that everything started happening right after Janis Sheridan called your home, that first time? That's when all the other calls started. That's when Meredith started having all these blood pressure problems and..."

"Mother, she was pregnant. Pregnant women have blood pressure problems."

Laura fixed him with an exasperated glare. "Yeah, well forgive me, Mr. Hot Shot! I know you've been brushing up on your reading, but while you're busy talking down to the rest of us, and being such a know-it-all, Satan is having a field day with your wife! I swear, Joel Etheridge, you have the discernment of a turnip!"

Joel narrowed his eyes and looked her closely. "What are you talking about?"

"I'm talking about the fact that there's a Heaven and a Hell! I'm telling you that there's God and then there's Satan. There are people who serve and worship God, and then there are people who serve and worship the enemy! Get out of the physical realm, Joel, and look around at the real world... the *spiritual* world! God uses people to accomplish His purposes and so does Satan. Joel! Didn't I teach you anything at all?"

He held her incredulous stare with one of his own.

"Mother, are you telling me that Janis Sheridan..."

He didn't finish so she helped him out. "I'm telling you that there's enough witchcraft happening around here, to scare every cat in Nashville!"

Something moved in the back of his heart, that made him squelch the sarcastic retort he had been about to make.

"Witchcraft..." he echoed vacantly.

He pushed open the door and stared back at his wife's motionless body. She suddenly seemed more vulnerable and helpless than ever. He moved swiftly into the room and sat down on the edge of the bed, bending over her protectively.

Laura followed him in, and watched his white face with a pang of compassion. She laid a gentle hand on his arm.

"Sweetheart, all I'm saying is this. You're Meredith's covering. You need to do more than just sit and wait. You need to stand between her and the enemy, and take authority over him, through Jesus. You've been given charge to watch over your household."

Joel nodded slightly, his breathing becoming shallow and uneven. He raised his blue eyes to Laura's imploringly.

"I could use some help."

"You don't even have to ask. We'll mix our faith and begin to intercede. I'm calling everyone who knows how to pray in faith."

Joel reached out one arm and pulled his mother close. "I love you, Mom."

"Yeah? Well I happen to love you too, which is why I don't whop you good upside the noggin, you impossible brat!"

He laughed softly, and gave her another affectionate squeeze. "You're a violent little thing. If I didn't hate the enemy so much, I'd warn him you were coming. Hardly seems fair."

Laura gave him a wide-eyed look for a second, before realizing that he was joking. "Yeah, well, he asked for it!"

Joel chuckled again and reached a loving hand back down to Meredith's cheek.

"Then he shouldn't be too surprised when he *gets* it!"

Chapter Twenty-Three

Darcy raised her head up from the pillow she'd been trying in vain to take a nap on, and held her breath, listening carefully. A hesitant knock sounded again.

She pulled herself up off the bed and hurried over to look out the peephole. She felt her adrenaline kick in with a jolt, as she fumbled clumsily with the lock and threw the door open to admit Craig and Donna Holt. Words failed her, and she stood there in dumb silence.

"Darcy, may we come in?" Donna's meek voice stirred her out of her stupor.

"Please." This was surreal. "Yes, please. I'm sorry." She moved back and gestured them in.

Craig moved stoically in behind his wife, failing to meet Darcy's eyes. He stood staring past her at nothing, a quieter, less agitated version of his former self. Donna reached for his hand encouragingly.

"I told you, Darcy, that it would have to be up to Craig whether or not we could help you."

Darcy nodded, but said nothing.

"We've talked things over," she continued slowly, "and Craig has decided we should meet with you, and say what needs to be said."

Craig lifted a silencing hand, and looked up with a baffled expression. "Darcy, who exactly is Neil?"

She stared at him, confused. "You asked me that before. What do you mean, who is Neil? He's your brother-in-law."

He closed his eyes and let out a muted oath.

"Craig," Donna reproved gently. She met Darcy's eyes and offered a trembling smile. "Could we sit down?"

Again, Darcy was suspended in a daze. She shook herself mentally, and hurried to lead the way to the small sitting area. She opened the drapes to let in the sunlight, and motioned for them to take chairs.

They all sat still for a moment, as if unsure of who should begin.

"I don't understand," Darcy stammered finally. "Why don't you know who Neil is?"

Donna and Craig exchanged quick glances.

"Because we've never met Neil," he replied. "In fact, we've never even heard of him."

His wife took in Darcy's shocked face and leaned forward to touch her hand. "Darcy, we've never been to Tennessee, or rather, *I* haven't. Craig was there, a few years ago. You know about that, but it was only for a few days. Being so far from Madeline... well you never knew more about Madeline, than she wanted you to know. There was never any mention of Neil.

"Madeline left home when she and Craig were just teenagers, and pursued a music career that finally took her to Nashville. No one was ever able to have contact with her, unless she initiated it. After Craig and I married, we'd get an occasional note or a call, but then, only every year or so, and never very informative. Craig and Madeline's parents have been dead for a number of years, and what little family is left, is scattered all over the country."

"Madeline never told us she was married," Craig cut in. "*When* was she married? Where is he?"

"Why haven't you asked Madeline?" Darcy questioned, a strange feeling creeping over her. "Why are you asking *me* this?"

Donna looked away and left Craig to field this one, on his own.

He returned Darcy's gaze as intently as she gave it. "Madeline's dead."

Darcy couldn't figure out how she was supposed to feel. It didn't occur to her to be relieved. It didn't dawn on her that if Neil's wife was dead, he was free to love her. She just continued to sit there, with a blank face. It was the last thing she had expected to hear.

Questions rushed to her brain from every conceivable angle, and she wrestled to get them into some kind of order, but it didn't matter. She couldn't string two words together.

Donna recognized her dilemma. "Madeline died two years ago this February," she explained. "We didn't know there was anyone else to tell, Darcy, and certainly not a husband." She shot Craig a swift glance. "Plus, she made us swear not to let it get out."

Darcy eyed them both sharply. "Not to let *what* get out? What are you talking about?"

"Donna," Craig interrupted, softly. "Let me." He studied his hands, as if this were a test, and he had the answers written on his palms, before he looked up and scanned Darcy's face.

"First, tell me what you know about Madeline. Better yet, tell me about this marriage. That might help."

"I know that they were married about six years ago," Darcy began, not missing the surprise in their faces. "It was..." She stopped herself and let out a sigh. "I don't want to say anything negative about your sister, Craig."

"Just tell us the truth," he suggested impassively.

"Okay." She took a deep breath. "Then I may as well tell you straight out, that Madeline was pregnant, when she and Neil were married."

This was the one time she expected a strong reaction, and she got nothing. It seemed obvious that they already knew. Darcy pursed her lips, then forged ahead.

"Neil didn't know about the baby until their wedding night. It... well, it wasn't his baby. Anyway, the sum of it is that he decided to remain in the marriage anyway, and try to make a go of it. He loved her, even though he knew she didn't really love him. Your sister miscarried just shortly after they married. During their second year of marriage, Neil went to Mexico, on a mission trip. When he got back, Madeline was gone, along with all her things. He hasn't heard a word since then."

"Why didn't he divorce her?" Donna wondered out loud.

"It would have only needed to be an annulment." She understood their astonished expressions completely. Hers must have looked that way, when Neil explained things to her.

"It ended up being a marriage on paper, only. But, you see, Neil's a minister. He still felt bound by their vows and, like I said, he loved her. He kept hoping she'd love him and then, after she left him, he kept hoping she'd come back. He didn't know how to go about finding her. He did try, just not successfully. I wouldn't have had any luck either, if I hadn't discovered that a friend of mine was doing studio work with her, about the time she left."

Craig had been staring at her attentively, throughout her revelation.

"A minister," he echoed, in disbelief.

"Yes." She sat quietly a moment and let them absorb everything. Finally she sat up straight, and brought them to the question they were dreading.

"How did Madeline die?"

Donna met her husband's eyes. "There's no point in keeping this secret any longer, Craig," she ventured.

He looked away without speaking, and his wife decided to spare him.

"Madeline's death was slow and tragic. It still seems fresh to us, because of the toll it took on Craig and me and also, because of the kind of death it was." She cleared her throat and blinked rapidly, as emotions began to close in. "Madeline had AIDS."

Darcy gasped softly and sat back, a look of disbelief shadowing her pretty face. "AIDS!"

Donna nodded, her eyes brimming. "I know that, socially, AIDS doesn't seem to have the shock value that it once did but still, *we* were. Shocked, I mean. It was horrible, what it did to her, Darcy. She called Craig, it sounds like right around the time her husband went to Mexico, somewhere in that time frame. She just told him she was in a bad way, and desperately needed his help."

"Madeline was always so closed and independent that I knew it was serious, or she wouldn't have called," Craig added, with a grim shadow in his eyes. "I took the first flight out to Nashville, and met her at the studio she was working at. I was there for a little over a week, before she finally told me what was wrong.

"First of all, she talked about the pregnancy and the miscarriage. It turns out the father was a married guy. Some record producer."

"Kirby Yeager," Darcy said quietly. She had heard Meredith say the name to Joel, when they'd been together at

Ross and Hailey's home, and the look that had passed over Joel's face now rested on Craig's.

He clenched his jaw and nodded, then glowered at the floor before continuing. "She said he pretty much washed his hands of her, when she came up pregnant. Not long after the miscarriage, he showed back up, full of apologies, and excuses, and promises to leave his wife. My sweet, but stupid sister bought right into that, and started up another relationship with him. She was seeing him right up to the time she called me for help.

"She realized something serious was wrong with him. She found out he had been HIV positive for long while, and that it had developed into full-blown AIDS.

"The devastating and criminal thing was that he had known about it all along, throughout their relationship, and never told her. Anyway, after she started having some issues breathing and becoming easily fatigued, and kept losing weight, she finally had herself tested, and found out that she also had AIDS. She begged me to let her come back to California with me. I couldn't just leave her there. Maddy and I used to be very close before she left home, and..." Craig's voice began to crack. "I loved her very much."

Donna stroked the back of his hand tenderly. "Craig called me and we both agreed to bring her here for whatever she needed. What she needed most was a lot of love and reconciliation to the Lord. God was able to use us in Madeline's life. When her time came, I know she left at peace with God, but... well, if only she could have made peace with her husband..." Her voice trailed off.

Craig lifted eyes to Darcy that pleaded for her understanding. "She wasn't a bad girl, Darcy. What she did to Neil was harsh, I know that. But I knew my sister. She was just deceived, and had to have been filled with remorse. Once she found out she had AIDS, she wouldn't have wanted to shame him, especially if he was a minister, and especially if he was a kind man, and it seems clear that he is."

Tears flooded his eyes and he blinked them back furiously. "You'd have to have known her like I did, to see that. She would have thought that it would have been easier on Neil, for her to just up and leave, than to have him find out what she had done, and how she ended up. I'm not saying that shame didn't play a large part in her decision, but I'm also convinced that she did what she did to him out of kindness, not because she wanted to hurt him. Please believe me."

Darcy nodded slowly. "I do believe you," she replied in a hushed voice. She bowed her head, and moved everything around in her mind to its proper place.

"I suppose the guy is dead, as well," she speculated. "The producer. My friend said he 'dropped off the radar'. I guess that's why."

"Yeager?" Craig shrugged. "I wouldn't be surprised. I mean, he was beginning to show signs of deterioration. That's how Maddy found out. I would imagine he's dead, by now, yes. I never met him. Maddy wouldn't allow it. She knew I would do something stupid."

Darcy nodded again. Suddenly, it was all she seemed to be able to do.

"Darcy."

She looked up at the sound of Donna's voice.

"Craig and I were wondering... well, it's not fair to saddle you with anymore of this. We'd like to be the ones to tell Neil, if you don't mind."

"We'd like to know him," her husband added. "When you mentioned Neil to Donna and she came to me, we were stunned. Finding out now that Maddy was married explains so many of her decisions, and her insistence that no one find out about her. That was one of the reasons we felt we had to come here today, to learn more, to have some old questions answered."

He folded his hands together and rested his forehead on them, taking a moment to think. "We had just assumed that she didn't want the Christian music industry to find out about her, and we didn't question that. No one can be more brutal to a Christian, especially one who's messed up, than another Christian.

"But finding out about Neil... I believe I know what she was thinking, now. At the same time, it's still hard to believe that my sister would have told me so much about her past, but deliberately not mention that she was married."

"Maybe she thought you'd find Neil and bring him to her," Darcy suggested quietly.

"I guess so. I probably would have, not to expose her but to help her, if I could. I think that if Neil could have come to her and hopefully forgiven her, that her passing wouldn't have been so... I think she could have passed more peaceably, than she did."

He reached for his wife's hand and gave it a squeeze before glancing back at Darcy.

"Would you object to our flying back with you, on Monday? This really should come from me, Darcy."

She hesitated briefly.

"You have to realize that this is going to hit him hard," she pointed out. "It's one thing for him to think she just took off out of spite, but it's another to suddenly have to mourn her death."

This hadn't occurred to either of them. Darcy could tell, by their faces. She watched them sort through this before finishing.

"But I think... it would help him, somehow. I mean you're family. Maybe you could help him make sense of things."

"We'd like to try," Craig said, smiling sadly. "It seems the very least we could do, under the circumstances."

"Darcy, let us take this off your shoulders," Donna added, in her kind, soft way. "Not just for you, but for Madeline."

She offered them a smile of gratitude. "I think it would somehow end up meaning more to Neil, if it did come from you. I'd appreciate it, if you flew back with me."

Joel turned around with a question on his somber, handsome face, as the door was pushed open. Meredith had been rolled out for another CT scan and he had used his time alone to engage in a little restless pacing and praying.

Dr. Chambers had assured him that he simply wanted to assess her current status more definitively, but being separated from Meredith made him jumpy, and ready to pounce on anything or anyone that moved. Relief and pleasure washed over him, as the pediatric nurse grinned and lifted the small bundle on her arm up to him.

"Someone wants his daddy," she announced with a cheerful smile.

Joel beamed down at the miniature of himself, and took him carefully. The nurse waited until his hold was sure, then offered him the bottle of formula that automatically accompanied Kaylan, every time he was brought in.

"You're so good at this, we've just decided to let you handle it, from now on," she informed him, as she turned and headed back to the hall. "Just remember to get a good burp. I'll be back in a bit. Call if you need anything."

"Thank you," Joel said, gazing down with awe at the beautiful little creature in his arms. He lowered himself into a chair and cradled his son close, while he pulled hungrily at the bottle. Joel's heart was about to burst.

"Hey, little man," he breathed in hushed tones. "Wait 'til Mommy gets a load of you, huh? We did good, didn't we? Yeah... we did *real* good!"

He studied every facet of Kaylan's face, almost unable to believe that God would bless him like this.

He had really believed that his past actions had opened a door for the enemy to harm his son. He thanked God again in his heart, for His protection and for the strength He had used Iris to bring to him.

"We'll be taking you home soon," he murmured. "You'll love it there. Mommy and Daddy and Kaylan. And Hook. Let's not forget about Hook."

He grinned and shook his head. "Wonder what ol' Captain Hook's gonna think about you, Son? 'Cause you know, after all, it really *is* his house. He just lets us live there."

Joel laughed softly and lifted his son up onto his shoulder as Laura and Gary opened the door and smiled in.

He nodded to them and arranged a towel over himself, in case Kaylan wanted to send anything back.

Laura wasted no time in rushing over and planting her face in front of her grandson's.

"There him is!"

Gary chuckled and rolled his eyes. "Why is it that every woman in America loses her command of the English language, the minute a baby shows up?" he demanded.

"Beats me." Joel continued patting his baby lightly, a look of utter contentment resting all over him. "But you make a good point. Mother, stop that silly, gushy baby-talk around my son."

"You hush!" she returned with mock severity. "I'll have you know, I fully intend to exercise every right that comes with being a grandmother, which happens to include silly, gushy baby-talk."

Kaylan signaled the end of round one with a loud burp. Laura laughed with delight, and held out her hands pleadingly to Joel.

"Oh, alright." He gave in. "You win every one of these power plays of yours, anyway. Why fight it?"

He passed the baby to her good-naturedly, and let her take his chair and the bottle.

"She's in her element, now," Gary commented with a broad smile. Joel nodded and looked up quickly, as the door opened again. Meredith was rolled in, as still and as lovely as ever.

Gary stepped back out of the way. "I'll just be outside, until they get her back in bed," he said, closing the door behind him.

Joel hovered anxiously, while the aides maneuvered their patient carefully into position. A nurse followed them in and held Joel at bay while she took Meredith's vital signs and recorded them in her chart.

She finally took her leave with the flash of a smile, and Joel wasted no time in rearranging the covers and his wife's gown to his satisfaction.

He stood back and viewed his handiwork with a critical eye, before something tender crept into his face and he reached for his son.

"Here, Mother, let me take Kaylan for a minute."

She gave him up reluctantly, then watched as Joel laid Kaylan next to his sleeping mother and wrapped her arms around him. He stepped back and stared at them, a large knot forming in his throat. Kaylan blinked his blue eyes in momentary confusion, then turned his face into Meredith, and rested there complacently.

Laura gazed in wonder, as her grandson seemed to recognize that this was his mother, and the place where he belonged.

Something light seemed to hover around Meredith's mouth, for a fleeting second... a passing sensation, almost an expression, something very close to the ghost of a smile.

Hope burned in Joel's eyes, as he sat down on the edge of the bed, convinced that his wife knew she was holding their child. He glanced up as Gary slipped in, and grinned.

"Pretty picture, huh?" he asked.

"As pretty as you'll ever see!" Gary agreed stoutly.

"Look at Meredith's face," Laura whispered, taking his arm and resting her head against his shoulder.

He stood watching with one hand laid across Joel's shoulder, taking it in with a full heart. Something was there, a blush of feeling, almost. Certainly not the blank, lifeless veil she'd worn for so many days. Meredith's baby was talking to his mother in his own way, and Gary felt she was hearing him.

He had thought of Meredith as a daughter for so long, that Kaylan seemed as naturally his grandson, as if he had been born to his own Bethany, who had left this world as a small girl years ago. He caught Laura's understanding smile, and returned it lovingly.

"Joel, Laura and I are having another prayer meeting at my house tonight." He spoke softly, studying Joel's expression, as he watched his son nest placidly within his wife's arms.

"Others are joining us. We believe we've got a better idea of what we're dealing with, and we're taking it to God. I know that God will answer our prayers. I know it."

Joel looked up, with a glad smile. "Thanks for that, Gary. It helps to know people who love us are looking out for us." He glanced back down fondly at Meredith. "You and Mom, both, have always come to the front when Merry and I needed you."

"To the front," Laura repeated. "That's a pretty good analogy, because this is a war, that much is certain." She grinned up at her fiancé.

"But we've got Man O' War, here, leading the troops. Who knows? By this time tomorrow, Meredith will most likely be outside, yelling at traffic!"

Joel caressed his son's face and laughed quietly. "We'd better call Ross, then," he advised. "I've seen her in action, and poor traffic's gonna be unarmed."

Gary stared in playful consternation. "Joel! I thought you *liked* Ross!"

Chapter Twenty-Four

Janis Sheridan stepped back in obvious dread, and shivered involuntarily, as the two men pushed past her.

"You certainly took your time about answering the door," Warren Patrick observed coolly. "Aren't you feeling well, dear?"

Oliver Sullivan snorted at his lack of sincerity, and motioned toward the bar with an imperative gesture.

"I'm fine," Janis returned, her eyes following Warren's large form across the room. "I was on the telephone."

"Oh, indeed?" Oliver inquired in thick, polite tones. "Anyone we know? I understood that the past recipient of your many calls is no longer available to come to the phone." He paused and narrowed his eyes slightly. "Was I misinformed?"

"I was just calling the... room service."

"Don't you mean the airport?" Oliver took the drink Warren offered him, and sank down onto the sofa. "That *was* what you were about to say, wasn't it?"

"No!" She couldn't hide the panic in her voice. "I meant what I said."

"Indeed?" Oliver waved her toward a chair. "Sit, Janis, darling. Would you like Warren to mix you a drink?"

She shook her head and lowered herself nervously, until she felt the chair's support.

"No?   Oh, well then, if you're sure." He nodded to Warren, who filled his own glass, and came around to join them.

"Miss Sheridan, you wound me, you really do. I had begun to feel that we were becoming fast friends, and now you deliberately try to deceive me. Of course you were calling the airport. Do you take me for a fool?"

She gripped the edge of her seat, saying nothing, and Oliver gestured slightly.

"Warren?"

Warren Patrick obligingly retrieved a notebook from his jacket pocket and flipped it open with a nonchalant air.

"Sherry Janson, flight 1281, departing Nashville 8:20 p.m., one hour and ten minute layover in Atlanta, arriving... what's this? Dallas? Then Dallas to LAX? LAX to..." Warren laughed wickedly. "Well, my, my! LAX to London! Going to red-eye your way to see the queen, Janis?"

Janis blanched and began wiping her sweaty palms on her skirt.

"Janis, sweetheart, you look positively ghastly!" Oliver pointed out. "Oh... was this a secret? Did Warren just go and spoil everything?"

"I don't know what you mean," she tried lamely.

"Nor do I know what *you* mean," he mused. "Imagine, choosing to travel under an alias, and then picking one so transparent! Janis Sheridan, Sherry Janson. Not very bright, my little dove."

"I didn't..."

"Sure you did!" Warren cut her off. "Just like you did, back during your college days, when you earned extra money by dancing in those seedy nightclubs you weren't even old enough to patronize. Did you think we didn't know about that... Sherry?"

She drew in a sharp and difficult breath, and did all she could to appear unaffected by his words.

"Warren, where are our manners?" Oliver chided. "We're keeping Janis chattering away, and she hasn't even finished packing."

Warren got up and sauntered leisurely over to the table beside the bed. He picked up the remains of a black candle, and held it up with a dramatic flourish for his companion's inspection.

"Tools of the trade?" Oliver smirked unpleasantly. "So, Miss Sheridan. I bring you here to do a job, and you dwindle away your time playing with matches. I'm afraid this won't do. It won't do at all. Warren, see if you can accomplish getting the rest of Janis's things together, there's a good man."

"Why?" She laid a hand on her chest to calm her heartbeat. "What are you going to do?"

"Do? Why, we're going to drive you to the airport, of course." Oliver grinned slowly. "I've decided to overlook your trying to steal away without so much as a good-bye, thoughtless as that was. But all is forgiven. Just relax and we'll take care of everything. Are you sure you wouldn't like that drink?"

Janis closed her eyes and leaned her head back. *Just play along,* she told herself. *They're just trying to scare you, to teach you a lesson. They've done it before. That's all this is.*

She lifted her head and managed a smile. "No, thank you."

Oliver shrugged, and flashed a wordless question at Warren.

"All set!" he responded, snapping Janis's luggage shut and throwing her suit bag over one shoulder.

"Well then, we'd better be on our way, if you're going to make that flight, Janis." Oliver smiled unpleasantly, and opened the door with exaggerated courtesy. "Shall we?"

She picked up her purse and briefcase, and led the way from the room on shaking legs.

They passed through the lobby and out to their waiting car, all too soon for Janis.

Oliver tucked a generous tip in the valet's pocket, and thanked him warmly for holding the car, before they took their leave. Only someone who knew him, as Janis and Warren did, would be able to see the condescension beneath his polished veneer. The valet was still waving, as they pulled out into the evening traffic.

"Silly snit!" Oliver commented scornfully. He turned around and leaned forward to the front seat where Janis sat belted in beside Warren, who was driving.

"Comfy?"

"I'm fine," she said in a small voice.

"Delighted to hear it." He sat back with a placid expression, and pretended to take in the passing scenery, that the setting sun behind them was reaching out to, with the day's last light, as Warren merged onto Interstate 40 and headed east toward the Nashville airport.

When he passed the exit for their own hotel, Janis let out a sigh of relief. She had been right! They had just been trying to unnerve her, after all. When they put her out at the airport, Oliver would more than likely hiss a few ominous warnings at her, and suggest that she stay out of the country, once she left it, along with some dark ultimatum. Well, that much she could handle.

She leaned back and tried to relax, not catching the triumphant look Warren sent through the rear-view mirror to Oliver Sullivan. She half-closed her eyes, and mentally prepared for the long, arduous travel ahead.

True, she would liked to have seen the fruit of her labors first-hand, but she knew enough to feel reasonably sure that Meredith Clark was on her way out of this world, and that was why she had been summoned here, in the first place. She couldn't deny feeling a pang of regret, at having Joel Etheridge slip through her fingers so completely, but that couldn't be remedied now. Time to move on and the sooner, the better.

She shifted her weight in the seat and looked casually around, not realizing, at first, that the exit Warren took was not the one for the airport. Comprehension gradually began to dawn, and she sat up straight and craned her neck to see where they were.

"This isn't right," she said faintly, as a sick feeling crept over her.

"Hmmm?" Oliver raised one eyebrow sardonically. "Pardon me, did you say something, Miss Sheridan?"

"This isn't the right exit! We need to get back on the freeway!"

"Are you sure?" He fashioned a solicitous attitude. "After all, you're not from here. You could be wrong."

"I'm *not* wrong!" She looked back and forth from Oliver to Warren with wild eyes. "We have to go *back*!"

Warren said nothing but continued following a road that was gradually becoming more and more rural.

Janis felt hot tears sting her cheeks. "Warren, this isn't funny! I'm going to miss my flight!"

"Yes, Janis, you are," he agreed quietly.

Janis gasped, as she understood what was happening. She unfastened her seatbelt and grabbed for the door handle.

"Don't you just love technology?" Oliver purred from the back seat. "Child-proof locks; what will they think of next?"

He laughed at her dismay when she reached around to manually lift the lock, only to find his hand firmly clamped over it.

"Let me out!" she screamed. "I mean it, Warren, stop this car!" He fastened his eyes on the road ahead as if he were deaf. *"Warren!"*

Janis grabbed his arm, and received a sharp blow to the head, for her trouble. She fell back against the door, in dazed horror. All hope that they were pushing a joke too far, to make a point, was gone. This was really happening!

Warren slowed the car down with a clear intention to turn right onto a single-lane dirt road, that meandered along a dark river bed.

She lunged at him and grabbed the steering wheel in a panicked attempt to stop him. He snatched the wheel from her grasp and she took hold again, pushing it back to the left with all her might and stamping the accelerator with her left foot.

Janis's scream and a loud blaring horn pierced the air as the lights of an oncoming log truck blinded them and tried in vain to keep from plowing headlong into the swerving black Mercedes.

The deafening crash, and crunch of metal and glass seemed to last forever, before all was silent.

Dr. Chambers handed the chart back to his nurse before tapping lightly, and opening the door to Meredith's room. He stopped and took in Joel's drawn countenance with a thoughtful eye.

"Joel! How's it going, man?"

Joel lifted his head from his hands and sat back in his chair with a feeble smile. "Fine. I'm fine."

"Yeah you *look* it, too," the doctor returned with marked sarcasm.

He came over and laid a hand on Joel's shoulder. "Well, you were on top of things for a while, but this must be crash day. I've seen it before. Let's take stock.

"You've got a new baby, and Lynch says Meredith is healing well from the C-section. Her scans look fine. She hasn't opened her eyes, but she's breathing good, she's made some responses, vitals are great, swelling's gone. There's no physical reason why she can't make a full recovery. I know you've got a lot to cope with, Joel, but sooner or later, we all hit a wall. Anything I can help with?"

"Can you wake my wife up?"

Dr. Chambers met Joel's level gaze with one of his own. "No. But maybe you can."

Joel blinked at him, not understanding.

"Joel, I never knew Meredith before her accident. I mean, I know who she is, of course, everyone does. But I didn't know her personally. I have, however, heard enough about her from Beatty and people who are close to her, to know that Meredith is... well, let's call it what it is. Stubborn."

Joel smiled involuntarily and nodded.

"I believe strongly that people in comas can have an awareness of things," he continued. "I've interviewed a few people who have awakened from brief to fairly long periods of being comatose, and many claim to have heard various things that were said to them, while they were unable to respond, things that family and friends could verify.

"Anyway, with that in mind, Joel, think about this. What is it that Meredith responds to? I understand that, along with being her husband, you're also her manager. So, manage her. Get her to do what you want. You know how."

He leaned over and raised one, then the other of her lids briefly, and made his evaluation, before looking back intently at Joel.

"Think about it." He winked and let himself out quietly.

Joel reached for Meredith's hand, and laid his head down onto the mattress beside her. He closed his eyes and let the doctor's words pass back and forth in his mind, but it all seemed beyond him.

"Oh, God." He breathed out a prayer, lifting his head and staring at his wife with a full heart. "Why won't You let Merry wake up? I'm just so tired, I don't know how to pray, anymore. I can't come up with any new words. I know you heard me the first time, but I keep asking. I know You dote on Meredith, Father."

He cleared his throat roughly. "I don't blame You. If I were You, I would want to just keep her. But, Father, You're gonna have her forever and ever. Can't Kaylan and I just have her here with us, a little longer? I promise to take better care of her, to be a better covering."

After a long while, and feeling that his words and his bargaining were bouncing back off the ceiling at him, he raked his hands through his hair roughly, and shot out frustrated words, harsh and bitter.

"How long does this crap have to go on? What am I supposed to do, God? *Wrestle* you for my own wife?"

Joel crumpled over onto Meredith's shoulder and lay there for some time, rubbing his dull, throbbing head.

"Missy," he whispered in broken tones, "I love you so much. I wish you would just open your beautiful eyes and look at me. Please don't sleep anymore, baby. Meredith, I need you. Kaylan needs you.

"Do you hear me? We have a baby boy and he needs his mother! Merry, please wake up!"

Anyone coming into the room, a full hour later, would have found an anguished and lonely man, still pleading with everything he had, for the one he loved most to come back to him.

Finally, Joel sat up in anger and slapped the bed, and his tender loving eyes took on the same steely glint of temper that Meredith used to evoke effortlessly.

"You little idiot!" he fumed. "Just *lie* there, then, like a roll on a buffet! You're a selfish brat! You know exactly what you're putting me through, and you don't even care!"

Little by little, he left off grating out his frustration in hushed fervor, and his voice rose in anger.

"What do you want from me? Are you punishing me? I've had it, Meredith! If you think I'm gonna raise Kaylan all by myself, while you just lie there, soaking up glucose, then you're badly mistaken! Wake up, you insensitive little jerk! You've slept enough!"

Joel sagged back down and buried his face in the sheets, his body shaking slightly with sleep-deprived fatigue, and some leftover tears that he shoved into the mattress.

"I love you, stupid," he moaned brokenly.

He lay there weeping quietly into the covers for only a few moments more, before he felt a lock of his hair being twirled. He threw back his head and stared openmouthed at a beautiful scowl and half-opened, breathtaking gray eyes.

"I... I love you, too... stupid..." came the breathy rasp of a whisper. "But who, the heck... can sleep... with all that racket?"

Chapter Twenty-Five

Gary Brenner stepped out of the elevator with a grim, worried shadow on his usually cheerful face. He paused momentarily, before pushing open the door to Meredith's hospital room, then squared his shoulders and tapped his intention to enter.

"Gary!" Joel looked up from his wife's side and smiled warmly. Laura rose from her chair and came to receive a hug.

"Well, look at you!" Gary planted himself next to the bed and did just that, taking in Meredith's smiling face with deep joy. Kaylan peeped up from her arms, then closed his eyes, as if too content to be bothered with company.

Gary was about to put words to his elation, then stopped short and gaped at Meredith's head of full, long, dark hair.

"How did you..." He broke off and continued to stare in confusion.

"Hey, Preach." She grinned up at Joel's pleased expression, before answering. "It looks real, doesn't it?"

"It looks... you mean it's not? I mean, it looks just like your hair always looked. It looks like your own."

"That's because it *is* my own." She paused, for a little dry cough. "This husband of mine made them save my hair and had it made into a wig. I may just keep this man." She held Joel lovingly with her eyes and he held her back. "I'm probably not supposed to wear it *all* the time, but my incisions feel healed to me, so I'm going to ask Dr. Chambers if I can keep wearing it while I'm waiting for my hair to grow back. I can tell it's already started to grow."

"Merry's something of a miracle, according to Dr. Chambers, Gary," Laura informed him, joyfully. "He said that usually, when a person wakes from a coma, there's a period of confusion, and it takes a while to begin feeling better or for memory to return, depending on what caused the coma to begin with. Of course, Meredith wasn't in a coma for as long as it felt to us, but still, it's as if she was completely healed, before she was given back to us."

"All but this froggy voice," Meredith inserted, with a grimace.

"Maybe we can do something with that, Sister Clark," Joel teased with a grin, referencing an old joke that made his wife giggle and lightly slap his leg.

"I still can't get over all of this!" Gary beamed down at her with delight and touched her hand fondly. "I know I talked to you last night on the phone, but I had trouble this morning with whether or not it was a dream."

Meredith grinned lazily. "Oh, I'm sure there'll be days when you'll wish it was." Joel rolled his eyes and she giggled again, apparently at another private joke between them.

"Well if it is, it's the best dream I ever had!" Gary declared. He clapped a hand on Joel's back and looked at him casually, but without disguising that he had something on his mind.

"Hey, old man, how 'bout stepping out with me for a minute?"

Joel drew his brows together, clearly reluctant. He tightened his hand on Meredith's shoulder and glanced down at her, conflicted. "Well, I don't know..."

"Oh, go on," she admonished. "It's not like I'll pass out again, if you leave." She could tell he didn't think that was funny, so she laced her fingers into his and sent him a look that she had always kept reserved, just for him. "It's okay," she said softly. "I'll be fine and Laura's right here."

"I'll watch her like a hawk," Laura promised.

Joel hesitated, then stood up to go out, but not before laying a kiss on his wife's lips. "Okay," he sighed. "But I'll only be a minute."

Gary moved toward the door and waited, and he grudgingly followed.

As soon as they were in the hall, Joel placed his hands on his hips and leveled clear blue eyes on his pastor's face. "I don't like to leave Merry, if I can help it, Gary. Is this important?"

"Very!" He returned Joel's steady gaze. "I was called in by the hospital's chaplain to visit some of the patients, since he couldn't get here this morning. I stopped by the emergency room first, to check on what might be a priority." He watched Joel's face for the reaction he knew was coming. "They brought Janis Sheridan into the ER late last night."

Joel rippled his jaw muscles but remained silent.

"I know how you feel about her, Joel. I understand the absolute horror she's brought to you and Meredith, and I also know about your episode with her at the office. But I want all that put aside for the moment."

"Put aside." Joel voice was flat, bland, and layered with coldness. "You want 'all that' to be... put aside."

He turned to walk away and Gary caught his sleeve with uncharacteristic roughness.

"Stop and hear me out."

Joel looked back at the door impatiently and Gary could tell he was deciding to go back in to Meredith.

"Wait! Listen to me, Joel. Janis Sheridan is in a bad way, severe, irreparable damage to her liver and spleen and a lot of internal bleeding. She's drifting in and out of consciousness and the emergency room doctors are saying she'll be gone within the hour."

"Good."

Gary blanched white. "You don't *mean* that!"

Joel's face was like granite. He looked away from Gary, which was just as well. Gary wouldn't have wanted to witness what was churning in those eyes.

"Why are you telling me all this?" He was openly agitated.

"Because she kept saying Meredith's name over and over. I stood close and listened, and she just kept repeating again and again that she was sorry. So I bent down and told her that I'm Meredith's pastor, and asked her if I could pray with her. She could barely get it out, but she begged me to ask you to forgive her."

Joel seemed taken aback. This was obviously not what he had expected Gary to say. He shook his head in an attempt to clear it. "She's dying?"

"Yes, and very soon, if she hasn't passed already. She was with two other men, when their car crashed into a log truck. They were both killed instantly. The truck driver walked away, but Janis isn't so lucky. She's fading fast. It's clear that she knows that, and she's asking for forgiveness.

"Joel... " Gary placed a detaining hand on his sleeve. "Come with me to the ER. Just for a minute, that's all it'll take. I believe we can lead this woman to Jesus."

"You *do* realize what this woman is?" Joel demanded sternly.

"No more and no less than we were, when we were enemies of the cross," Gary insisted. "I know all about her occult activities. She's been deceived, Joel, and trapped by

Satan. We can help her get free, before she enters eternity. You're not *really* thinking of saying no to me, are you?"

He planted a challenging look on Joel, and waited.

Joel ran an impatient hand through his hair, in a show of exasperation. He stared down at the floor for a minute, before letting out a breath, and an incoherent mutter.

"Fine," he grunted. "Let's just get it over with!"

Gary started immediately for the elevators with Joel on his heels, speed only important as a means of getting back to his wife and child quickly.

Gary was acknowledged and nodded in by the RN on duty in the emergency room, and he hurried over to a bed behind a curtain and to what was left of Janis Sheridan. She was a pathetic, swollen mound of flesh, unrecognizable as her former self.

"She's full of pain meds," the RN advised, as she turned to leave. "She probably won't understand much."

"Janis," Gary called softly. She moaned from somewhere far away. "Janis, it's Pastor Gary. I've come back, and I brought Joel Etheridge with me."

Her eyelids fluttered in vain as if she would try to see him. "Wh... where?" She could only just breathe out a response.

"Right here!" Gary grabbed Joel with an iron grip and pulled his resisting form around to the side of the gurney.

Janis tried to focus on his face but he was growing dim and watery. Darkness was rushing toward her.

"Jo..."

He looked away, and tried to balance his outrage with the strange compassion that rushed to the surface of his heart. He wanted to hate her for what she had put his beloved Meredith through, but standing here at the last moments of her passing, he was suddenly unable to fan the flames of his loathing.

"Jo.." Her breathing wasn't enough to accommodate the effort she was trying to make. "Sorry... so..."

Talking was too much of an ordeal for her. She tried again. "Sorry... forgive..."

Joel surrendered to the influence of the Holy Spirit, and yielded his stubborn heart.

"I forgive you," he said quietly. "I forgive you, Janis."

Rare and wonderful tears coursed their way down her cheeks, and she felt Gary take her limp hand in his.

Joel swallowed hard at the lump in his throat, and wiped back tears of his own.

"Janis..." He looked briefly at Gary before continuing. "Janis, you need more than *my* forgiveness. You're leaving this world. You know that, don't you?"

She wept silently.

"I know you've been serving someone other than your creator. I know you've given much of your life as a follower of Satan. Where has it gotten you, Janis?"

She began to shiver, and her weeping became a soft, painful moan.

Joel reached down and took her other hand, a gesture that completely surprised Gary, but one that rescued Janis.

"You can't afford to leave this life without Jesus," he said calmly. "You already know that the time you spent in darkness was wasted. But it's not too late to redeem that time, Janis. It's never too late, not while there's a breath in your body."

"Can't..." she gasped. "Dirty..."`

"We're *all* dirty," Gary answered tenderly. "Even our righteousness is dirty. We all have to pass through the same Blood to be clean." He caressed her fingers.

"Hard as it is to understand, Janis, it really is as simple as believing that Jesus is the Son of God, the *only* God, and that He's the only way to be saved from eternal death and to have eternal life. Let us help you do that."

She closed her eyes as the blackness threatened to engulf her and Joel shot a worried look up at Gary. Death was imminent.

"Janis!" He squeezed her hand with quiet urgency. "Please don't go, without accepting Jesus."

She struggled to force open her eyes. They failed her almost immediately, but the brief expression in them was one of wistful longing. "Want... want me..." All she had left were shallow gasps. "He...want..."

"He wants you!" Gary insisted. "Pray with us. Just repeat what I say and mean it with all your heart." He leaned over, taking Joel's other hand in agreement and gently led Janis to the Cross.

Her lips trembled with the faintest smile. "See... I see... I... see..." she gasped with difficulty.

Joel leaned down over her and laid his hand on her forehead. "What do you see, Janis?"

"Beauti...ful... He..."

"Yes," he said, in a rough whisper, tears finding their way onto his face.

Gary smiled through his own glad tears, that were spilling down his fatherly cheeks. "He is. Very beautiful!"

Joel drew in a quick breath, as Janis slipped away from her mangled body, and followed the One who beckoned to her. He reeled from the many different emotions assaulting him, and lifted his eyes away from her empty remains.

"Thank you, Gary. Thank you for making me do this."

Gary and Joel stepped back, as a physician and his nurse responded to the monitor's flat line and pulled the curtain shut around Janis Sheridan's lifeless form.

"It had to happen," he said, giving Joel a soft pat on the shoulder. "And I knew you would do the right thing."

They made their way back to Meredith's room in mutual silence, each lost in his own thoughts and feelings.

Laura was helping Meredith change Kaylan, and they both looked up curiously, as the door opened.

Gary motioned for Laura to come, and Joel crossed over to claim Meredith's kiss and to help her tend to their son.

He smiled down lovingly at her, when they were left alone with their baby and each other. "Hi."

Meredith gazed up at his emotional face with intuitive eyes. "What's going on, Mister Man?"

Joel tossed a rolled up diaper into the wastebasket and stood watching her tie the drawstring in the end of Kaylan's gown.

"Baby, I'm so sorry I didn't listen to you, when you tried to tell me what was going on. I mean, with Janis Sheridan." He reached down and took his son's miniature fingers in his own large ones.

Meredith wrinkled her pretty brow. "Okay, you go out with Preach, then come back in here, and now we're talking about Janis Sheridan. *Why* are we talking about Janis Sheridan?"

"Because we need to."

She studied him quietly. "Okay."

Joel swung his leg over the top of the mattress, and sat down slightly behind her, pulling her back to rest against his chest, and securing her in his arms. "Do you remember the day you and Hailey took Darcy to youth camp? Then you went to look for a baby bed?"

She took a moment to think it through, then nodded slowly. "I guess, maybe. Some of it. Okay, wait, I do."

"I worked late that night. You knew that, at the time. Anyway, while I was looking over some contracts, Janis Sheridan showed up at my office unannounced, after everyone had gone. She claimed she was on her way to a meeting, and that she needed me to look over some data she was presenting, for the documentary she was supposed to have been working on. The thing is... she was never really working on a documentary, at all."

Meredith nodded again, but resisted the urge to point out that she had been telling him that, all along.

"Meredith, she tried to come on to me."

He waited for some sort of response but she wasn't surprised. She remained still.

"I didn't see it coming, I really didn't, but all at once, she came around my desk, and was trying to kiss me."

"I don't blame her."

He was being serious and her teasing got past him. She decided to let it go.

"Anyway, I jumped up and threw her out of my office. I never saw her again, or heard from her after that. I wanted to tell you about it that night, but you were already pretty emotional and I was waiting for the right time. Then you had your fall..."

"Joel..." Meredith left off smiling down at Kaylan, and turned her head to look up at him. She reached up and stroked his handsome face softly. "Why are you telling me all this now? Is she back?"

"She's dead," he said simply.

Meredith widened her eyes in surprise. "What do you mean, she's dead? When did she die?"

"A few minutes ago. Downstairs in the emergency room. She was in a wreck with two other people. They were killed right away, and she was injured beyond repair."

The door swished open and an aide swept in busily. "Time for Master Etheridge to join his little buddies in the nursery," she announced, with a big smile. "Hand him over peaceably, please!"

Meredith had been fighting all morning with anybody who had even suggested taking Kaylan back. Now she nodded passively enough, and let the astonished aide lift him up.

"What? Just like that?" She cuddled Kaylan close and grinned. "I was thinking of asking for hazard pay, coming in here like this. You should see the nursing casualties, piled up at the door!" She directed this to Joel, with a teasing wink.

"Don't get too used to it," Meredith grumbled. "I want him back here, as soon as possible!"

"Yes, ma'am!" The aide chuckled, and hurried along, before Meredith could fire off another round.

She gazed at the door for a moment, as if wanting to go out and retrieve her son, then looked back up at Joel, as he brought her back to himself and wrapped his arms around her again.

"He'll be fine," her husband assured her gently. "Kaylan needs a bath and some sleep. Let them do their job. Baby, we need to finish this conversation before more company arrives."

She just looked at him, so he plodded ahead.

"Gary came and got me because Janis Sheridan was downstairs, in the ER. He said she kept saying your name, and talking about how sorry she was."

Meredith retained a blank expression, just waiting.

"Merry, you were right to have reservations about her. It turns out that Janis was involved in the occult."

Her face registered her dismay. "Was she..."

"She was targeting us, yes. Targeting *you*, actually, but that automatically means the both of us. Mom and Gary managed to put two and two together, and called in some intercessors to stand in the gap for us. Anyway, for whatever reasons, Janis was in that car crash last night, and was barely hanging onto life, when they brought her in."

"So you went down there?"

"Yes. Gary said she was asking for forgiveness. I didn't want anything to do with it, I'll admit it, but he wouldn't let me off the hook, so I went with him downstairs."

He raised her chin with his fingertip, and studied her with sad eyes. "She was a mess, Merry. She tried so hard to ask for forgiveness, even though she couldn't get all the words out. I don't know how I was able forgive her, but something just drove me to do it."

"Good," she said softly.

Joel brought her hand up to his lips and smiled. "That's just like you to say that. I wish I had your mercy."

"You do have mercy, Joel. You forgave her."

"But I knew she was dying. You would have forgiven her, while she was trying to slit your throat."

"Hi, I'm Meredith. Have we met?" she grinned and he responded with a little laugh.

"Okay, *eventually* you would have, then," he amended.

"Joel, did you guys ever figure out how you got her card that was in your wallet?"

He shook his head in resignation. "I have absolutely no idea."

"Well, it might have been during the last NAMM show. You know how crazy that gets," she pointed out. "People just shove stuff in your face, all day long."

"Maybe. Not that it matters, anymore," he said, leaning his head down and dropping a kiss on her forehead. "Here's the happy ending. Gary and I were able to lead Janis to the Lord, before she died. And I literally mean *just* before she died."

She reached up, and drew her fingers softly across her husband's chin. "Joel, I'm so glad, I really am."

"She saw Jesus."

Meredith drew back and stared, in wide-eyed delight. "She did! What did He look like?"

Joel laughed at her enthusiasm. "Well, she didn't describe Him, she couldn't. All she could say was 'beautiful' before she died."

"He is. I saw Him, too."

It was Joel's turn to stare, not with excitement, but with raw pain. "Did you see Him, sweetheart? Were you that close to leaving me?"

She captured his face in her hands. "I pitched a fit and He let me stay with you. Okay, I'm just kidding about that part, Joel," she hurried to add, when he seemed to believe her.

"To be honest, I'm not sure I'm going to be allowed to fully remember everything I saw. A lot of it's gone, already. But Father was there, that much I'm sure of. I can't recall His face, exactly, but I remember being very happy with it. I'm looking forward to seeing His face again, someday. It's like Janis said. It's beautiful."

She looked off into the invisible with a longing in her eyes. "I just wish I could remember," she whispered softly.

Joel traced her lips with his thumb. "I've missed you so much, little one. And I'm so sorry I wasn't a good covering for you."

"What do you mean?" She sat up straight and drew her brow in disapproval. "Why would you say something like that?"

"Meredith, it was Mom and Gary, and the others who dug deep to find out what was going on, and then went head to head with the enemy, for you.

"I just sat here, like a ghoul, and grieved over you. I didn't fight, like they did. I didn't take authority. About all I accomplished was crying like a faucet. Some covering I turned out to be," he sighed.

Meredith popped him lightly. "You stop that, Joel Etheridge! You're exactly who Father picked for me. Are you saying He messed up? *You're* the one who called me back. You're the one I kept reaching for. You did what came naturally. You brooded and searched for the rest of yourself, and wouldn't stop until you found me."

"Well, you got the brooding part right, anyway."

"No, listen to me, baby." She wanted desperately for Joel to hear her. He rested his eyes on hers and waited.

"You remember in Genesis how the Bible talks about the Spirit brooding over the earth? That's because part of Him was down here... under all that water and darkness. He wanted us, He longed for us. He looked for us, He found us. What you did wasn't so different."

Joel considered all this quietly, before grinning down at her. "That's quite a powerful picture you're painting. Did Father tell you to say all that to me?"

Meredith looked around. Her throat was dry, from talking so much, and she reached for the glass of water on the overbed tray and took a sip, to wet it. She looked back at him, with a serious face. "No. He just said to tell you hi."

"Hi," Joel repeated, in measured skepticism. "The Creator of the universe took time out from running an entire planet, not to mention the whole galaxy, to tell Joel Etheridge 'hi'. Anything else?"

She was quiet for a moment. "Well... one other thing, but I don't know what He meant by it."

"Oh yeah, what's that?" Joel asked flippantly, taking the glass she offered and helping himself to a drink.

"Something about challenging Jehovah God to a wrestling match being understood, but ill advised...

"Joel!" She yanked the sheet over her head as a spray of water hit her in the face.

Chapter Twenty-Six

Neil McCallen sighed and hung up his telephone with a disappointed cast to his dark eyes. Bett Greer had been her usual patient, kind self but could offer no more news of Darcy's return than she could the other two times he had called earlier today.

He threw one leg over the arm of the sofa, and stared vacantly at the ceiling. Where was she? And why was she so adamant that Bett not tell him? He thought back over their last time together, and tried to remember what he had done to cause her to feel she had to leave without a word.

"What do you *think* you did, idiot?" he muttered darkly to himself. "Maybe she has this thing about falling in love with married men. Isn't that reason enough? It would serve you right, if she never came back."

Surely that wouldn't happen! No, he decided, solely on the basis of Darcy's integrity. Bett was right. She wouldn't just bail on her kids. Besides, Bett fairly promised him that Darcy was due back sometime this evening.

He pulled a pillow over his face, and tried to quiet his impatient reasoning. There was nothing he could do, but wait for her call.

It wasn't much longer until a knock finally did interrupt his scattered thoughts, and he somehow knew it was her, even though he was surprised that she would come here. He threw the pillow across the room and hurried to the door.

"Darcy!" Neil made a move to take her into his arms, then stopped short, as he saw the couple standing just behind her.

"Neil," She looked back nervously at Craig and Donna Holt, then up into his eyes. "These people have something they need to talk to you about. It's really important, so I brought them straight here, from the airport. When they're done, would you please take them back to their hotel?"

"I... of course." He made no effort to conceal his bewilderment, but tried to recover.

Perhaps Darcy ran into some friends at the airport, and they were in need of counseling. But why didn't she take them to Pastor Lynwood? He quickly rejected this possibility, not believing that she would have brought anything likely to become complicated to his door tonight, of all nights, not when they had so much to say to each other.

Neil focused and struggled to maintain some level of courtesy.

"Please come in." He opened the door wider and stood aside to admit them. Craig and Donna smiled and stepped past him, but Darcy remained out on the porch, obviously not joining them.

"Please have a seat and I'll be right with you," Neil instructed kindly. He pulled the door closed between them, and stepped toward Darcy, with a look of urgency in his eyes.

"Darcy, where have you been? Why did you just take off like that?" He took her by the shoulders and pulled her close.

She braced a hand against his chest and stepped back. "Don't, Neil. Not yet."

"But you don't understand," he began, reaching for her again. "Things are different."

"No, just wait, okay? Just wait. You need to hear from these people first, and then we'll talk. Later."

He searched her eyes and found his own love reflected back at him. Her nearness was wreaking havoc on him.

"Neil, please. Just go in and we'll talk later. Please."

"Who are these people?"

"They'll tell you that, themselves. Listen, I'm sorry about the way I left, but I didn't see any other way. It had to be done. You'll understand when you're done here, and then we'll see about things."

"Things between us?" He slipped a hand behind her neck and hovered dangerously close. "Things between *us*, Darcy?"

"Yes," she breathed. "Don't, Neil. Don't look at me like that. Not yet, it's not time. I have to go now."

"Go where?" he asked quickly. "Where will I find you?"

She smiled up at him and gave his hand a squeeze. "I'm just headed home. I'm not leaving again. I'll be in, all evening."

"When we're done here, I'll come over. There's so much I want to say."

"We have plenty of time for that. Right now, the most important thing is waiting for you inside. I have to go."

He resisted her effort to reclaim her hand and gave her a disappointed smile. "So, not even a hug, then?"

She hesitated. "Let's wait on that, too. I just... things are still unsettled, right now."

"But not like they were." He reached to stroke her chin, and studied her thoroughly.

"You're right," he finally relented. "But we have to talk tonight. Yes?"

"Yes," she whispered.

"Okay, then."

He watched her get into her car and drive off, before he opened the door and eyed the strangers inside curiously.

He came around to take a seat and offered them a friendly smile, then froze as something about the man's face caught his attention. Had they met before? He looked so familiar...

Darcy pulled into her driveway with a mixed sensation of relief and dread. Relief won out, as she was spotted and claimed by an ecstatic Wally.

"Deck!" He hurled himself at her and she was almost thrown off balance by the impact.

"Hey, fella!" She wrapped him up tight in her arms and planted a kiss on his cheek, something he normally shied away from, but now seemed to welcome.

"Hey! You here to stay?" he demanded anxiously.

"Well, sure! Why wouldn't I be?"

"Well, you snook off like you didn't want to be here no more."

"Sneaked off and any more," she corrected, presenting him with a garment bag. She dragged her suitcase out of the trunk and fished out an overnight case. "And I didn't sneak off, sweetie. I just had some business to take care of and it couldn't wait. It sort of came up all at once."

"Was is somethin' to do with that Neil guy?"

"Why do you ask?" She stopped and looked at him in surprise.

"'Cause he was here almost every day, askin' Mom where you went, and when you was comin' back," Wally informed her, matter-of-factly. "I told Mom we should just tell him and put him out of his misery, but she said if I did, I'd catch heck, so I just kept my mouth shut."

Darcy smiled after him, as he lugged the garment bag to her door. She had really missed her little buddy!

The Greer's screen door slammed loudly and Bett hurried down off the porch with open arms and a big grin.

"Hey, girlie! Come here, you!" She bundled Darcy up in her arms and gave her an exaggerated squeeze.

Darcy patted her cheek and laughed. "I missed you guys! I was ready to get home anyway, then when you called and told me about Meredith waking up, it's all I could think about."

"She asked about you," Bett said. "I told her you'd be home today."

"Well, I wish I could drive to Nashville to see her this evening, but I'd fall asleep at the wheel if I tried, it. I did call her, though."

She had put her things down when Bett came out, and now watched Wally trying to impress her, by attempting to pick up too much at once, then thinking better of it. She couldn't suppress a little laugh, before resting a hand on his mother's shoulder.

"Thanks, Bett, for keeping this a secret. Wally told me that Neil tried to wrestle it out of you."

"Have you seen him, yet?" Bett placed her hands on her hips and shot Darcy a demanding look.

"Yes. But only for a minute. We didn't get a chance to talk. He'll probably come over later."

"Hmmm!"

"What does that mean?"

Bett's mysterious smile widened. "Never mind! You'll find out soon enough."

She stared at her, in amazement. "What do you mean by that, Bett? Listen, I don't think I can handle any more surprises. Do you know something that I don't?"

"Forget it, sister!" she advised staunchly. "I'm sworn to secrecy. Anyway, it may turn out to be meaningless, depending on how your trip panned out... which I want the low-down on, as soon as you're rested up."

"What may turn out to be meaningless?" Darcy wondered out loud.

She was ignored.

Wally had piled a second load at her door and then wandered back over to join them.

"Deck, you know somethin'?" he asked, his blonde hair whipping around in the cool, early autumn breeze. "I been checkin' while you was gone, and we was right about God havin' wings!"

"Were we?" She smiled down tenderly at his cute little face.

"Yep. I found a whole passel of wings verses. What's He want with 'em, do you think? I never heard of Him flyin' or nothin' like that! Foster said He pro'bly flaps 'em, when He wants to whip up a tornado or somethin,' but I don't think so. I said, I think they're probably more like tents or somethin'. What do you think?"

"Tents?" She thought about it. "Well, you might be right, Wally. That makes a lot of sense. Tents hide us from storms and protect us. You just might be onto something."

He flushed with pleasure at being validated by his favorite adult, relations not counted, and hurried to inform Foster that his doctrine needed a little work.

Darcy and Bett watched him go with big grins on their faces.

"I just love that little guy!" Darcy declared warmly.

"Well, get in line," his mother advised. "There's a whole bunch of us that are rather fond of him."

She walked alongside Darcy to her apartment.

"You weren't around here much, before you left for California, so you missed it, when Wally's dad found out about the dam he and Foster built."

"I meant to ask about that. Big fun, huh?" Darcy sent her a knowing glance.

"Stan acted all bent out of shape about it, but after he sent Wally to his room, he got down on the living room rug and just rolled. Then he called his folks up and told them all about it."

She took Darcy's keys from her full hands and unlocked her door. "That smell did finally make it over here, but I think we've managed to clear it all out."

"Oh, thank you!" Darcy shoved her things inside the door and took her keys back. She hesitated briefly.

"Go ahead, I know you're tired and probably want to freshen up." Bett made it easy for her. "Have a little rest, and then come on over for some coffee and fill me in." She gave her a little wave.

"Okay, that sounds good." Darcy smiled gratefully and closed the door, glad to be left alone to gather herself.

She disciplined herself to at least pile everything into one corner of her bedroom, and out of sight, before stepping into the shower and standing there, until she had used up all the hot water. She slipped into some gym shorts and a baggy sweatshirt and fell across the bed heavily. She knew that Bett was probably watching and waiting for her to come over, but she just needed a few minutes.

A few minutes turned into hours and when Darcy finally rolled over and opened her eyes, the room had grown dark. She pulled herself up slowly into a sitting position, switched on a lamp and rubbed her eyes.

"I can't believe Bett hasn't pounded my door down, by now," she mumbled.

As if on cue, a sharp rap sounded on the heels of her remark. She smiled at Bett's impatience, and stumbled over to open the door, not yet fully awake. It was because of this, that she stood blinking stupidly at Neil, for quite some time.

"Aren't you going to invite me in?" he asked softly. She took in his red, swollen eyes and bleak smile, with a sharp stab to her heart.

"Come in, Neil," she said quietly, moving back so that he could. She led the way anxiously over to the sofa, and sat down, noticing that, as Neil joined her, he kept a respectable distance between them.

He interpreted her quick look and gave her a sad, tender smile.

"Don't read anything into that," he advised. "It's just that the things that have to be said are too important to be clouded by our emotions."

Darcy nodded slowly and waited.

Neil leaned his weight onto his knees, and stared down at the floor. "Craig and Donna are back at their hotel," he explained needlessly.

She made no reply.

"They're nice people, aren't they?" He flashed her a sideways glance.

"They're very nice," Darcy agreed. "Except, you didn't come here to tell me that."

"No."

She watched him study the floor for another moment, before reaching across and laying a tentative hand on his arm.

"Neil, just say it."

"I'm not sure I know what it is I want to say."

He gave a scant, bitter laugh and rested his head in his hands. Finally, he turned and gazed at her, with a bit of irritation evident in his demeanor.

"Darcy, why did you do this? Why did you just take off, and not tell me what you were doing? I was very clear about not wanting to look for Madeline anymore!"

She widened her eyes in surprise. It had never occurred to her that he would be upset with her, once he knew the truth. If she had returned with nothing, she might understand it, but she would have supposed that finally having answers, after all these years, would somehow override his previous misgivings about finding Madeline.

She bit her lip and struggled with her response, feeling a sudden burst of quiet indignation.

"I did it for me, not for you," she said in a tight, controlled response. "I'm sorry, if you seem to think I was trying to force something on you that you didn't want. But I had to know. I couldn't live the rest of my life, in love with a man I could never be with."

Her temper mounted and she made no attempt to suppress it. "To be honest, Neil, you really hurt me when you didn't seem to care enough about us to pursue this matter yourself!"

He jerked his head up quickly and stared at her.

"I mean, if you were just going to leave things the way they were, then what right did you have coming in here and kissing me, not to mention telling me you love me?"

Her eyes flashed with anger as she jumped up. "Do you wanna know what Meredith said about you? She said you were a jackass!"

She clapped a hand over her impulsive mouth, and flooded with color.

Neil stood up and grazed her with an unreadable look, but with a tiny hint of sardonic amusement playing around his mouth. "So, I'm a jackass, am I?"

He came close and looked down at her. She made a move backwards, and he caught her firmly around her wrist.

"Where are you rushing off to?" he taunted, noticing that temper did beautiful things to her eyes. "Don't you want to stay and tell me what else I am?"

She jerked her hand free. "Maybe I'm sorry I said it, but that doesn't make it any less true!"

Neil winced slightly but maintained his composure. "Are you always in the habit of blindly accepting everything your friend Meredith says as the truth, without discovering the facts for yourself?"

"Why do you think I hopped a plane to California, if it wasn't to discover the facts?" she fired back. "It's more than *you* did!"

"Ah, we're back to that."

"We never left *that!*"

"You..." Neil blew out a loud breath, in frustration. "How do *you* know what I did or didn't do? You certainly didn't make yourself available to find out! Bett's been dying to tell you, but I decided if you were just going to high-tail it out of here with no explanation, let alone a goodbye, then you could just find out on your own!"

"Find out *what?*"

"That I filed for the annulment!"

Darcy was surprised, but it didn't show in her face. She even managed to roll her eyes.

"I realize it's a moot issue, but there it is! Did you really think I could just let it go, once I'd found you, and fallen in love with you?" he demanded harshly. "I might be a jackass, but at least I'm not an idiot!"

"No, you're an ingrate!" she blurted out, still fuming over his response to what she'd done.

"It has nothing to do with gratitude! You didn't give me time to find out if I was going to leave things as they were, or try to resolve them!

"If I couldn't have been granted an annulment, then yes, I would have asked for help, and done anything I could to find out what my marital status really was, but I didn't believe it to be necessary, once I spoke to my attorney. And I could have *told* you that, if you hadn't gone traipsing off and demanding that it be kept a secret!"

"So you're just mad because I stole your thunder!"

"I'm just mad, because you did all this behind my back! You should have told me!"

"Why? So you could order me again to leave it alone? Well, I wasn't *going* to leave it alone. I did it for me, not for you! It was *my* time and *my* money and I didn't need *your* permission!"

"No, you just needed to leave me here, thinking that you were done with me!"

"Well, if that's what you thought about me, then we might want to revisit whether or not you're a jackass!"

They locked glares and stood there as if frozen in time, before Neil surrendered to the fact that he was utterly charmed by her, and love softened his eyes. He finally pulled her to himself, and trapped her with his kiss. She made a half-hearted effort to pull away, and he secured her with a tighter grasp.

"Stop that!" he ordered lightly. "Now I have to start all over again."

This time she submitted completely, and Neil held her there for several long moments before relaxing his hold, and cupping her face in one hand.

"You're a feisty little thing but I believe I can take you."

"You think so?" she challenged breathlessly.

"From this day forward." He smiled at the picture she made in his arms.

"Neil..." Darcy clasped her hands around his neck and searched his face. "You weren't just upset at *me* when you got here. Craig and Donna... I can only imagine how hard that hit you."

"Cried like a baby," he admitted simply, pulling her back down to sit beside him on the sofa. "I won't try to deny it. I guess maybe one of the main reasons that I didn't want to keep searching for Madeline, is because I had an instinct that she might have met with an unhappy end.

"I can't explain it," he added, catching Darcy's raised brows. "It's just that Madeline always had an element of... I don't know... rebellion. She never quite abandoned her infatuation with the man she had been seeing. I didn't know if she was acting on it or not, but I knew she was still hung up on him. I had heard all kinds of things about the guy, and I tried a few times to warn her. It was a mistake. For all I know, she hated me for it."

He laid an arm around her shoulder, and drew her into a closer embrace. "I have to wonder if I didn't drive her right back to him... putting her in a position to constantly defend him, I mean."

"You can't take the responsibility for that," Darcy soothed, curling up against him. "From what her brother told me, Madeline lived for Madeline. She was going to do what she wanted, regardless."

"Craig was right about that. I tried everything I could think of, to get her to stay and make her happy. She just wouldn't."

"Then let it go," she whispered.

Neil looked down at her intently. "I need for you to know this, Darcy. I know now that I've never been in love before. What I had for Madeline wasn't love... not like I have for you, anyway." He traced her lips gently. "I love you with everything that's in me."

"I love you, too," she returned huskily.

"Enough to audition for Mrs. State Youth Director?" He grinned playfully.

"I don't know. How stiff is my competition?"

"Well, tell me this, little lady. Can you fry chicken?"

"Like the colonel!"

"Then you *have* no competition."

As he found her mouth again with his own, poor Bett realized that she might as well turn out the kitchen light and go to bed.

Chapter Twenty-Seven

Laura threw open the door in response to the bell, and beamed a welcome at Neil and Darcy.

"Look who's here!" she announced over her shoulder, to the others throughout the house.

"I'm the official greeter," she explained, guiding them through Joel and Meredith's usually quiet, large, stately home, now filled with friends and family.

Hailey made a beeline for her sister-in-law and future brother-in-law. "Hey, you two! You're late!"

"I have a good excuse," Darcy explained, smiling up at Neil.

She held out her left hand and Hailey squealed with delight. She immediately latched hold of Darcy's arm, and steered her over to the couch, where Meredith lay propped up on a pile of pillows.

"Hey, baby!" She grinned lazily and lifted her arms for Darcy's hug. "Whatcha got there?"

She pulled Darcy's hand down and inspected the beautiful solitaire.

"Just a token of affection from a jackass," Neil quipped from across the room, with a faint smile.

Meredith grinned and winked at Darcy. "Well, might outta clean out a place in the barn for the ol' boy, then," she advised dryly. "You should probably hang on to him, I guess, as long as he's passing out goodies like this."

Neil rolled his eyes and cast a pleading look in Joel's direction. "Isn't it time for her nap, or something?"

Joel laughed softly. "If I so much as catch her *thinking* about a nap, I'll poke her with a fork! I've had my fill of that Sleeping Beauty number."

"Well, is *Kaylan* asleep?" Darcy asked, looking around. "You know, we still haven't seen him."

"Mom?" Joel raised questioning brows.

"Gary's got him out in the den," she said. "I'm not sure who's rocking who. Hang on and I'll see if I can pry him loose."

"These are pretty!" Darcy bent over and fingered the leaves on a small bunch of violets.

"There's a card," Meredith retrieved it from the table next to her and held it out with a tender expression.

Darcy read it silently, her eyes misting over:

Mis Merry,

We new you wood wake up.
Hope you are feeling better and
good to here about the new baby.
Love,

Your frends on the river front.

"Pockets and his friends from the shelter?" She fanned her eyes. "Oh, Meredith, that's so sweet!"

"What's sweet, is that I know they went to a great deal of trouble and personal sacrifice to be able to send them," she remarked, with a soft smile.

"I have a lady coming tomorrow who professionally preserves flowers. I want to keep these forever." She tucked the card back into the little pot, almost reverently.

Darcy looked around with a full heart at Joel and Meredith's other friends and family, and thanked God for the answers to prayer that brought them all together. Things could have ended so bleakly and tragically, if Father's wings hadn't covered them all.

She knelt impulsively on the floor next to Meredith and took her hand. "

"You remember Wally?" she asked, with a smile.

"Little blonde explosion, with eyes like chocolate kisses? You bet!"

"Well, before I left for California, he and his little friend Foster were arguing about whether God has wings or hands. You know how kids are!"

Meredith made a face. "Not really. I'm just a rookie."

Darcy grinned. "As soon as I came home from the airport, he met me in the driveway, and informed me that not only does God have wings, but He uses them like tents to cover up His kids. Yesterday, he told me he wasn't sure, but he thinks Jesus might be a big bird of some kind. I asked him why, and he whipped out that 'Oh, Jerusalem, Jerusalem' scripture."

Meredith burst out with a little laugh, and raised one arm up under her head for support. "Wings, huh? I like that," she said, raising her eyes to her beloved Joel, who was listening in.

"Me, too." He lifted up her legs to settle down with her on the couch, and held her feet on his lap, absently rubbing them, and smiling to himself at the image Wally had conjured up.

"Look who we've got here!" Marshall Edwards put down his coffee and lifted Kaylan right out of Laura's arms.

"Hey, no fair!" she pouted.

"Oh, dry up, you get him all the time!" Marshall's wife, Bobbie, leaned close and chucked the baby under his chin. "Who's a cute wittle ting?"

Gary shot a meaningful look at Joel, and the two men snickered over something they both found funny.

"Knock it off!" Laura admonished. "And you give me back my grandson!" She turned to Marshall and Bobbie with playful malice.

"Bobbie's right, Laura," Delores chimed in. "You've had your turn. Give somebody else a shot!"

Hailey and Darcy both hopped up and sprinted across the room to Kaylan.

"I want one!" Hailey wailed, taking a tiny little finger, and wearing an expression of longing.

Ross, who had been chatting quietly with Neil over in a corner, looked up quickly with startled eyes, and the room erupted into laughter.

Darcy reached out a tentative finger and stroked Kaylan's satiny skin. "Oh, Meredith!" she breathed, with shining eyes. "He's just so beautiful!"

"Like his daddy," Meredith replied. She nudged Joel's hands with her toes, and they exchanged a look that might have embarrassed anyone who'd happened to be noticing, but Kaylan was commanding everyone else's attention. The moment belonged to them, alone.

"He'll look even better in his Grammy's arms," Laura insisted, reclaiming her little bundle with unbelievable swiftness.

Gary moved to greet a new arrival and swept the door open with a flourish.

"Not so fast, Grammy!" he called. "Aunt Iris and Uncle Jack are here to dispute your claim!"

"Ooh!" Iris sailed right past everyone and zeroed in on her nephew.

"Look out," her husband warned Gary, with a grin. "She's got an agenda, and a mean left hook."

Meredith and Joel watched everything quietly from their comfortable old couch, with peaceful smiles resting on their faces.

Joel reached down and scooped up an annoyed Hook, who had finally mustered up the fortitude to wander in, and was quite put out with what he'd found. He hadn't invited any of this ruckus over, and as far as he was concerned, they could all take it right back out with them. Unless...

His nose twitched with anticipation, as Meredith took the bottle of formula Delores brought her, and reached for her son.

"Sorry, Hook, old man," Joel laughed. "You're stuck with canned tuna and kibble."

He settled down on Joel's lap with a disgruntled air, and closed his eyes in boredom.

Gary led Laura across the room by the hand, and motioned to a loveseat near the fireplace. "You can never invite a pastor to any kind of get-together," he began with a grin, as they sat down. "Sure as you're born, he'll come up with something he feels he just has to say. You might as well all get comfortable."

Neil gave him an understanding nod, and patted a place next to himself for Darcy.

Everyone else took Gary's advice to get comfortable and quieted down, to hear what was on his heart.

"To begin with, I just want to thank God for this woman here." He reached down to take Laura's hand and gave it a little squeeze. "I couldn't have asked for a better partner in life. She's got built-in radar, too!"

Laura smiled fondly at her fiancé.

"I shudder to think how things might have turned out, if she hadn't kept bugging all of us to get to the bottom of things, and intercede until the enemy was exposed and stopped. No one here wants to even imagine what life would be like, without Meredith Etheridge in it."

"Amen." Several voices chimed in softly around the room.

Joel swallowed the knot that swelled in his throat. His eyes traveled to his son, cradled in his sweetheart's arms, then up to her face. He found what he needed there.

"I hear we've got yet another wedding in the works." Gary grinned at Darcy and Neil. "But you'll just have to wait your turn. We're next. Once October is gone, you two can have at it!"

He waited for the muted laughter to subside. "I guess the main thing I wanted to do, is to ask you all to join me and offer up a prayer of thanksgiving, for the way God has delivered us out of the hand of the enemy. I overheard you, Darcy, a few minutes ago, telling Meredith about little Wally Greer's concept of Father's wings. Nothing could better describe the way we've been watched over, and cared for, these past several weeks and months."

He smiled broadly at the joy around him. "Let's just let the Lord know how much we appreciate Him."

Others followed suit, as he bowed his head, and their whispered sentiments were deep and fervent, as Gary put into words what they all felt. It was several moments, before throats began to clear, and eyes and noses were wiped.

"I'd like to say something." Joel's deep voice was rich with emotion. "I know I've been pretty much unbearable for quite some time, now. I've yelled at most of you, cursed in front of some of you, and ordered you around, as if you were my servants. I want to apologize deeply for my conduct, during our stay at the hospital."

He waved away the beginnings of protests. "You all have extremely short memories," he continued, with a wry grin. "But Mom and Sis here, will confirm that I was a beast. All I can say is that I was a frightened, and grief-stricken man, which is really not much of a defense.

"Marshall and Dee, I can't say enough about the way you took over things at the office, so that I didn't have to do anything, but be with Meredith. It was above and beyond, and I can never repay something like that."

"It's not like you've never done anything for either of us," Marshall declared stoutly.

"Still..." Joel held up an interrupting hand and favored his good friend with a warm smile. "I want you two to know how much I appreciate it. All of you were such a source of strength, for me to draw from. There were times, when I just didn't have any belief left. All I could do was pull from what you had."

"That's one reason God puts other people into our lives," Gary said quietly. "We sometimes have to borrow from each other."

"The stronger, receiving the weaker," Joel said, smiling over at his sister Iris. She gave him a secret wink.

There was a long reflective silence that began to linger, until Kaylan suddenly pierced it with a resounding burp. Hook looked up in startled alarm, then beat a hasty retreat to the kitchen, his departure accompanied by giggles and belts of hearty laughter.

Meredith lifted her little man up, and turned him around to face their guests, with a proud grin. "Like I said," she repeated to Darcy, with an impish light in her eyes, "just like his daddy."

Joel held out his hands and took him, unable to keep the love and excitement off his face.

His wife laid back and viewed them with quiet satisfaction. She let her gaze float around the room, from face to face.

"I saw Father," she said, barely above a whisper.

The quiet conversations around her ceased abruptly, and all eyes were riveted on her, expectantly.

"While I was in the coma, I guess. I can't remember everything," she added, with sad regret. "And I can't recall His face clearly anymore, but I remember thinking how beautiful He was. He smiled a lot. He said He was excited about the time I'll come back to stay with Him for good, but that He wasn't through using me down here, just yet. I assume He meant to straighten Joel Etheridge out."

There were a number of appreciative grins.

Meredith smiled, as some of the memories and visions she had thought were gone, began to surface. "I wish it was as clear today as it was then," she murmured wistfully.

"Most of it seems dreamlike. But I am sure about some things. Like, for instance, the way things that seem so important, and rankle us, and grieve us down here, aren't even remembered there. Father said we shouldn't give so much time and thought to things that are so temporary.

"And I'm sure about the way the angels can't take their eyes off Him. And who could blame them? He's... He's just really so breathtaking. And Darcy..."

Meredith rested peaceful gray eyes on her husband and a special something passed between them.

"Tell little Wally Greer he's right. Father *does* have wings."

Coming soon from

Rhonda Hanson
and
Grace Under Pressure Publishing

Father's Song
Book Three in the Father Series

Expected release February 2024

Also by
Rhonda Hanson

Father's Choice *(Book One in the Father series)*
Father's Wings *(Book Two in the Father series)*

The Adventures Of Pahwoo And Her Friends
(a seven year long continuing bedtime story)

For more information, visit
graceunderpressure.com

Grace Under Pressure Publishing
P.O. Box 337
Bell Buckle, TN 37020

www.ingramcontent.com/pod-product-compliance
Lightning Source LLC
Chambersburg PA
CBHW060900140726
47996CB00001B/60